L O V E SHRINKS

JULIE SINGLETON

LOVE SHRINKS
First published in Australia by Julie Singleton 2024
www.juliesingleton.com

Copyright © Julie Singleton 2024
All Rights Reserved

ISBN: 978-0-6484105-2-2 (pbk)

Prepublication Data Service details available
from The National Library of Australia

Book cover design by Publicious Book Publishing© 2024

Typesetting and design by Publicious Book Publishing
Published in collaboration with Publicious Book Publishing
www.publicious.com.au

For my father, Gong Gong.

To Jennifer Thommeny, thank you for your support, research and encouragement.

Love Shrinks is the second novel by Julie Singleton, and sequel to her first novel *Love Bites,* published in 2018. She lives in Sydney, Australia, is a proud mother of four children. Julie was admitted to practice as a lawyer in NSW in 1990, working mainly in the area of family law. Julie has worked in the media providing legal commentary on radio, television and in the news.

www.juliesingleton.com

Contents

Sarah

Chapter 1

I was eleven years old when I decided I wanted to become a lawyer. From that moment on, if anyone asked me, that's what I adamantly said I'd set my heart on. I suppose it came from believing even when I was eleven years old, that I should have had a say in what happened to me in my life after my parents died, which I did not.

My parents were immigrants to Australia and my father was a firm believer that education was your main path to improving your life. He would always say to me, "Learn as much as you can, because no-one can ever take that away from you. They can take away everything else, but not your knowledge." My father had immigrated to Australia from Malaysia during the guerrilla war. His bodyguard had been shot protecting him and the British Embassay had advised us to leave. We left a prestigious life, with my father at the time being the head of a major rubber plantation. We lived on the estate in a mansion with household staff and a driver. We had to leave all of this behind to immigrate to Australia.

As a new immigrant, and with four children and a wife, my father had to quickly find a new way to earn a living. His agricultural degree and experience running rubber plantations limited his job prospects. He found a job in real estate, but with no qualifications in that area he only earned the minimum wage. He attended classes at night to obtain a real estate license. My mother, even with her limited English managed to start a small restaurant. My grandmother looked after us while my parents worked seven days a week. That work ethic eventually resulted in their early demise; driving home late from work and my father falling asleep at the wheel of the car, was how the coroner's report explained the accident.

I have been lucky and unlucky in my life, but I achieved my goal of becoming a lawyer. I was the fortunate recipient of a scholarship to attend a private boarding school for high school, after my parents died in a car accident. During my university years, I lived on campus. I dreamed of being able to afford my own home, a security and sanctuary which I had lost when I was only eleven years old.

After graduating from law school, I decided that the area of law I wanted to specialise in was family law. Numerous people, especially my lecturers tried to talk me out of it. They said it just involved overly emotional clients who more often than not became hysterical, difficult, and ultimately ungrateful. It was also the field which I believed had the most potential for me as a lawyer; it was complicated, and so was I. It involved not just law, but trying to guide your clients into making the right decisions when they were usually in their worst head space. I had experienced my whole life doing just that.

I am stubborn; I will admit that. The more negative feedback I got, the more I thought Family Law was for me. My father had often said to me as a little girl, "Always do the job that everyone else does not want to do. That way, you will get ahead much easier because there will be less competition." I tested his theory on volunteering as a library monitor at school. No one else wanted to do it. I spent my lunch hours with the library teacher, who helped me with my homework every day. My marks went from average to top of the class. My dad was right. He was ahead of his time.

My first job was with a boutique legal firm. I worked with them for five years until I started my own firm. During the five years I had been employed at the firm, I mainly practised in family law. Occasionally, I assisted one of the Commercial Law partners if they needed assistance. One of those occasions was for the firm's most important client, a property developer Bobby Briggs. I had been working on a property development project with him at the time his wife surprised him with asking for a divorce. Knowing I had also worked in Family Law, Bobby had explicitly asked if I could work on his case with our firm's divorce partner, Katrina Hicks.

Katrina was one of Sydney's leading Family Law lawyers. I was excited to work with her on what would be a very complicated matter

- due to Bobby's complex financial structure and high net worth. When Katrina had asked Bobby to explain his financial structure to her, he suggested that she consult with me, as I had a detailed knowledge of his financial affairs, having worked with the banks to secure loans for his last development.

Katrina hated me. The more I tried to get her to like me, the more she detested me. Bobby hated her because she hated me, which made the situation even worse.

However, as the saying goes, "Out of chaos comes shooting stars," I loved Family Law. Katrina did her best to turn my happy working environment into a daily challenge. After six months of extensive negotiations and the settlement of Bobby's Family Law matter, I went to lunch with Bobby and the senior barrister who had worked on the case. Both commented on the strained relationship I had with Katrina, and they colluded in suggesting that I leave and start my own firm. "You will at least have one client, which is one more than I had when I started my own business," Bobby said. It had been one of the biggest challenges of my life but one of the best decisions I had ever made. I knew the firm would not be happy that Bobby, their biggest client, was leaving with me.

I don't remember much about my mother, but I do remember her saying to me, "If you do not feel the warmth of life, the cold will kill you." I had to leave, or Katrina was going to freeze me out. When I struggled in the early days of running my own firm, I thought about my mother starting her own Chinese restaurant in Australia. When I looked back at the difficulties my mother must have faced starting her own business as a new immigrant, with four children, who could barely speak English; I realised how lucky I was.

Twenty years later, my firm and my daughter were my life. I spent almost every working day in the Family Court or getting ready to go there. I had a successful business with happy staff and the offices that I had always wanted. Thanks to my mother's inspiration, I took the risk and worked with all my heart to achieve the best I could for my family.

Some days were better than others in the Family Law Court. Most of the time that I appeared in court for my clients, I felt that the system worked effectively and fairly. Today however, I had been in Court via a video link in another State, and I was not only frustrated with the result but also surprised. Of course, I knew that the judge would question me about what he viewed as me assisting a mother who had breached her Court Orders.

My client had compelling reasons but the judge did not want to listen to them. Instead, he focused on the breach of Court Orders and said in a booming voice over the video link, "Make sure the mother is in Court next week Ms Walters, or you may both end up in jail in contempt of Court."

My client could not come to Court because the police would arrest her on sight, take her to the police station and charge her. If her son was with her, they would take him and give him to his father.

I knew at the next hearing when she did not turn up, the judge would order me to provide the mother's address so she could be arrested. I would rely on legal professional privilege as a reason to deny him that information. He could still decide to make a Court Order against me for contempt; I knew that, but I felt compelled to help this woman who had already been in hiding for two years to protect her son.

I enjoyed helping people in need. It was the most rewarding part of my job. I had a wall of photos in my office from several grateful clients of their children. The photos of Fleur always brought a smile to my face. Her mother had sent me a photo of her every year since I had helped them move to England from Australia. It had been a difficult extraction. That was ten years ago, and Fleur was about to start University. She was eighteen years old now, happy and healthy.

Next to Fleur's photo was the photo of my parents, taken the day before they died. I put their photo next to these photo's so that I could somehow justify to myself that their loss had made me the person I was today. On my desk was my grandmother's photo.

Without warning, just as it always did, anxiety overcame me instantly, and I had no control over it. It drew me and my childhood with me, down a long dark hole, like Alice in Wonderland.

I constantly tried to find a way to lift the emptiness and despair that consumed me during these attacks. When I felt like this, I became consumed with the disasters in my life like my divorce, my ex-husband facing criminal charges resulting in my daughter seeing him via supervised access visits.

I knew I had to act quickly before my emotions overcame me and caused me to black out with anxiety. Starting my meditation, I closed my eyes and held my breath for as long as I could; then I exhaled slowly. The stop in the flow of oxygen slowed down my heart, which in turn helped me slow down the chatter in my brain. As I breathed in slowly, I focused on picturing the sun shining rays of warmth and energy moving through each area of my body starting again with my toes, slowing moving each one, then each leg, finger, arm, and last of all my neck. Whenever a thought tried to enter my head, I threw it out quickly, like salt over my shoulder. After energising my body, I slowly worked on releasing the anxiety from each part of my body. I then took three slow, deep breaths before opening my eyes.

The alarm in my phone pinged and saw the reminder for my appointment. With relief, I picked up my handbag and walked out of my office to my consultation with Charlie, my psychiatrist.

Sarah

Chapter 2

I walked out of my office to the lifts in reception. As I pressed the lift button, I informed my receptionist where I was going. Her sympathetic comment, "I hope it goes well," made me feel embarrassed.

Despite my chaotic childhood, the perfect life I had managed to create had now become a public roller coaster ride. My ideal marriage seemed to have been a shopfront for my ex-husband's hidden sexuality and allegations of heinous conduct with Anthony when he was a minor. All I could do was to try and protect my daughter from the fallout of the allegations against her father whilst we established the truth of it all.

I leaned against the wall, nervously scrolling through my mobile phone so that I looked busy, desperately trying to pretend to escape what I felt was the constant daily scrutiny of eyes watching me as I slowly broke up inside. The lift finally arrived, and I stood as still and emotionless as a sculpture, staring straight ahead at the doors in case someone tried to speak to me during the ride down from the 55th floor. As soon as the doors opened, I walked briskly out of the building, stopping only momentarily to nod politely to the door attendant as I left.

I knew that I was walking at a pace that seemed abnormal. As though I was trying to escape from someone. I picked up my pace and headed towards the only person to whom I could unload the chaos that consumed my mind. The turmoil that I know I had brought unto myself, and if I had a choice, I would run away from it quickly. But now I had a daughter; she was also part of this chaos.

Now I had reached the stage of deceiving myself, with the utter incapacity to reason or understand what had gone wrong in my life.

It was now in complete chaos. The only answer for me was to see a psychiatrist. One who would help me find my way out of the emptiness I was feeling with my only motivation being that of obligation and service.

As I reached the old stone building on Macquarie Street, I leaned against the wall and pressed the intercom button to announce my arrival. It was not an unpleasant building. The hairdresser on the ground floor always seemed full of happy people, those working there and the clients having their hair attended to. Upstairs we had our heads dealt with differently.

It was the same routine for every appointment at the entrance to the building of my psychiatrist's office; to preserve his client's anonymity. After pressing the button on the intercom and announcing myself, I waited. Within moments, the door clicked open. I walked in and proceeded up the hallway, walked up the stairs into the waiting room and took a seat.

The same classical music was always playing as though it should be calming, but it annoyed me. I heard the door of my psychiatrist's room open and then the footsteps of someone walking past the waiting room and down the stairs. The design of the office was such that we did not see each other. There was always a patient before me; I knew that. I presumed there was always a patient after me, and I often wondered if they were listening to my footsteps as I left.

As soon as the front door closed, Charlie, my psychiatrist, walked into the waiting room to greet me and usher me into his office. I turned off my mobile phone before I sat down.

There were two chairs in his office, positioned across from each other. My chair always faced his bookshelf, which I occasionally scanned as a pleasant distraction during my sessions.

Charlie started the appointment by asking me, "How are you this week?"

"Worse than normal if that's possible. I have lost control to the point that I am constantly putting out fires. It's been chaotic, and I know I am not dealing with anything as well as I could be," I said.

"You are a perfectionist, Sarah. Control is very important to you, but you must accept that you can't control everything that happens to you."

"I accepted that and have worked hard to find stability. That's why I chose a career to help others fix the chaos in their lives. But lately, I am becoming annoyed at people coming to me with problems, instead of being patient."

"Give me an example?" Charlie asked.

"Well, this morning, I said something aloud that I have thought to myself many times but never said aloud before. After two hours of a client complaining to me about his wife being unreasonable in their property settlement, I just said to him. "For goodness' sake, you married your wife, in your own words, "for her extraordinary body and not her IQ", and now you are wondering why she is being ridiculous with her financial demands on you. You gave your Barbie doll wife an unlimited credit card, Ken's car, Ken's house, and Ken's boat, and then you wonder why Barbie won't give them back because you have a new Barbie."

"Did your client get upset with you, Sarah, or did he laugh?" Charlie said.

"Actually, he took it quite well and said I was right. But I never should have said it."

"These are signs. You get them to let you know you are getting tired and need a break."

"Remember, you have not only had to deal with some very stressful personnel issues in the past year, but you have also had to deal with your client's issues daily without a break. Eventually, endless stress affects you and your ability to cope."

"I don't have time for a break, and things are worse than ever with Peter. Whenever I think about him, it derails me. I have been here before and got out of it, but I don't remember how I did it."

"You usually cope with stress by working more, which distracts you from thinking about your problems. But that coping mechanism eventually creates more stress."

"I know that I can usually distract myself by working. I know I am spending too much time at work and not enough time with my daughter, but even working 18 hours a day is not helping anymore. I'm not sleeping, and I am just not a fun mum to be with right now."

"We can try and give you other tools to manage your stress, since a holiday is not an option."

"I have been trying to manage my problems with Peter, but he has made a mess of our lives with Anthony's expose' of their alleged inappropriate childhood friendship. You can tell me as often as you like that it's not my fault, but whenever I think about it, I can't understand it, and then I start blaming myself for not seeing it for all those years."

"Sarah, it's completely understandable. When you don't understand why people have acted in a certain way, you block it out. It relates to the shock of the death of your parents. You are then taken away from your grandmother and brother to boarding school. You were overwhelmed with emotion, but you didn't want to show your grandmother that. You blocked out your feelings and did what you were told to do. From that moment on, your sense of self and trust were violated. Your manner of coping with the vicissitudes of life has been shaped by your life experiences; you learnt how to adapt and survive which has created your personality disorder which we are working on."

"I know I have always found it easier to block out things if it hurts me than to think about them. I have no trouble processing things that don›t add up for my clients to work out the obvious, but why can›t I do that when it relates to me?"

"What do you mean, Sarah?"

"Well, I saw a client today who said her husband wants a trial separation. During this «trial separation," he would also like them to do a property settlement. He told my client that he thinks he is having a mid-life crisis. He wants to risk everything to grow his business rather than keep the family business safe and small. His accountant suggested that she would be better protected if she made a postnuptial financial agreement to put the family home in her name in case his business plans failed. She believes that he is just trying to protect her, and to keep the marriage."

"So, you are saying, because it›s happening to someone else, you can see the holes in his story?"

"Exactly. She doesn't, and she doesn't want to."

"Luckily, she went to see you."

"She came to see me, not for advice on whether the settlement offer was fair, but because he told her that she needs a lawyer to sign off on it, to make it legally binding for him."

"But if it's not fair, then you'll advise her against agreeing to the settlement, won't you?"

"I have, but she still wants to agree to it. She won't accept my advice because she loves him and thinks that this will help save their marriage. I see this in people all the time."

"I see the problem," Charlie replied. "They won't see what they don't want to."

"I feel like my job is at times half lawyer, half psychiatrist. I shouldn't have to try and work out why or how to change this woman's mind because of her emotions, should I? But it is my job to do just that."

"I can see that the dynamics of financial agreements can compromise you. You will have to learn to separate the legal and emotional implications."

"I can do that most of the time. This week I finalised a prenup during mediation. My client could not fathom why his fiancée's lawyer was vehemently against agreeing to it."

"He was funny?"

"The prenup terms were if they broke up that the fiancée received the ten-carat yellow diamond engagement ring, her Ferrari car, four weeks to move out of his penthouse and $200,000.00 to find somewhere else to rent. When her lawyer objected to the terms, my client asked if she had a ten-carat diamond ring, a Ferrari, and $200,000.00 cash. When the lawyer said, "No," he replied, "Well, maybe you should have signed one of these agreements, or were you never offered one? This agreement would give your client more money than she has ever had or may ever be offered, and your rationale not to sign it is what?"

The intercom to Charlie's office buzzed. This had never happened during one of our appointments. He looked concerned as he excused himself and left the room.

I always felt like I was back at school in Charlie's office. I started to get up to walk closer to the door to try and listen to who had just buzzed the intercom, but I sat back down as quickly as I had gotten up, knowing that was wrong. In that second of excitement though, I realised that I had somehow snapped out of my depressed state.

I didn't know why it was so important to Charlie that he kept all his patients apart and secret from one another, but it was. I heard Charlie speaking to a woman, and I could hear her crying. I heard Charlie explain he was in consultation with another patient. It was only a couple of minutes before Charlie walked back into the room and said, "Sorry about that."

"That's ok. She sounded like she was crying. Is she alright?"

"She will be fine. Now let's go back to focusing on you now. Let's talk about what you remember from 11 years old, after your parent's car accident."

Talking about my parents had the same effect on me as it always had. I suddenly felt like someone had taken a straw and sucked all the energy out of me as I slumped into the chair, feeling drained. The dizziness and nausea started seeping into my body, and I felt light, like I was drifting up and away and looking down at myself.

Anthony

Chapter 3

It has been six months since I was convicted and sent to jail. I can't get used to the noise and the constant echoing of voices from the extensive line of cells in our tunnel-like existence. The lighting in my cell is so dim that I can't even read to distract myself from the buzzing in my head. My roommate's constant leg tapping while he talks to himself, reading the bible, makes me want to hit him, but he is twice my size and covered in tattoos, so I refrain from it. The smell of urine and sweat constantly makes me want to heave as I lay in my bunk.

In the mornings, we are led out of our cells like cattle into the exercise yards, and the light blinds us with its sudden penetration and then leaves us as it struggles through the windows in the canteen. In a line, pushing trays along like children, we are given mounds of what is allegedly food but has no resemblance to the meat and vegetables it was derived from.

I had ruminated for the past six months over what had happened. If I had done anything wrong with Jessica, it was not my fault - I knew that. All I had ever done was love those who I believed loved me. I now knew that Peter didn't care about me. I had seen that in his eyes when I saw him at the coffee shop and the hospital. Unlike my feelings for him, his eyes showed no emotion when we saw each other again. He looked right through me, as though I did not exist.

I wanted Peter to know how it felt to be abandoned like he had deserted me without explanation. That's why I sent the letter with the photos of him and me together to his ex-wife Sarah, after the trial. I wished I could have been there when the tall and imperial snob opened the envelope.

I still don't understand what happened. I had been happily married with a beautiful home, a loving stepdaughter, and a successful business; now, it was all gone. The last phone call I had with my stepdaughter Jessica was to set me up to tape the call for the police so they could charge me; I would never understand it or forgive her for that.

Slowly but surely, I would get out of here one step at a time. My sister was now my biggest ally, feeling guilty and sorry for not realising what Peter had done to me at our home when Peter was her boyfriend. *She should feel guilty*, I thought to myself. Both she and my parents had thoughtlessly allowed Peter to sleep in my room without supervision or questioning. I was only twelve, and they had not protected me from him supplying me with drugs and alcohol whilst he explored his sexuality. That was all because they were too busy protecting Madeline.

The sentence was eleven years in jail, nine non-parole, but I knew I would get out of there before then. I had to. To help myself, I started a law degree to make sure I knew exactly how to structure my court appeal. I saw the jail psychiatrist twice a week to prepare a report on how my psychological state had not been considered during the court case or the sentencing.

How was I supposed to know I had psychological issues due to my childhood friendship with Peter? It was not until I met Anne that I allowed myself to get close to another person. My attachment to Jessica soon followed. Sam, my psychiatrist, said it had been good and bad, as I had allowed myself to feel love again. Still, unfortunately, my idea of love had developed from a broken and distorted basis.

I had found comfort in seeing my sister Madeline again and her children. We both wanted to keep that connection. It was a connection I had let go of for all those years, and although I had not understood it, I felt betrayed by her and my parents.

I looked up from my bed, squinting to read the words carved on the wall, "Man shall love a woman." I realised I had inadvertently read the quote aloud when my cellmate's head suddenly appeared, leaning down towards me from his bed above. "It's from the bible. I told them you just needed to be reminded with God's help. That's right, isn't it?"

"I don't know what you mean."

"What were you convicted of man? Did you, do it?" He asked me.

"I did nothing wrong, and I am appealing," I said.

"Go to Bible Studies. It will help you. If you don't, then I can't help you."

I realised what he meant and my survival instinct kicked in. I replied, "Sure. I will go tomorrow."

He lifted himself up, and I thought with relief that our conversation was over until he suddenly threw a book down to me. It was the bible.

"Start reading it now," he said.

Charlie

Chapter 4

One of the most difficult challenges of being a psychiatrist was seeing my patients in pain when they opened up to me. Watching the beautiful and confident Sarah Walters enter my office and transform into a broken child as we talked about her childhood was painful. I truly believed that I was the only person who knew how imperfect her perceived perfect life was. Her life was sabotaged by her childhood trauma. This was the reason for her success and the current emotional turmoil in her life. My challenge was to help her overcome the abject pain inflicted upon her as a child and which was now haunting her as an adult.

As Sarah spoke to me in our session, I could see that she started to retreat into herself as the memories became more painful. She now sat staring blankly ahead towards my bookshelf. This had happened before. I gently prodded her back by saying, "Where have you gone, Sarah? Please come back."

I watched as Sarah slowly redirected her gaze back towards me. As she turned her head, it was as though she had to refocus her eyes before she realised where she was before she asked, "Sorry, what were we talking about?"

"You told me about your mother, and then you suddenly stopped talking. I was talking to you, but I could see you had gone elsewhere."

"I'm sorry, Charlie, I don't know what happens. It only happens when I talk about my childhood. Do I really need to go back there and discuss it with you? My life is a mess, and I want to focus on trying to help Chloe rather than talk about my childhood."

"I know it seems a waste of time for you, Sarah, but to move forward, we need to work out what happened to you for you to get over it. If you don't work that out, you will keep feeling the pain you don't understand and make the same mistakes again."'

"I'm used to the pain, and I can push it away, until you make me relive it. Really, in the end, the end is the end, Charlie. We must all cope best living with what life throws at us."

Sarah reached into her handbag and took out her mobile phone, and as she did, she saw my look of disapproval. I said to her, 'Please try not to look at your phone. You are only here for 50 minutes, and we need that to be uninterrupted."

"I just need to check if anything is urgent," Sarah said. She was now agitated.

"You were on your phone as you walked in. You need to let go of worrying about others to focus on yourself for the 50 minutes we have."

I watched as Sarah put her mobile phone away like a disgruntled child. She was the epitome of a workaholic, which affected her life in ways she failed to see. The more chaotic her life became, the harder she would have to work to avoid it.

I asked Sarah, "What did you mean when you said, "in the end, the end is the end?" "It's quite simple, isn't it, Charlie? Life, as you know, it changes. There is an end to how your life was, and you need to start a new life. People die, they leave marriages, kids grow up and leave home, and we all must adapt to the changes without whining about it. We must forget about it and move on. That's what I mean."

"So, you mean when something ends, it doesn't matter how it ends?"

Sarah shuffled in her chair, nervously flicking her hair behind her ears, as she said, "I mean, for example, that Peter won't accept that because our relationship is over that we will not be playing happy families anymore. He keeps telling me how disappointed he is when I take Chloe to see him, that Chloe is missing having a family because we are divorced. He won't accept that part of our lives is over and that we must develop a new relationship as co-parents. He says he still loves me. Why does that matter anymore?"

"Do you know when you stopped loving him?" I asked.

"No. I don't know when I stopped loving him. I can't pinpoint it to an event or moment in time. I often wonder, did my love for him shrink over time, disappear overnight or was it just an illusion to start with?"

"That's an interesting question Sarah. Research has found that in most relationships, there is the initial honeymoon period, and then after that, love grows, or in your words, shrinks over time. Unfortunately, it may not be the same journey for both partners, and that's when the relationship issues start."

"I only know it's over, and I don't get why Peter doesn't accept it."

"How long have you been feeling frustrated with Peter?"

"It's only been recently, and it's not just about Peter."

"Sarah, as I have been saying to you for a while. I am bandaging a wounded soldier to send you back to war before the stitches have healed. Eventually, you will need to take some time out to allow yourself to recover from what life has thrown at you."

"Charlie, I know it's getting worse. Lately, when I look at the photo of my grandmother on the wall in my office, instead of seeing her smile inspiring me, I feel the pain of when she let them take me away to boarding school. The pain is so intense; I am back in that moment. I remember running away from the lady who had come to pick me up and hiding from her. Then my brother came to get me from under the bed."

"When did this flashback last happen?"

"Last night. I don't remember how I ended up on the floor, but I woke up in the foetal position. When I got up and looked in the mirror, my eyes were red and swollen. I must have passed out."

"How often does this happen?" I asked.

"Not often. I don't understand why I have these emotional tsunami's when I know my grandmother thought boarding school was the best thing for me after my parents died. But no one asked me first. I wanted to stay with my grandmother and my brother."

"What did you do after you saw your reflection in the mirror? Did it make you feel anxious that you did not recall what happened?"

"Momentarily, I was confused. But I recovered quickly. I know I have been lucky that none of my staff has witnessed one of my meltdowns?" Sarah replied.

"Was Peter ever with you when you had a meltdown as you described it?"

"Not that I know of."

"I don't think you shared many of your emotions with your husband, and conversely, you didn't allow him to share his with you."

"What do you mean?" Sarah asked.

"Peter told me that when he tried to talk to you about times when he felt upset, you were not interested."

"I told him I can't do emotion when I get home from work. I have been doing it all day since then, and all I want to do is see Chloe and relax. He always seemed to want to talk about his bad days on the days I had a particularly challenging day – that was all."

The timer on my phone went off and alerted us to the session ending. Sarah looked relieved when she heard it. As she stood up to leave, I said to her, "Before you go, and while we are catching up about your former clients, I have been meaning to ask you, have you heard anything about Geoffrey Pemberton? Was he charged over Amber's death, or did the coroner find it to be suicide?"

"That man has more lives than a cat. The coroner ruled it to be an accidental death – that Amber had drowned in the bathtub due to an accidental overdose of Valium. The coroner didn't think it was a critical issue that Amber just happened to be the second girlfriend in a succession of Geoffrey's who had accidentally died within the last couple of years, both whilst he was in a relationship with them."

"I didn't know that about his other girlfriend. Did she commit suicide by way of overdose too?"

"Howard told me about it. He had acted for Geoffrey as his lawyer about that matter too. She allegedly had a fatal allergic reaction while on his boat with him at sea—all too much of a coincidence. Amber was no angel, but she didn't deserve how he mistreated her. He abused her right up to the end. You know the paramedics walked in on him having sex with Sally, Amber's best friend, in the bathroom on the vanity, while Amber lay blue and lifeless in the spa bath next to them. His response to the paramedics when they asked how he could have sex with another woman while his girlfriend was unconscious was, "What else were we supposed to do while we were waiting the 30 minutes for you to get here? Play marbles? This is what I do to relieve my stress."

I burst out laughing before immediately regretting my inadvertent response to hearing about Geoffrey's appalling behaviour. Apologising to Sarah, I said, "Sorry, I laughed."

"You weren't the first one who laughed," Sarah replied.

As Sarah reached the door to leave, I opened it and said, "All I can do for you is triage you each time you come in to get you back out there to work again. It's not the long-term solution, though."

"I know that. I hope to deal with it in this lifetime, but until then, triaging my madness will have to do. I appreciate it, you know that."

"You are not mad, Sarah, far from it."

"Thanks, Charlie. It always helps to talk to you. If nothing else, you can reassure me that I am not mad even when I sometimes find myself blacking out and lying on the floor."

"PTSD is not madness. It's a condition triggered by an event."

"You are handling it well under the circumstances. When you have time, more intense therapy away from the other pressures in your life would help you even more."

"I know I have issues, but at least I know it. Geoffrey keeps killing women and getting away with it. See you next week Charlie."

Mark

Chapter 5

I was at a time in my life when I should be the happiest. I had been happily married for over 25 years with two great kids. I am a successful oncologist and surgeon, and I am respected by my staff and colleagues. Since I was a child, I have wanted to become a doctor and help sick people get better. I had devoted myself to becoming a surgeon and a leader in my field of oncology.

However, my life is a nightmare. For the past three years since my wife left me, my lawyer Sarah Walters has dictated my every move, both financially and personally. At fifty-three, I did not see this coming. I thought my wife was happy, but I was very wrong. Instead of respecting me, I discovered that my wife had despised my dedication to my career and patients for the last 25 years. As far as she was concerned, my dedication to my work resulted in my neglect of her as a wife and as a father to my children.

I had unfortunately found out way out too late to save our marriage, how my wife had felt about our marriage. Not a word of complaint from her while we were married. She drove a new luxury car every four years, and the kids went to private schools. It was only when she had decided to divorce me and claim the significant share of our assets, that my wife expressed her displeasure with my apparent neglect of her and our children. My wife was unhappy with my performance as a husband. This was due to the time demands of my career as an oncologist.

How was I supposed to be a leading specialist at a teaching hospital without sacrificing my personal time with my wife and children? Why did I have to defend myself in Court when I was applauded for the same sacrifice at work? It was not as if I was at the pub with the guys or even playing golf on the weekend. I was at the hospital working, doing what I had to do as a specialist in my field, to save lives or at least give more time to those who had cancer to sort out their affairs and goodbyes.

Since the court case I had dreaded checking my emails. My days were now invaded with correspondence with requests from my ex-wife's lawyers. Although I knew that I was in the best legal hands that I could be, I felt like I was at war with no guarantee of survival. The feeling of vulnerability of being at the mercy of the legal system was one I would not wish on anyone. The only bitterness I now felt towards my ex-wife was her effect on my ability to work. How I was supposed to be able to respond to all the requests for information and answer all her Affidavits whilst running a department at a major hospital didn't matter to her. I could not ignore it.

As I stand outside the Family Court this morning, I can't help but stare at the building I am about to enter. "The Palace of Crushed Dreams," my lawyer called it, because of its decadence. The marble and glass building were adorned with gold embellishments. A tall sculpture over the entrance depicted a man and woman looking in opposite directions appearing angry, under a thundercloud.

As I stood staring at the building, a lady walking past me asked me if I was ok. I told her I was. She said to me, "Don't overthink it, is my tip. Just walk in. You will have your case adjourned anyway. Mine was adjourned because my ex didn't show up the last three times." She then walked into the building.

I stood on the footpath and watched more people in suits walk into the building. Not a smile to be seen. Heads down, dark clothing, luggage bags being wheeled full of legal folders, no doubt containing affidavits detailing how couples believed their relationships had gone wrong. What they had contributed, what they deserved, and how their children wanted to be with "them", not the other.

I pulled out the sheet of paper from my pocket on which I had scribbled where my lawyer had told me to meet her. Looking at my scrawled handwriting, it read: Monday 8.30 am, Family Court, Level 6 Courtroom 3B.

I started walking up the steps of the building, feeling more anxious with each step. It felt more like walking into an interrogation room than a courtroom, where I was presumed guilty. The whole concept was so hard to comprehend. How could someone I had never met before, who was ridiculously dressed in a gown and wig, decide if, how, and where, I could see my children. And how much of my assets I could keep when I had done nothing wrong except work hard, become a leader in my field, and provide well for my family. That was one of my biggest mistakes.

I was advised by my barrister that the more extravagant the lifestyle you provide for your wife and children during your marriage, the more chance your wife will have in court of getting the funds for it to be continued after separation. I had said to my barrister in response to that advice, "So, The Family Law Act really affirms the saying, "No good deed goes unpunished."

I followed the rest of the people moving into the building like sheep. I approached the security checkpoint, and I obediently emptied my pockets, took off my belt and placed it with my mobile phone and wallet in a tray to go through the scanner. I walked through the scanning arch, and the security guards greeted me by saying, "Good morning." I had heard that every time I had been here over the past three years. I know they were being polite, but it always made me want to ask, "How could this be a good morning when I am at the Family Court?"

"Have a nice day," the guards continued with their monotonous pleasantries to each entrant of the building. I nodded to acknowledge their kind gesture, the best I could, as I gathered up my things from the tray. I kept walking towards the lift and stood in the crowd waiting for my turn.

After the usual wait of two to three lifts stopping to open their doors, I could finally shuffle into an already crowded lift with several other people. I wished I could be anywhere else; even the dentist was better than here. I pressed the lift buttons and saw that level three was already pressed. With my back to the lift, I stood close to the entry doors. Just as the doors were about to close, a hand suddenly appeared in the middle of the doors pushing at the side of one of them, and the doors jolted open. A couple rushed in, looking flustered as they pressed their way into the already crowded lift.

As soon as the doors closed, I heard a woman from the back of the lift shout, "I can't believe you brought that bitch to Court, you bastard. You are unbelievable, Kevin." The couple who had just gotten into the lift turned around and appeared shocked. The man said, "Please, Patricia, don't do this. Don't embarrass us all."

"Do what, Kevin? Embarrass you by letting everyone know you had an affair with our baby's nanny, whom you left us for?"

"It›s been two years now and being hysterical is not good for you."

"Oh, of course, "I" am being unreasonable and hysterical because you want to sell the home your son and I live in, so the two of you can move on with your lives. I can't believe that I am so selfish."

Unperturbed by his obvious unpopularity in the lift, Kevin continued speaking as he stared at her and said, "Patricia, we need to sell the house because we all need to move on. Our marriage is over, and we need to divide what we have. You can't keep the house and leave me with nothing. That's not fair."

I looked around the lift; everyone looked uncomfortable.

The woman stood up stiffly. She lifted her head whilst wiping away the tears from her red puffy eyes with smudged make-up. She said to the two women beside her, "I'm ok."

"Let me help you," one of the ladies said to her as she dabbed at the mascara running down the woman's cheeks with a tissue.

With just the touch of gentleness shown by others, Patricia seemed to instantly compose herself enough to say to Kevin, "Move on. How do I move on from what you did? You were having an affair with the nanny looking after our baby while I was at work. When I suspected the two of you and confronted you, you denied it, telling me I was being paranoid. It wasn't until I hid a baby monitor in our bedroom and the baby's room to record the two of you while you thought I was at work that you had to confess the truth to me."

Kevin looked contrite as he replied, "How could we tell you we had fallen in love? We didn't plan it – it just happened. We were going to tell you when you had settled back in at work, and the baby had settled into day-care in a couple of months. We tried to be sensible and wait until everyone was in a routine."

The whole lift felt the anger rise in Patricia. The tears were now streaming down her face as she screamed at him like a maimed animal in terrible pain. "That's rubbish. You wanted to wait until I was back at work because "I" am the one earning money to fund our lifestyle and pay for our house. You were not being sensible. You encouraged me to go back to work so you could both have the house to yourselves whilst I funded you both."

He replied, "No, it was not planned. It didn't happen that way. We just fell in love so gently and naturally when we should have been together as parents with our baby. Strolling through the park and talking about everything from what schools we were thinking about to politics. It just developed, and then we fell in love."

Finally, the lift doors opened and everyone walked out swiftly except Patricia. I saw her slumped against the back wall with tears streaming down her face. Walking from the lift towards the couple, I heard them discussing what had just happened. She was clearly annoyed and said to him, "I told you that trying to settle with Patricia was a waste of time. She is not going to agree to sell the house. You will need to move forward and get court orders to finish this. I am not going to put up with any more of her abuse."

I saw the look of guilt and conflict on Kevin's face, and I felt sorry for him. He clearly felt guilty but was also trying to appease his new wife. I heard him trying to defend himself, "This is the process we must go through. We go to court, and while doing that, we attempt to settle to show the judge we are trying. We will have to go to mediation; if that fails, we will get a schedule to prepare for a hearing. It takes time, and it's hard on us all. I am sorry about that, darling."

I walked briskly away from them without appearing as though I was running. Somehow the incident made me feel better about my divorce, which up until now, I had thought was the worst divorce in the world. I started to look for the numbers next to the various double doors at the front of the courtrooms and eventually found Courtroom 3B.

Sarah

Chapter 6

I had completely adjusted to life as a single parent until Peter created chaos again. So many things had changed because of our divorce, and I got over them, but Sunday had been up to now my favourite day of the week. Now, every second Sunday, I had to take my daughter Chloe on a supervised visit with her father. Although the venue varied, the feelings I felt seeing Chloe with him didn't. Chloe had no idea of the situation's complexity, and the visits always made me feel anxious before and physically exhausted afterwards. My psychiatrist said these feelings were natural, but what was normal about taking my child to a supervised access visit with her father?

Today, as we drove through Centennial Park on the way to Sunday lunch, Chloe said, "Mummy, look at everyone having picnics. One day, can we picnic here with Daddy instead of going to the restaurant? It would be so much fun."

I felt like a traitor, not telling Chloe why things were the way they were, but right now, she was too young to understand. Instead, I did what my psychiatrist advised me to do; I deflected her question and said, "Of course we can. A picnic is a lovely idea, darling."

"Yes, Mummy, that would be so much fun," she squealed. Relieved by her response, I continued to drive to the parking lot of the café. As we left the carpark, I held Chloe's hand and headed towards the café to meet Peter. Strolling through the park, we seemed surrounded by happy families walking together, riding on bikes, or having a picnic.

Looking to my right, I was drawn to a young couple who were sound asleep under a tree. He was lying on his back, and she was lying on his chest, nestled into him while he had his hand protectively on the small of her back. *I thought to myself that pure, deep, unconditional young love is just so beautiful.* I wondered how relationships that started this way could evolve into the destructive state that required lawyers like me to step in to unravel them.

I suddenly felt Chloe pull my arm, and I realised she had seen her father standing in front of the restaurant. She ran towards him and hugged him. I watched them, wishing I could turn back time so that their lives could be as they were before Anthony reappeared in Peter's life.

As I approached Peter, he stared directly at me, his eyes begging and pleading for forgiveness. I smiled as always, and we walked into the restaurant to sit for lunch. Anyone looking at us would have thought we were just another happy family having lunch in the restaurant. I felt like I had suddenly become one of the people I disliked, the parent playing the role of being happy; to keep the peace and family lifestyle intact.

Peter told me that he had been regularly attending a psychiatrist. We had also been going to counselling together to help us co-parent Chloe. The more I learned about Peter's childhood, which led to his relationship with Anthony, the more I wished I didn't know. His childhood relationship with Peter had more twists, turns, and complications than a twisted root growing in a drainage pipe. I tried to remain calm whilst Peter explained what had happened between them during counselling. But I could not control the devasting rage I felt when he discussed it, to the point where I had to leave the room before I became apoplectic. How could anyone, even a teenager, regard that conduct as normal? I asked myself.

I watched Chloe and Peter, and they were animated in their discussion about Chloe's week at school. I looked around the restaurant from time to time to see if I recognised anyone, but to my relief, I did not. Although these lunches were always trying, being in such a tranquil, happy environment made it easier for all of us. I reminded myself that a change of scenery and seeing that everyday family life existed for most people was good for me.

As we got to Chloe's favourite part of lunch, dessert, she excitedly went through the choices on the menu with her father. The close bond between them was evident. At times I felt guilty about this. Peter had spent more time with Chloe in the early years of our marriage, from when Chloe was a baby until she went to preschool, as the stay-at-home parent. He had been the obvious choice between us. His income wasn't even a quarter of mine then, and he enjoyed staying home. The reality was that Peter knew that it hurt me when he said it. I did not enjoy being a mother to a baby. Whether it was the baby's total dependence on me, the lack of mental stimulation, and/or my guilt at not being at work, I was not good at it.

When the time came for lunch to end, I could never tell who was the saddest, Chloe or Peter. They were both reluctant to leave. At times like this, I felt I was the only adult in the family. Peter would have let the lunch drag onto dinner and then breakfast the next day if he had his way. "We need to go soon," I said to Chloe and Peter as I handed my credit card to the waiter to pay the bill.

"I thought this week was my week to pay," Peter said as he looked at me despondently. He had accused me several times at counselling that I had emasculated him by taking control all the time, like when I paid the bills at restaurants. I could still not see how this made any difference when I paid his credit card bills, but the counsellor did.

"Sorry Peter, I promise, next time it's yours," I said, as the waitress brought the card machine to the table.

As we walked out of the restaurant and back to our cars, Chloe ran towards a group of children standing at the pond's edge and said, "Mummy, look at the mummy swan with her babies." Chloe's face lit up when she was around animals. It reminded me that I needed to take her to see Hillary soon.

As we walked to catch up to Chloe, Peter said, "Sarah, I was waiting for the right time, but I need to tell you something without Chloe hearing." We both looked at Chloe, about twenty metres in front of us, standing with a group of little girls cooing over the baby swans.

I walked over to Chloe quickly and said to her, "I will just be over there sitting on the bench talking to Daddy and watching you, darling." Chloe nodded but did not look away from the pond. I walked back towards Peter and sat down. "What is it?"

"The police have called me to come in and see them. Anthony has officially made complaints, and they are investigating them. I have arranged for one of my barrister friends to go with me to see them tomorrow, but I wanted to let you know."

Although I knew Anthony was angry at Peter because of the letter he had sent me with the photos of them together on the day he was convicted, this still came as a shock. "Are you concerned about this?" I asked him.

"Of course, I am. Anthony is an angry man, caged in prison, trying to hurt anyone he can. The police must investigate all allegations, even ones fabricated by a convicted criminal with nothing better to do in jail."

I stared at Chloe, who was innocently watching the baby swans. I did not want her to experience her father going through a criminal court case. As Peter saw the look on my face, he touched my arm and said, "I'm so sorry."

I inadvertently flinched. I looked at Peter and then started to walk away, calling out to Chloe, "We need to go home now, darling." Chloe recognised my voice, turned around and obediently walked back towards me. I said to her, "Give your dad a hug goodbye."

I took Chloe's hand, and we walked back to my car without looking back at Peter. I didn't trust Peter, and I did not trust Anthony. Why could the two of them not sort out their adolescent unfinished business? Why did they have to involve everyone?

Driving home, I felt nauseated. As I watched Chloe sitting happily in the car's back seat with her headphones on, I wondered what I should do. I needed to get over my anger at what should be and get on with making things work the best they could for us.

As I pondered my options, I felt Peter didn't deserve my help. Feeling confused, I thought I should get some advice. I would call Howard, and then Hillary. Having Hillary now in my life for emotional support, made me feel like I had a mother again.

As soon as we arrived home, to Chloe's delight, I put a movie on TV for her and went into my study to call Rupert.

"Hi Sarah, it's not like you to call me on a Sunday. What's up?" he said.

"Peter told me that the police want to interview him. Anthony has made some allegations against him and…"

Rupert interrupted me, "Sarah, before you say anything more to me or anyone, I want you to think about where you stand in this situation. If he is charged, the police will want to talk to you. You are his ex-wife and the mother of his child. What you have to say is important to Peter. It would help if you thought about how this will affect you and Chloe first and how it affects Peter last. "

"What do I do, Rupert?"

"When in doubt, say nothing, Sarah. If they contact you, you contact me and say nothing until we discuss it first. I am sorry to say this, but it is in your best interest that I act for you and not Peter. I could not act for both of you as my position would be conflicted."

"What do you think will happen now?"

"Anthony must have some evidence to back up his allegations if the police are investigating them. Do you have any idea what they are?"

"Yes, I do. Anthony had a letter with photographs delivered to my office the same day he was convicted. The letter contained information that Peter had a relationship with him from the age of twelve, at his home, over several months."

"Did you ask Peter about this?"

"Yes, and we are going to counselling to deal with it."

"You know the prosecution will subpoena all of that if they find out about it?"

"I do now."

"Please have the letter and photos delivered to my office tomorrow morning. I don't want them in your possession."

"I will have Kate do that first thing."

"I will try to find out what I can, Sarah, but my interests are to protect you and that's even at the expense of Peter."

"Thank you, Rupert. Sorry to do this to you."

"I will let you know what I find out."

Poor Chloe," Sarah said.

"She has you, Sarah, so she will be ok. Leave this with me for now. Don't beat yourself up: most importantly, do not call Peter."

"I know you are right. I will leave this with you."

"Just changing the subject, I saw your client Geoffrey Pemberton yesterday. He asked about you and said he was going to call you."

"Really? That's all I need."

"I thought you would feel that way. That's why I wanted to give you the heads-up before he contacted you."

"Is he involved in another situation involving a girlfriend who died accidentally?"

"No, it's nothing like that. He got a few too many speeding fines and has lost all his points. It's just a traffic appeal this time."

"Well, there are small mercies. How did I come up in your conversation, pray tell?"

"He just asked how you are. He also asked if you were still single."

"You didn›t tell him I was, did you?"

"He is only human, Sarah. Anyway, I have got to go, but call me if you need me."

The call to Rupert had made me feel more anxious. All I needed now was Geoffrey Pemberton stalking me again. I called Hillary and asked if I could quickly visit her after work tomorrow. She told me that she would love to see me.

As Chloe was happily doing her homework, I went into my study to email Kate to arrange the delivery of Anthony's letter to Rupert's office in the morning. As soon as I turned on my computer screen, several urgent emails appeared, making me smile. Chloe walked into my office and asked me, "Why are you smiling, mummy? What's funny?"

I hadn't noticed that Chloe had walked into the room. I looked up at her and said, "Hello, darling. I am smiling because it's funny how everyone sends me emails on Sunday for my urgent attention and expects me to be working on a weekend."

"But you always work on weekends, Mummy. You work every day," Chloe replied.

"Do I really?" I replied to Chloe.

Chloe genuinely looked confused as she replied, "Yes, Mummy. You work every day."

"Give me a hug, darling," I said. "I do work every day, and I am so grateful that is ok with you."

"Why would it not be Mummy? That is what you do?"

"It›s definitely ice cream time," I said as I took her hand and we walked towards the kitchen.

Emma

Chapter 7

Even though it was 7 am on the weekend, I was in bed alone. My resentment grew as I stared at the other side of my bed, looking at where my husband should be and where he was spending less and less time. I loved him, but I had given up everything for him, and he was still living his life as though nothing had changed after our marriage and our pregnancy.

It was impossible to not feel rejected when my husband chose to leave me in bed at 5 am every morning to go to the gym without fail. I had begged him yesterday morning to delay his training until later on weekends. But he was adamant that his 5 am training regime was essential to his daily routine. Clearly, it was much more important to him than me.

More and more frequently I found myself bursting into tears without warning. I was unsure if it was my pregnancy making me feel so emotional or the realisation that married life was not what I thought it would be. I knew I should be happy: I was married to a man who loved me. We had a beautiful home and we were financially secure. I was pregnant with our first child. *Why wasn't I happy?* I would question myself repeatedly.

Knowing that wallowing in misery would only make me feel worse, I picked up my mobile phone. I called my best Sofia, who, to my relief, answered quickly. "Hi, can you please come over? I'm feeling emotional again. I don't know if this is because of the baby hormones, but I can't stop crying."

"Emma, you need to pull yourself together and do it quickly. You decided to marry Bruce and knew what you were getting into. Life will be lonely at times, stressful and sometimes even confusing – but you knew all of this. I warned you. In fact, we all warned you, but you fell in love, and we understood that. We will go through this again, but the reality is that you are married to a difficult man who is either wonderful to you or a nightmare."

I started crying as I listened to her. She then said, "Look honey, you are pregnant and full of hormones causing you to feel more emotional than normal while you try and navigate your new life. I'm sorry."

"I am trying, Sofia."

"I know you are struggling because this is a huge change for you."

"Is that it? You really believe that?"

"Honey, your new life is a life that most other women dream of. You married the love of your life, live in a beautiful home, are pregnant, and have help to cook and clean for you. You must adjust to all the changes you have been through, from a successful businesswoman to a devoted wife."

"I wish I was adjusting better than I am and more quickly."

"Emma, promise me that you will not tell anyone else but me that you are unhappy. You must look and act to everyone else as though you are the happy princess everyone thinks you are, or they will tell Bruce, and he will react badly. He thinks what he has given you would make any woman happy. Get dressed, and I will pick you up to go to lunch and waft around the shops. That's what a wife like you is supposed to do when she needs cheering up."

I knew she was right. No one else would understand that I wanted to go into my kitchen and make some toast with vegemite and a cup of tea instead of having a housekeeper waiting to make my breakfast. No one else would understand that I wanted to go to work like I had done for the last 12 years in a business I had created and loved. I missed my clients and my staff. I missed the happy atmosphere at my salon. I missed being wanted like Bruce used to want me.

I said to her, "You are right. You are always right. I'll stop feeling sorry for myself and pull myself together, and I'll get ready."

Sofia sighed with relief and said, "I have been worried about you, Emma. Giving up your career and being a full-time wife is difficult for you. Still, Bruce does need you and being his wife and the mother of his children will be your biggest achievement."

"You are right, and you always help me to see everything in the right way when I lose sight of things. I love you for that."

After hanging up the phone from Sofia, I jumped into the shower to get ready. Sofia arrived an hour later, and I was ready as promised. I felt normal again, to my relief. As I got into Sofia's car, I knew I had recovered. As usual, we would have a fun day, with Sophia enticing me to buy designer-label clothing, shoes, and handbags.

"So, where should we go for lunch, babe? I was thinking of the champagne and oyster bar at David Jones, so we can go to the designer floor straight after," Sofia said as I got in.

"Great idea. I have got to meet Bruce tonight for dinner on a client's boat, and I can't fit into any of my clothes. I'm only three months pregnant now, but I'm already showing. Look at my tummy!"

"What tummy?" Sofia said. "You can't see a thing! But then again, what a great excuse. Yep, huge tummy it is. It would help if you had something fabulous to wear tonight. You need to keep the romance in the air, honey; even when you are pregnant, you can't drop the ball. We will also need to get you booked in for hair and makeup. If this is a business dinner, then there is no excuse that you feel bad about charging it to Bruce's credit card."

After settling into the restaurant and enjoying our oysters and champagne at lunch, Sofia took me shopping. We spent hours choosing a new outfit for me to wear to dinner. Sofia was relieved I was not protesting her suggestions as being too expensive. She knew that Bruce wanted me to look fabulous, and today I would let her do her best to make sure I did.

While trying on clothes, Sofia made a hair and makeup appointment for me. After I left the store, I had my hair and makeup done, and I felt beautiful for the first time in a long while. When we arrived at my house, I got out of the car with all my shopping bags and said to Sofia, "I could not have done that by myself today. You picked me up, lifted me up, and made me happy again. Thank you. You know I love you."

"That's what friends are for, darling. You look beautiful. Have a great night and call me in the morning to tell me how wonderful Bruce said you looked."

Sarah

Chapter 8

As I was driving to Hillary's home in Bowral, I was surprised at how happy it made me feel to be seeing her. In a short period of time she had become a very important part of my life, mostly due to the fact she had been in my life without me even knowing it. When she had revealed her role in my life as the benefactor who had secretly funded my high school education, it had felt as though she had thrown me another lifeline. The look in her eyes had shown me that her role in my life had not just been an act of charity; she really cared about me.

I was surprised at how light the traffic was on my drive. When I reached the turn-off to the freeway, I pulled over and stopped the car to lower the roof on my convertible to enjoy the wind in my face and the smell of the country air as I drove the rest of the way.

Driving along the streets of Bowral, lined with magnificent trees and beautiful gardens, I drove slowly to admire the homes in the area. As I waited outside Hillary's majestic wrought iron gates to enter her property, I immediately thought of Chloe and how I would love her to see the house.

The large imposing gates that guarded Hillary's home were impressive, grand, and welcoming. The house was visible beyond the gates. A grand two-storey Victorian mansion from a bygone era. After announcing myself via the intercom, I had just enough time to admire the workmanship of the two beautiful peacocks on each side of the gates, cast in iron, before the gates opened to allow me to drive in.

The driveway wound around a large pond with water lilies and a prominent stone water feature. The pond was framed by blossoming pink crab apple and crepe myrtle trees with coloured flowers. I stopped my car next to the largest tree to enjoy the scent of the blossoms. As I looked at the tree, I was surprised by the unusually bright shade of pink flowers. They were bright fuchsia, and when I saw so many flowers had fallen to the ground, I got out of my car and quickly picked up a handful to take with me to give to Hillary.

As I drove further along, flowering rose bushes lined each side of the driveway until I reached the garden surrounding the house. The last time I visited Hillary, she had told me that she had started her garden after losing her daughter thirty years ago. Hillary said she had started slowly and methodically planting flowering plants around the house and then a vegetable patch. The garden soon turned into a passion, and she realised in time that gardening was fulfilling her need to nurture while allowing herself to grieve the loss of her daughter. With that in mind, she created the pond and installed the fountain with a memorial garden of pink flowering trees and shrubs.

Hillary told me she often sat on the garden bench inside the open shaded pergola in the front yard. Bordering the front of the house, she planted crepe myrtles, tea olives, boxwood, and nandina. On the south side of the garden, Hillary grew her cutting flowers to ensure her home would always be filled with fresh flowers of peonies, gerberas, daisies, weigela, wisteria and verbena. She planted her vegetable garden on the north side, which supplied her kitchen daily.

As I pulled up to the front of the house, I saw Hillary sitting on the veranda. As soon as she saw me, she smiled and waved. I reached over to my passenger seat to pick up the pink crepe myrtle flowers that I had collected and walked up the stairs. I placed the flowers on the table before her as I sat down. She immediately picked one of them up to smell it. "Aren't they the most divine colour," she said as she placed the flowers back down with the others on the table.

"Yes, they are. That's why I stopped to pick them up. The tree was ablaze with colour, and some flowers had fallen and lined the road beautifully as I drove by. It was just the most stunning picture as I drove in."

"I am really touched that you did that my dear," Hillary replied. "I have been trying different fertilisers with my gardeners and I think we have created the perfect colour this year."

Hillary poured us both a cup of tea. She then handed me the delicate milk jug as she said, "I am always too heavy-handed with my milk pouring. Better if you do it yourself, darling."

I smiled as I watched Hillary sipping her tea while marvelling at her flowers. She was a woman of extraordinary achievements, having been a Queen's Counsel before becoming a Judge of the Supreme Court of New South Wales. But here she was, clearly enjoying the simple things in life, having a cup of tea on her veranda and discussing her perfectly coloured fragrant crepe myrtle flowers.

I said to Hillary, "Every time I am here, a peace transcends upon me that I cannot describe. It starts almost immediately after I enter your gates."

"I'm so glad you came to see me, Sarah. I always love seeing you, but what was on your mind last night when you called?"

"I'm so sorry I keep coming to you with my problems. I feel quite selfish. You have your own problems, and I keep dumping my never-ending issues onto you."

Hillary leaned back in her chair and said, "I enjoy so many things in my life, and one of them is being here for you, my dear."

"My problem is with Peter. Yesterday when we were leaving lunch, he told me that Anthony had made a complaint to the police and that they would interview him. I am not managing this at all well."

"That's come out of the blue, hasn't it?" Hillary asked.

"Yes, it has. I know it's an act of revenge by Anthony."

"We can all clearly see that. I am surprised the police are taking any action at all, surely they see it for what it is."

"The trouble is that Anthony has all the time in the world to work on the revenge he seeks against those he believes put him in jail, and Peter is the easiest victim. I should try to help him, but on the other hand, I want to stay out of it as I don't need this in any way reflecting on me. Is that selfish?"

"I can see what you are saying. If you don't help him, you feel you are letting down the father of your child, but if you do help him, you feel you're forgiving him for the hurt and pain he has caused you and Chloe?"

"That is exactly how I feel, conflicted and angry. Then I feel guilty about feeling that way."

Hillary leaned forward and touched my hand as she said, "I don't think there is any reason you need to get involved in Peter's problems right now. They are his creation, and he has legal friends to help him with that. Your only concern should be you and Chloe and how to protect the two of you while he has this battle. I think you should discuss this with your psychiatrist, Charlie and get his advice on how we work through this. There is a fine balance between protecting Chloe by not telling her everything and being dishonest by not telling her the truth. Charlie needs to help us with that advice so that we do the best thing by Chloe."

"I don't know why I always feel guilty if I don't help, Hillary."

"I know, Sarah, and that is why you need to work on that. It is an admirable quality in you, but others have abused it for too long. It is time you looked after yourself and Chloe and had some fun too. On that note, have you received any flowers lately from admirers?" Hillary asked.

I smiled, and as I did, I felt better. "Thanks for changing the subject. No, I have not received any more flowers, but thanks for asking. I am not sure what to do with that man either!"

"Enjoy his silliness. It is a much-needed distraction for you right now. Please don't take it seriously and enjoy it. A man being attracted to a woman and showing that by sending flowers should be appreciated, not worried about. Savor the attention while it's fun; if it ceases being fun, you stop it. Obviously, Phil is not going to be the one for you, but he certainly sounds as though he will be entertaining for a while. I enjoy waiting to hear what he will do next to try and impress you."

"You are right. I am taking this all too seriously. I will lighten up and see what Phil has next up his sleeve. One thing is for sure, whatever Phil does is not boring."

"It's when you get to my age Sarah you realise that for way too long in your life, you took things far too seriously. If you do that, you can miss enjoying things that come up spontaneously just because it is fun. Embrace what life gives you; you will always work out what you should keep and let go of."

"Do you have regrets about anyone in your life?"

Hillary smiled as she sat back in her chair and said, "I do have a couple. I will tell you about both of them when you have time."

"Both of them!" Sarah exclaimed. "Now, I really need to hear about that."

The time passed quickly as we had been deep in conversation. I realised that I had to leave shortly, and said to Hillary, "I can't believe we have been chatting for over two hours."

Hillary looked at her watch in disbelief. "I can't believe it either."

"Thank you for the tea and your advice. I almost feel normal again after talking to you."

"You are always welcome. I am always happy when I see you. Please give Chloe a big hug from me."

"I will call her as soon as I get in the car. She always says that I look happy when I talk about you and I have promised her that I am going to bring her to meet you very soon."

"That's so sweet, I can't wait to meet Chloe. Now you drive safely," Hillary said.

I hugged Hillary and then walked down the stairs towards my car. I looked back and saw that she walked inside the house. As soon as I got in my car, I wished I didn't have to leave. I drove slowly down the driveway, enveloped in the garden's serenity and the smell of spring in the air.

Even though I had only recently become friends with Hillary, I felt like I had known her all my life. Apart from Hillary, I had little memory of my parents and had always been a loner. My attempt at marriage with Peter had been a disaster, and apart from my work and Chloe, I did not allow much more into my life.

I was overwhelmed when I discovered that Hillary had been my secret sponsor for boarding school. During all those years, Hillary had sponsored many girls, expecting nothing in return, which inspired me to do the same thing, starting with Jessica. I had already learned so much from Hillary, and I just hoped to learn so much more before losing her to her illness.

My mobile rang as I exited the gates, jolting me out of my thoughts. It was Phil calling again. I answered, and he said, "Hi Sarah, how was your friend?"

"She is well, thanks. I am just leaving her house."

"Before you cut me off like you usually do, I wanted to ask you if you got my email about the ball?"

"Sorry if you felt I cut you off. I was going to call you back very shortly. I don't recall seeing an email about the ball, but I will check as soon as I get home."

"When I saw how amazing the event was going to be from the invitation, I wanted to send it to you straight away. I knew you were busy, but I thought it was an event that you and your staff might enjoy."

Phil sounded contrite as he bumbled his way through his apology. I suddenly felt terrible for being so curt with my response and said to him, "I am excited about the ball. I was visiting a friend and was distracted by a couple of things. As soon as I get home, I will have a look at the invitation."

"Thanks. I also copied Kate. I hope you don't mind. It was just a habit, as I did with all my emails to your office when you acted for me."

"Well, if you have emailed Kate too, then as soon as I arrive at the office in the morning, I will no doubt hear about it. Kate loves attending functions and has already told me this ball is a great charity function and is in the news every year." I smiled as I realised Phil clearly had no idea that Kate did not like him.

Phil said, "Well, I wouldn't invite you to anything I didn't think you and your staff would not enjoy. It will be a fun night."

"I am sure it will be."

"Drive safely and let me know what you and Kate think of the invitation. I'll let you go; Goodnight." Phil said as he ended the call.

I felt relieved that the call had ended on a lighter note than it had started. I was still unsure whether it was a romantic gesture on Phil's part, but then I remembered that I had agreed with Hillary to stop worrying about Phil's attempts to woo me and to just enjoy it. I put aside my concerns and decided to go to the ball.

It was now starting to get dark so I pulled over to the side of the road and stopped to raise the roof back onto my convertible before I continued my drive home. Whilst waiting for the roof to lower and lock back into place, I thought about the irony of Kate planning to lure Phil into a trap of revealing his true self. At the same time, she took full advantage of his generosity at a charity function. I had to wonder who would win in the Kate vs Phil battle.

Once on the freeway, I called Chloe to tell her I was on the way back and would be home for dinner.

Debbie

Chapter 9

As a working married mother, I enjoyed catching up with my girlfriends when I got the chance. I regularly had lunch with them on my monthly rostered day off. I was the only one who worked, so they fitted in with my day off and had done so for the past five years.

Today was the day that I was having lunch with my girlfriends. The rest of them went to lunch together at least once, if not more times a week, so it was not as special an event for them than it was for me. They thought I was jealous of their freedom, but I never was. I appreciated our time together and enjoyed working; the arrangement was perfect.

I loved our lunches. I would always plan our next one, and as soon as lunch ended. Sitting on the veranda of the waterfront café today, we discussed the usual topics, men, kids, and gossip. I always found discussing my friend's relationships entertaining, however today they had decided we should discuss mine, and I was not enjoying it.

The girls said to me that that over the past few months, they had noticed that I was not as happy as usual. They asked me to confess why. I knew that once the door to my suspicions was opened to my friends, there would be no turning back. I had been a co-conspirator on many occasions regarding their partners, So I knew they would feel compelled to jump into action when I told them about the nagging thoughts I was having about Jim.

The past few months had been different, and I was worried there was someone else. I had no tangible evidence; it was just a feeling or intuition which I had tried to dismiss as paranoia. Trying to dismiss my concerns by just putting them down to being over-suspicious was getting harder and harder for me. I knew it had started affecting me, and now I knew that my friends had noticed it. After a few wines and their constant prodding, I spilled it all out to them, revealing my fears and concerns. Over lunch, they devised the plan's first step to finding out what was going on with Jim, if anything.

The girls decided I should do some detective work as soon as I got home from lunch, as Jim usually got home before I did. When Jim left for work this morning, I had yet to tell him it was my flex day like I usually did. In the past few months, we weren't as communicative anymore, so I hadn't bothered.

My friends told me I should no longer ignore the signs concerning me, like why he was acting distant but happier lately. It really concerned me when Cassie said to me that her husband had complained to her only last week Jim had not been to drinks with the guys for ages, but Jim had told me for the previous few weeks when he was out, that he was going to drinks with the guys.

I had believed up until now that I had the most stable marriage of my group of friends. Although I had watched many of my friend's relationships and marriages break up, call it denial, I never thought mine would. I had dated many attractive and charismatic men before meeting Jim. Still, I married him because he seemed stable, honest, and dependable. Some of my friends had described him as dull when they first met him. But the routine and the stability in our lives were what I had longed for and loved about our marriage.

I met Jim at work ten years ago. I had been working as a local real estate agent's secretary for five years. Jim was a builder who had been looking to buy an investment property to renovate in the area. When he walked into the agency in his work clothes, I was mesmerised. I was tongue-tied when he first spoke to me, but he quickly made me feel at ease with his wicked sense of humour. I couldn't believe my luck when he told me he was single. We had connected instantly, and our phone calls grew longer and longer each time he called, and they were not just about properties. He asked me out for dinner to celebrate the purchase of his first property, and we were married a year later.

The girls pushed me to leave lunch today before Jim got home from work. With their encouragement, I got an Uber home to start my investigations. When I pulled up outside our house, I thought I saw Jim through the lounge room window. I got out of the Uber and walked up to the front door. Through the glass, I could see him. I went inside and asked him, "Why are you ironing, Jim?"

Jim looked up and was surprised by my early arrival home. He had his ear pods in his ears and had not heard me walk in.

"You startled me, Deb. What are you doing home so early?"

"Why are you ironing? You never do the ironing," I replied.

"I got home early, thought I'd help out with the laundry, saw the pile of ironing and thought I would surprise you by doing it." "The ironing," I said.

He walked to the table, picked up his car keys, headed to the front door and said to me, "I'll go pick up Ashley now from school, or will I get in trouble for that too?"

I felt terrible. I had arrived home early to sneak a look into Jim's laptop and desk and go through his jacket pockets. That's where the girls told me to look for signs that he was having an affair. They said to look for emails and receipts. But instead, I found Jim home doing some ironing to help me before he went to pick up our daughter from school. Sitting on the lounge, I wondered how I would patch things up with him when he got home with Ashley. I didn't want her to see us upset with each other.

I walked into my bedroom to get changed, and the doubts and questions kept going on in my head. I wondered if I had drunk too much wine and if that had made me more suspicious than usual. As I took off my dress and reached for my track pants, I remembered that I was supposed to go through his pants, jackets, and desk and look for receipts.

As though the devil had gotten into me, I suddenly became obsessed and went through all of Jim's jacket pockets. I found pens, coins, and parking meter receipts, but nothing incriminating. Then I looked at my dresses. They were bunched together in one section, and I would never do that. Below, my shoes had all been rearranged too. *Was I imagining this? Had Ashley been playing in there?* I asked myself.

My mobile rang, and it was Jim. "Debbie, I love you. Please don't be grumpy. I'm sorry if I sounded cross, but you startled me when I was trying to surprise you," he said.

"I love you too. I'm sorry. I drank too much at lunch and what I said just came out wrong."

"That's Ok, honey. We'll be home soon," Jim replied.

As I hung up, I felt relieved. I finished changing and tidying up my wardrobe, noticing more than ever that everything seemed out of place.

Anthony

Chapter 10

I had been sent to jail for something I was not guilty of. I had not sexually abused my stepdaughter. We had a loving relationship that some people may have found hard to understand. It was not child sexual abuse. My ex-wife had forced my stepdaughter to have me charged so that it was easier for her to take my assets and lead the life that I had given them without me. I had underestimated how clever my ex-wife was and how stupid a jury could be, the result of which was me languishing in a jail cell until I found a way out.

I was informed this morning that my psychiatrist had requested to see me today and that he was bringing someone with him. I guessed who it would be, but I wanted to stay calm in case it wasn't who I thought it was.

The correctional officers arrived at my cell to take me to the visiting room. I sat in anticipation, waiting for my visitors to be escorted in to see me. I was used to waiting now. I had lots of time to wait. It seemed to take forever, but I eventually heard the key in the door. As it opened, I saw the security guard first, then my psychiatrist, who I recognised from our online skype sessions. He was with a police officer. They walked in and introduced themselves, and we all sat at the table. The guard remained but stood in the corner of the room near the door. I was now excited that my plan had worked. With the help of my psychiatrist, the police were now seriously considering my complaints against Peter.

"It's good to see you in person, Anthony," my psychiatrist said as he reached out to shake my hand.

"I am so happy to finally meet you too. I can't thank you enough, Sam. You have taken the time to help me with my case and come in and see me today. I am very grateful."

Sam introduced the police officer who was with him, Sergeant Thommeny. She shook my hand before saying to me, "Hi, Anthony, Sam came to see me to discuss your situation, and he asked me to come and see you in person. I have a copy of the statement you drafted with Sam." She then placed a typed written statement on the table in front of me.

Then she said to me, "The allegations made in the statement are very serious. Before I proceed any further, are the contents of that statement true and correct per your recollection?" she said.

"Yes, they are," I replied.

"I need to ask you why you are making these allegations now, almost thirty years after they happened and while you are in jail?"

I knew that the police were going to ask me that question. I had practised the interview online with Sam several times, so I appeared calm when I replied, "Because I was a child when it happened. I had not even realised at the time that what we had been doing was wrong. It was not until I started seeing a psychiatrist, Sam, that I was told that as a twelve-year-old child, I was too young to consent to what I had been doing with an older boy who was 19 at the time."

Sergeant Thommeny made notes as I spoke. She said, "You mention your sister in your statement. I will need to contact her to speak to her. Are you ok with that?"

"Yes, but as I said in my statement, she didn't know what Peter and I had done. I didn't tell her about it until last year."

"I understand that. But she can confirm the circumstances that put you and Peter together in the same house and room when the offences occurred. The evidence from her can help to corroborate your facts." *That had been the reason I had included my sister in the statement,* I thought to myself. "I have written down her contact details for you," I said as I slid the piece of paper across the table."

"Do you think there is enough in my statement to charge Peter?" I asked.

"Anthony, I am here so we can work out what evidence we have and if that is enough for us to charge Peter with. I need to go through every paragraph of this long statement with you. Then, I will need to speak to Madeline and then Peter. After that, we will decide whether we have enough to charge him."

I wanted more than anything to be there when Peter was questioned. I wanted to see how he would manage being treated like a criminal by the police, just like when they looked at me as if I was a monster when the police questioned me about the allegations Jessica had made. What had happened between Jessica and me had been nothing more than what had happened between Anthony and me. Why shouldn't Peter be, too, if I was put in jail for it?

I picked up the copy of the statement handed to me and said, "Ok, let's start then. I am ready to go through it with you."

Sam looked at the security officer standing at the door and said to him, "Do you have to stay and listen to all of this?"

"There is nothing I haven't heard, Doc. I am required to stay present the whole time," he said.

Sergeant Thommeny picked up her copy of the statement, asking me if I would like a copy. I indicated that I would, and we painstakingly went through the statement sentence by sentence. When we had finished two hours later, Sam asked the Sergeant, "Now do you think there is enough there for you to charge Peter?'

Sergeant Thommeny sat back in her chair, shuffled her notes together and then looked up at me before responding. "I am deeply sorry for what you have been through, Anthony. Your statement is compelling, and if we speak to your sister and she can collaborate the circumstances of when this occurred, I believe we may have enough to take this investigation further. Historical charges are complicated to prove, and it does not help that you are incarcerated. But we will do our best to investigate your complaint."

"That's all we can ask for," Sam replied. "Thank you for your time, Sergeant."

I wasn't as thrilled as I could be with the response from the Sergeant, but Sam had taught me the virtues of being patient. I shook the Sergeant's hand and thanked her for her time as she stood up to leave.

The security guard opened the door to show them out of the room. As he was leaving, Sam touched me gently on the shoulder and said, "I will skype you tomorrow for our session at the usual time."

I felt a mutual attraction with Sam when he walked into the room. It was the first time that we had seen each other in person. The simple act of touching his hand had sent sparks through my body, and I felt alive again, even excited. It had been so long since I had felt this way that I was shocked.

After they left, I sat down, waiting for a guard to take me back to my cell. I smiled, wondering if I had just met the next stage of my new life. Sam knew my history and what I had been convicted for, and he had still offered to help me. I would not have to hide anything about myself or my life with Sam. If he felt the same way about me, I could be with someone who loved me, without secrets, for the first time.

Like a reflex action, my mind quickly flicked back to Peter. I was suddenly disappointed when Peter stopped visiting our home without explanation. He had never come back. I sat, staring into space with tears welling in my eyes as the security guard came back into the interview room to get me. "It didn't go well?" he asked.

"Yes, it did," Anthony replied. "My mind is just scrambled right now." "I get it," he said. "But I need to take you back to your cell now." I got up, and he cuffed me to walk me back to my cell.

Sarah

Chapter 11

The drive home from Hillary's house went quickly. I chatted to Chloe on the phone the entire time about what she and Maria, our housekeeper, were making for dinner tonight. She had squealed with delight when I said I had just pulled into our building and would be upstairs in a moment.

When I walked into our unit, I could smell the delicious aromas of dinner baking in the oven. Chloe ran to me and excitedly hugged me as she talked about the meal she had helped prepare. She had even set the table for us, complete with candles. As Maria started to walk towards the table, I watched Chloe run to Maria to help her. I realised how lucky I was to have such a wonderful woman help me with Chloe. Maria hugged Chloe before she said to me, "Enjoy your dinner. I can't wait to see you in the morning to get a review of our creations."

"It all looks amazing, Maria. You and Chloe have done a super job. I feel very spoilt. Thank you."

After dinner, I helped Chloe with her homework before putting her to bed. I then went to my study to check my emails, and thoughts of Peter crept back into my mind. I worked until 3 am, trying to distract myself unsuccessfully from the position he had placed us all in.

Unable to sleep, I lay in bed, wide awake. By 6 am, frustrated from insomnia, I was even more anxious than the night before. I did not want to call Hillary when I felt so agitated, so as Hillary had suggested yesterday, I called my psychiatrist, Charlie. The enormity of what Peter had said to me and how it could affect Chloe consumed me. I was relieved when Charlie answered quickly, and I said, "I am sorry to call so early, Charlie, but I saw Peter yesterday, and he told me the police are going to question him about Anthony. We discussed the possibility of this happening, and I thought I would be prepared, but I am not. I couldn't sleep, and I don't know how I can ever explain this to Chloe when I don't understand it myself."

In Charlie's calm and soothing voice, he said, "Remember what we discussed, Sarah. This is not your fault, and you cannot control this. These events happened long ago; before you met Peter. You had no idea about these events in his childhood. We need to deal with this as the issues arise, and we will handle them. It may sometimes be hard to cope with, but you will."

"But Charlie, I am not coping. I feel lightheaded whenever I try to stand up, as if I might faint. I must get ready to go to the office, but I can't. I don't know what's wrong with me. My emotions are so extreme that they are affecting me physically, and I need to understand how this happens and how I can control it."

"Sarah, you need to breathe deeply and slow down. Remember what we did in our sessions; breathe slowly and deeply. Remember, we discussed that this is what happens when you get emotional. Your self-protection mechanism slows down your blood pressure so that when you feel faint, stop, and lie down. Listen to your body. Once you stop thinking and panicking, you will calm down."

I started to take deep breaths as Charlie continued to speak to me. "I can hear you, Sarah, that's right, Sarah, breathe in slowly and then exhale slowly. I will wait and I will not speak for a little while until you feel calmer. When you do, let me know."

After only a couple of minutes, I said to Charlie, "I don't know how that works, but it does. I feel so odd when I am like this. I am so embarrassed."

"Please don't feel embarrassed. I have the same reaction to stress, Sarah. That's how I know how you feel."

"Really? I wouldn't wish these feelings on anyone else. I'm sorry."

"It started for me when I was a child, and I went to many school counsellors who thought I was acting when I said I felt dizzy and often fainted. I lost count of the times I was sent to the hospital for brain scans and nerve testing. Eventually, after the tests showed nothing, the psychiatrists told my mother that they thought I was just attention seeking."

"That's just awful. Do you know what triggered it for you?"

"It started after my mother married my stepfather. From that moment, she left my life, and I started to feel unwell."

"She left your life?"

"My mother fell in love and was obsessed with her new husband. Until he came into her life, she had been struggling financially and after she married him, that all changed. She married a very wealthy man, and as a result, we moved into his beautiful home. At first, we both thought it was like a dream that had come true. I had my own bedroom, and Mum had the help of a full-time housekeeper. But it soon became my worst nightmare."

"How did it go wrong?"

"There is always a price to pay. After the wedding, they went away on their honeymoon for six weeks. Mum and I had never been separated before this; being apart for that long was devastating. I counted every day until she got home, but they went away again and then again as soon as she came home."

"Was your mum upset having to leave you all the time?"

"I don't know who cried more the first time she went on her honeymoon – me or her. But after that, when they went away – sometimes for months – she seemed to have adjusted. My stepfather would stand by looking incredibly pleased with himself each time they said goodbye to me."

"Were you scared when she was gone?"

"I was more heartbroken than scared. I never knew my father, so my mum was all I had. I was too young to understand that my mum was finding it hard to cope financially, so when she found a man who married her and offered to take care of her and me, she thought she was doing the best for us."

"That is so sad. Who took care of you while she was away?"

"They left me at home with a series of housekeepers. My stepfather justified the travelling by saying he was working and needed Mum. When I told him I needed her too, he laughed at me and said, "When you pay the bills, you get a say if she stays with you or me.""

"What a mean man."

"I was upset that my mother chose him over me and that he ignored my love for my mother. In my first year of psychology, I studied that this is normal in males. They are bred to dominate, alienate, and even kill the offspring that are not theirs so that the female wants to breed with them."

"Did you say anything to your mum about how much you missed her because she was away so much?"

"Yes, of course I did. She told me that I was lucky to live in a comfortable home with housekeepers, instead of being sent to boarding school like many other kids and how generous it was of my stepfather to do that for us. I couldn't believe that I was speaking to the same woman. Somehow, he had changed her into someone I now didn't know anymore and who didn't love me."

"You really believe that she stopped loving you?"

"Sarah, there was my mum and me for the first ten years of my life, and then she was gone. I no longer mattered. I was just a problem dealt with by housekeepers now."

"And your father?"

"Mum told me he had been a mistake that she would never talk about. I never found out who he was."

"Did you try to find him?"

"No. I had had enough rejection by then. If he hadn't enquired about me, I figured, why would I try to find out about him."

"Did you ever get close to one of the housekeepers?"

"Not really. I didn't want to get close to anyone in case they went away too. Of course, that resulted in me developing issues, which is why I became a psychiatrist after getting therapy for years without it helping. I eventually found a psychiatrist in my late teens who worked out the problem. I was so grateful for his concern and commitment to helping me, that I decided that I wanted to study psychology to help others who had felt as abandoned as I had."

"I didn't know that you had gone through all of this. I am so sorry."

"Is your Mum still alive?"

"Yes, she is. They live close by, but I rarely see her, and she never calls me anymore."

"Do you see or hear from your stepfather?"

"Never. I refer to him as "him", and I will never give him a name because he doesn't deserve one."

"When did you discover your symptoms were linked to your trauma?"

"After working with my last psychiatrist. He specialised in childhood trauma. He told me that our minds would only let us deal with what we can cope with. When it gets too much, we learn to stop the pain. With you and I, we go faint, which makes us stop thinking and stop doing. We are forced to stop and thus calm down. Our minds go blank, and we stop thinking until we can cope with it again. Our minds are amazing when we think about it and understand it."

"That makes so much sense. I hope I haven't caused you any pain by reliving your childhood. I am sorry that happened to you."

"I'm grateful I can help you when you are in pain, Sarah. That is what I wanted to do with my life after I realised what effect he had on me and would have continued to have had on me had I not been helped."

"Charlie, you help me more than you could know."

"That's what makes me love my job. I have you booked in later this week but let me know if you need to come in earlier."

"I will. Thank you. I feel so much better now."

"I am always here for you, Sarah. Remember that."

"Thanks, Charlie."

Sarah

Chapter 12

I had just walked into my office when my secretary, Kate, walked in with my coffee. As she placed on it on my desk, she said to me, "Your new client, Con Habib is here early. I will take him into the Conference Room and get him settled until you are ready."

After quickly checking my emails and messages, I walked into the conference room as Kate was pouring a glass of water for Con. He stood up immediately to greet me. This was the first time we had met, and he was staring at me intently as I introduced myself to him. As he sat down, he seemed to collapse into his chair as though life had broken him. As he placed his large, weathered hands on the table, I could tell he did not have an office job. I could also tell he was proud, neatly dressed, and well-groomed. His head was bowed, and he seemed hesitant to speak.

I had been through this with many clients, and I knew to wait until the wave of anguish had passed before I spoke to him. Con composed himself, sat straight, and looked up at me. Suddenly something in his eyes changed. The sadness had left and been replaced by a steely seething resilience that pierced right through him as he said, "I am sorry about that. I am not myself lately."

"I completely understand. Please take your time. I am here to help you when you are ready."

"My wife has left our daughters and me. She has gone with another man and has told me our marriage is over. She wants me to sell our home so that we both share the money.'" He then paused, and I could see the emotional distress he was going through.

After a moment, he said, "My wife told me that she had seen a lawyer who told her she would get at least half of the house and everything else I own in our divorce. When I told her that could not be right as the house was in my name, she told me her lawyer said that did not matter. She then handed me this letter from her lawyer, which lists everything I own, including my home and superannuation. The letter says that because we are now separated, the house should be put up for sale. Why is she saying these crazy things? How can she get anything in my name and which I paid for?"

"Can I please see the letter, Con?" I asked.

Con handed the letter to me. I could feel his eyes intently upon me as I read through it. When I had finished, I looked up at him and said, "Con, do you agree with the list of your assets and the values in this letter?"

"I do not agree with the values, but the list of what I own is right."

"Can you please tell me about your relationship with your wife, Con? When you met and when you were married and all about your daughters."

"We married thirty-five years ago when I was thirty, and my wife was eighteen. We have three girls who are twenty-three, twenty-five and twenty-seven. They still live at home because they are not yet married. When we married, we had nothing, and I have worked all my life for my wife and my children to give them a good life. We are a happy family. My wife was a good wife who cooked good family meals every day and cared for our daughters and our home. We had nice holidays, and the girls had everything they wanted, nice clothes and shoes. I am a good man and father."

I could see that the marriage ending was still a shock to Con. I asked him, "So, you did not see any signs that your wife had been unhappy and wanted to separate?"

Con raised his head in indignation as he replied, "No, how could I know she was unhappy when she wanted for nothing? I took care of her and my daughters like they were princesses, and now she tells me that I was never home, so she got lonely and depressed. Because of this, her friends told her to do charity work with them. They are volunteer support staff at the hospital. She started to help a man whose wife died by looking after his young children. She said they have grown close and fallen in love over the past few months and that she wants to be with him."

Con then paused, and I could see he was still in shock by the situation he had been placed in. I admired his wife for being honest about what had happened. Many people were not and hid their new love, giving reasons for the separation as a midlife crisis or menopause, believing the lie was easier for the other person to manage than the truth.

Con said, "She told me that with him, she feels like an equal, not just a wife. My daughters will not speak to her. They are hurt and angry that she wants to leave us."

"I'm sorry they are feeling hurt and angry. This is never easy for children caught in their parents' separation."

"I need you to write her a letter to tell her that she is wrong. She must know that the law cannot give her the right to claim half of what I own and my home."

I knew my response would disappoint Con, but I also knew that the sooner he knew it, the sooner he could accept it. I said, "I would have to go into this in further detail, but right now, from what you have said to me, your wife will have the right to a reasonable percentage of the assets that you own. At this stage, 50 per cent does not sound out of the question."

Con stood up and paced the room, saying, "I will tell you now, I will not sell my daughter's home to give half to my wife so she can live with another man. My daughters do not deserve to lose their homes because of their mother's insanity. I am now sixty-five years old, and I will never be able to make this money back and give my daughters the home they have now and support them. I am retired. I love my wife and have asked her to stop this craziness."

I felt for Con. He had an old-fashioned outlook and values. The reality of how he stood legally was shocking and upsetting to him. I said to him, "Con, I know you are upset, but you made your home in Australia with your family, and because of that, you are governed by the laws here. I am sorry to upset you with this information. I suggest I speak to your wife's lawyers, who wrote this letter, and then we meet again after seeing what I can do for you?"

Con replied, "She says my daughters are old enough to move out of our home now. This man has poisoned her mind and stolen her from us to help him look after his children and take my money. He tells her she is young and entitled to a happy life when she is fifty-three. I don't know my wife anymore. How does someone change after thirty-five years of marriage and become another person? Her children do not even know her. She is scaring them with all this talk."

"Your children may be upset with your wife, but she is their mother, and they need her. This is a difficult situation and one that would benefit from professional counselling to help you and your family to understand what has happened and to adjust to it."

"Yes, we need help. My wife needs to stop being so crazy and be told to come home and be with her family. She must care for her children, not this other man's children."

"That's not exactly what I meant. I suggested counselling for you and your girls to help you and your children deal with this situation."

"I will not give my wife what she wants. She has raised her daughters to be women with her beliefs, and now she tells them their beliefs are wrong and to become a western woman because she has found that life is better. She cannot do this because it suits her now."

"I'm sorry Con, I cannot say anything to make you feel better. There are not two sets of laws for people of your faith and western families in this country. I understand how you feel, but legally I cannot change what your wife is entitled to. Are you sure I am the right person to act for you?"

"Yes, you are, because I heard from my friends you can help me to stop her from getting my money. You can stop her from selling the house and my assets until a court hearing, which can take years. At that time, she will see she is wrong. The man may leave her because she has yet to get the money he wants. That is what you can do for me."

I never liked it when my clients wanted to use the family law system to delay or complicate resolving their family law matters. But it was my job to do what was in my client's best interests. I said to him, "I can certainly help delay selling the house for you. You can take your matter to court and ask the judge to decide what your wife is entitled to if you cannot accept my advice. It could cost you hundreds of thousands of dollars, be very stressful for you, your wife, and your children, and take up to three years before we get to a hearing. I never recommend that course of conduct as, in the end, it is more destructive than productive to both parties, but ultimately the choice is yours."

"That is what I want. I want this to take time, so my wife can come to her senses. In time she will stop this insanity and come home to us."

I was surprised. Although it was not the first time a client had told me they would prefer to spend money litigating, it was the first time I had a client prefer to drag the matter out so that their ex would return to them. I was not a person who engaged in litigation for reasons other than what I thought was in my client's best interests, so considering acting on Con's behalf was something that I would have to think about. I saw that he needed time to accept his legal position. For now, I agreed to act for him in the hope that I could eventually get him to see that his proposal was not a sensible solution to his problem.

I stood up and said, "I will do my best for you. But I also have a duty to the court. If you are willing to accept my advice to guide you on how I think you should best run your case, then I can act for you. If you stop accepting my advice, then I will need to stop acting for you."

Con looked confused as he replied, "So, you will act for me, and we will not agree to my home being sold, as she is asking now? Is that right?"

"Yes, you have the right to not agree to your wife's request that the home is sold immediately. Ultimately though, there will need to be a division of the assets of your marriage, and your wife will seek a percentage of the assets, or payment instead."

Con sat stiffly in his chair as he said, "I understand. I see that you are saying that in the end, I will have to pay her some money if she does not come home to us."

"Yes, that is right," I said, relieved Con had seemed to come to terms with the situation. I then said, "I will write a letter to your wife's lawyers, which I will send by email today in response to them. After receiving that, they will know that you have a lawyer acting for you, and they will correspond with me, not directly to you anymore."

"Thank you. That is good. I know this is the right thing to do."

"Con, I will email you a copy of the letter that I will email to your wife's lawyers. I will contact you when they reply to me, or in a week, whichever is the earlier, and we will proceed from there."

Simon entered the room, and I introduced him to Mr Habib. "Con, this is Simon Hamilton, a lawyer who works with me. You will be seeing him from time to time. Simon will now go through the paperwork we are required to give to you by law to retain our firm. I must go into another meeting right now, but I will be in the office if you have any issues with the paperwork Simon is about to go through with you."

"Thank you, Sarah," Con said.

I smiled and lightly touched Mr Habib on the shoulder before leaving the room. It was only that second after it dawned on me that it was inappropriate that I had done so. I smiled, quickly left the two men, and walked back into my office before Con could comment.

Emma

Chapter 13

I now started to worry. I was dressed and ready to leave for dinner with Bruce since 6 pm. He had reminded me when he left for work this morning that he would call me by lunchtime to let me know the time that the hire car would pick me up for dinner to go on one of his client's boats. When he hadn't called by 3 pm, I called his secretary, who said that she knew nothing about the dinner arrangements; but he had left the office hours ago. It was now 7 pm, and I was convinced that something was wrong.

I called Sofia and said to her, "I'm worried about Bruce. He didn't call to let me know the time the hire car was coming to pick me up to go to dinner, and he is not answering his mobile. I don't know what to do. Should I call the police station and ask if there has been an accident?"

"Calm down, honey. I am sure there is a simple explanation. Maybe, he just got caught up in a work meeting. Have you called his secretary?"

"Of course, I called her. She said she didn't know why he hadn't called me and that he left the office hours ago. She said that she had tried calling him too all afternoon, but his phone was off."

"Is that usual? Does he normally turn his phone off?"

"Sometimes he doesn't answer calls, but his phone is usually on. I don't know why he wouldn't have called me back by now."

"I'll come now, because that's unusual. His secretary always knows everything. I will stay with you until he calls, just in case you need me," Sofia said.

"You don't need to do that. I just needed to talk to you."

"I can tell that you need me, Emma. I am on my way."

"This is out of character for him. Even his secretary is surprised. I can tell in her voice she is both annoyed and also concerned that we can't contact him."

"I am sure there is a simple explanation, but I want to be there until he comes home because I can hear the stress in your voice. Try and stay calm. Remember you are pregnant, and stress is not good for you or the baby."

"Ok. You are right."

"See you soon. Stay calm, I'm on the way," Sophia replied.

Sofia

Chapter 14

I arrived at Emma's house in 30 minutes. When Emma opened the door, I could tell she had still not heard from Bruce. It was now 8.00 pm, and it was clear that either Bruce had gone out without picking her up or he had been in an accident.

Emma sat on the lounge, and although she was clearly worried, I could not help but notice that she looked stunning in her new outfit. She had gone to so much trouble to look beautiful for Bruce tonight. I hoped that he had an excuse for simply going missing and that he hadn't been in an accident.

"Are you Ok," I asked Emma.

"I know it's weird, I mean, I am worried sick about Bruce, but I am also starving," she replied.

Relieved that Emma wanted to eat, and for the distraction, I said to her, "It's not weird, honey. You are pregnant, for goodness' sake. We need to get you some food. Let's order Uber Eats immediately."

"What a great idea. Even if the hire car turns up for me, I would have to eat before I got into it because I'm starving," Emma replied. "I think Bruce has totally forgotten that I am pregnant."

Pulling out my phone, I ordered generously, hoping that by distracting Emma with food, she would calm down. Being pregnant and stressed was not a good combination for Bruce to place her in.

The food promptly arrived in 20 minutes. We had decided to casually eat whilst sitting in the kitchen. I was relieved to see Emma voraciously consuming the pasta and garlic bread. We started watching Netflix for further distraction, which was working. After an hour we moved into the living room and sat on the lounge. I was starting to wonder if I should call the police station when finally, two hours later, I heard someone at the front door. "I'll get it," I said as the noise of fumbled rattling keys, coupled with disgruntled groans, continued. It sounded as though Bruce couldn't get the key in the door and was getting frustrated.

I walked to the door, and as I opened it, Bruce stumbled through the doorway with a girl behind him. Her arms were wrapped around his neck as though he was piggybacking her. They were both clearly intoxicated, and Bruce was so unsteady on his feet that he almost fell backwards. Emma had walked behind me to the doorway to see what was happening. Unfortunately, it was too late to spare her the scene.

I looked at Emma and saw the devastation on her face. Bruce clumsily tried to explain the other woman's presence by saying to Emma, "Darling, this is Marci. She gave me a lift home."

Marci stood unsteadily on her feet and seemed to be trying to work out where she was. Clearly confused, she asked, "Who are you?" to me and Emma.

"I am his wife," Emma replied curtly.

Marci looked at Bruce and said, "Why did we come here? I thought we were going back to my place."

I was frozen. I had never experienced anything like this and watching my friend in so much pain before me was unbearable. Garnering my anger, I fought off the urge to slap Marci. Instead, I led her by the arm and said, "Bruce has a wife, so you must leave now. I will take you to the veranda, where you can sit and wait while I organise an Uber to take you away from here. I sat her down and then asked her, "What's your address?"

Luckily, Marci was so intoxicated that she was pliantly obedient as she gave me her address for the Uber. I then walked her out the door, gently guiding her. As we walked, I took the opportunity to ask her how she knew Bruce. "I met him at work," she replied.

"And you didn't know he was married," I asked.

"They are all married, but he is lots of fun," Marci replied.

As Marci was now settled on the veranda waiting for the Uber, I went back inside to check on Emma. As I walked inside the house, I saw Bruce. He seemed totally unruffled by the situation, and I watched him walk away from Emma in the living room towards their bedroom.

Emma and I followed him. Bruce walked towards the bed, and then we watched as he simply fell onto it, spread-eagled onto his face. He lay motionless. He was out cold and could not be awakened despite Emma's attempts. Emma sat on the edge of the bed and burst out crying.

She asked me, "What do I do? Do you know how to check his pulse? Is he ok?"

Reluctantly, I checked his pulse. As I held his wrist, Bruce murmured incoherently and pulled his arm away. I said to her, "He's alive."

I was so angry with Bruce, but I knew I couldn't show it in front of Emma. How he thought he had the right to treat anyone like this, let alone a woman who loved him with all her heart and was pregnant, was beyond my comprehension. Trying to calm myself down, I walked towards the wine fridge. Opening the door, I reached in and grabbed one of Bruce's bottles of Dom Perignon Champagne and a glass. After popping the cork, I turned to Emma, who was now staring at me.

"I will just be a minute," I said to her. My mother taught me that when you are in doubt, drink a glass of champagne. If the answer doesn't come to you, keep drinking until it does."

Emma frowned as she replied, "Has it worked before?"

"Never failed," Sophia replied.

As I stood staring at Bruce who was sound asleep on the bed, I suddenly had an epiphany. I said to Emma, "What a minute, I know what to do. I just need to get something out of my car."

Fearing the worst, Emma cried out to me, "Please don't get something to hurt him. I still love him."

I replied, "Don't be silly. I would never hurt him while you love him." I went outside to my car, and when I returned, I had a packet of coloured texters in my hand.

"What are you doing," Emma asked.

"I picked these up today to do some work on a mural. They are non-washable and will stay on for at least a few days." I sat on the bed bedside Bruce, who was still sound asleep. With his new buzz haircut, I could draw what I wanted to with my texters on the back of his head.

"Do you want to help?" I said to Emma as I handed her a texter.

"What are we drawing on?" She asked.

"Bruce's head," I said as I walked towards him. I had started the drawing with a large thick red love heart as the frame of the drawing along the outline of the back of his skull. Inside the heart, I had written the words "I love Marci." I then turned to Emma and said, "Now you it's your turn."

Emma and I continued drawing for about twenty minutes. When we had finished, we sat back and admired our handiwork. I led Emma out of the room before we both burst out laughing.

Emma had coloured in the spaces between the heart and lettering. "Better than a tattoo. Waterproof, so semi-permanent, but not permanent." I laughed.

Emma looked worried as she whispered back, "I just remembered; I am sure he has a meeting tomorrow."

"Too late now; it's done."

After Emma stopped laughing, she looked at me before suddenly crying. "What am I supposed to do? What has happened to my life? It's one thing suspecting there are other women, but it's another thing to have your husband bring one home."

I had always suspected that Bruce was a womaniser and player, but I knew Emma would never believe me, and if I said anything, it would just come between them. Men like Bruce could see a soft target and how easy it was to convince a girl like Emma that they were in love with them. I also knew why Bruce chose Emma to marry. He needed a girl like her as his wife to support him in his career – she was devoted, loyal, intelligent, educated and would make a great hostess to help his career. Now she was pregnant, he knew that she would put up with anything to keep the family unit together. He was right.

As though I was reading her mind, Emma said aloud in a tone that sounded like she was pleading with me, "I can't leave him; I'm pregnant. I don't know what to do next. I really don't."

I saw the complete despair in Emma's eyes and realised I had to say what she wanted to hear. "No, you can't leave Bruce now, not now. You must put this out of your head and concentrate on looking after yourself and the baby. Bruce will feel terrible and apologise, and everything will be ok again tomorrow."

"Thank you, Sofia. I'm relieved you understand. I'm exhausted now, I should go to bed. I promise I will call you in the morning."

I smiled as I walked towards the front door picking up my handbag. As I opened it, I turned and said to Emma, "I love you. Call me if you need me. Remember, I am never here to judge, just to support you."

Mark

Chapter 15

It was chaotic in the Family Court today. Walking around the crowded third floor, I continued to weave through crowds of people to make my way toward the courtrooms. I stood outside the entrance of a Courtroom and saw the sign above the door which read *Court 3B*. Next to the door was the hearing list:

10 am

Hay v Hay.

Property / Children's Matters / Spousal Maintenance

I felt a hand on my shoulder, and I turned around to see Sarah Walters standing in front of me. She smiled and said to me, "Hi Mark."

Standing with her was my barrister, Tim Bartlett. I was nervous and felt relieved to see them. Sarah looked at me reassuringly and said to me, "Let's go in."

Sarah appeared composed and calm, but with a deathly air of efficiency and professionalism. As a professional, I noticed how well she presented herself. She simply, but clearly, stood out from the others in her field. At forty-four, she looked years younger than her age, with the skill of being able to read people. She was not only intelligent but had a photographic memory. I would rate the statistics of finding someone with her combination of skills as being one in a million. I was relieved that she was on my side.

Although I hated being in court, I enjoyed watching Sarah in action. At five feet ten inches tall, with a solid but slim athletic build, she was daunting to most people, even before she spoke. Though she was taller than most men without shoes, she always donned the latest and most elegant designer high heels, which I knew was a psychological tactic as much as a fashion statement. My wife had always criticised me when I had commented on women's shoes, telling me that she thought it was odd that I noticed them. In contrast, Sarah always accepted my compliments on her shoes gracefully.

Sarah guided me to my seat, and I sat and watched both legal teams set up their laptops and folders on the bar table. Meanwhile, the court officers prepared the room, turning the microphones on and filling the water jugs. Shortly after that, the court officer approached the legal teams asking if they were ready for the Judge to commence. Acknowledging they were, the court officer walked up to the back door, tapped three times, and everyone stood, the court officer saying authoritatively, "This court is now in session," as the Judge entered the room towards the bench. We all bowed as on cue, and the Judge sat down. The hearing officially commenced.

Peter

Chapter 16

The whole time I was at lunch with Sarah and Chloe today, I had dreaded telling Sarah that the police wanted to interview me at the police station about Anthony. I had decided to wait until after lunch, when we were walking back to the car to tell her. I could still see her face; anger did not adequately describe it. I knew that I had to tell her today because my barrister, who was also my friend, Daniel, had told me that I may be arrested and charged in the next couple of days. He said it all depended on what evidence the police had, which we would not know about until the police interview. But he said that he had got the feeling that they felt they had enough to charge me with after his conversation with the Sergeant.

After I told her, Sarah had immediately ended our lunch with our daughter Chloe and left the park. I was clearly not going to get much support from her. I was relieved that Daniel, my friend and barrister had agreed to go to the police station with me for the interview.

After driving home from lunch, I sat on the couch with a bottle of scotch and my sleeping pills, hoping to knock myself out. Before I did, I set my alarm for 7 am with two reminders. Unfortunately, but predictably, the combination was a disaster. I was awake until 4 am and then slept through my alarm at 7 am.

I woke up again at 8 am, swore at myself and then jumped out of bed. I had a throbbing headache, but I threw on the clothes I had taken off and left on the floor the night before, racing out the door without shaving. There was no time for me to do anything else, or I would be late for the interview with the police. I combed my fingers through my hair as I sat behind the wheel of my car. Looking at myself in the rear-view mirror, I knew I looked terrible even before Daniel told me.

I parked my car and got out; I saw Daniel walking towards me. As he reached me, I held out my hand meekly to shake. He immediately started to reprimand me, "Don't tell me you went out last night? You haven't even shaved and look like you slept in your clothes."

"Sorry Mate, I thought it was more important that I got here on time, even if I didn't look pretty. I couldn't sleep all night, then at 6 am, I finally dosed off and slept through my alarm,"

Daniel was clearly annoyed with my presentation. He was pacing up and down the footpath. I could see he was thinking about whether he should go into the police station with me or not. I said to him, "I really want to get this over with. I can't do another night worrying about this, it's doing my head in."

Daniel stopped pacing and said to me, "Usually Peter, I would insist that my client go home and change before they go into an interview with the police. But as you knew better than to turn up like this, and you are now asking that we go ahead with it, why should I care when I am doing this for you as a friend?"

"I'm sorry. I've explained what happened. I will be ok in there. Let me say what I need to, and I don't think it matters what I look like when I am saying it."

Daniel glared at Peter, before placing his hands on his shoulders and said to him, "Peter, before we go in, remember that I am in charge today – not you. Let me talk, and you say nothing unless I ask you to. If you don't take my advice, I will cease to act on the spot and leave. Got that? I may be your friend, but today I am your barrister. If you stop taking my advice, I will stop acting for you and leave."

I reluctantly nodded in agreement and followed Daniel into the police station. Daniel asked for Sergeant Thommeny. Shortly after that, we were taken into an interview room. A constable offered us tea and coffee, which Daniel declined, and I accepted. Coffee was something I needed urgently.

Sergeant Thommeny walked into the room and introduced herself to us. She sat down and opened her folder, keen to start the interview. We sat on one side of the desk opposite her.

I got the impression Daniel was in a hurry. The Sergeant felt it too. I could see she was not going to let the opportunity of my barrister being in a hurry go.

Sergeant Thommeny was an imposing woman. She was confident and presented as serious but reserved. She said to me, "Peter, thank you very much for attending the police station about this matter. Before we start the interview, I must inform you I have reasonable grounds to believe that a serious offence has been committed, and this is your opportunity to give your side of the story. Just to let you know, I am required to electronically record this interview."

There was a knock at the door before another police officer entered the room. Sergeant Thommeny introduced him as Constable Coffey, before he sat down at another table in the room and said to me and Daniel, "Before this interview commences, I hereby advise you that it is being recorded." He then reached over to a video machine on the opposite table. I heard a click. The recording machine was on.

Sergeant Thommeny then said, "Before we start this interview, Peter, I have to caution you." I felt sick as Sergeant Thommeny commenced the caution. She continued, "Peter Walters, you do not have to say anything. But it may harm your defence if you do not mention when questioned something which you later rely on in Court. Anything you do say may be given in evidence. Do you understand this?"

I replied, "Yes, I do".

Following her introduction, names, times, and dates, Sergeant Thommeny said to me that Anthony Shaw alleged that I had a sexual relationship with him from the age of twelve for over six months. He alleged that this occurred on at least fifteen occasions.

Although short, the rest of the interview was a blur, I saw Sergeant Thommeny' s mouth moving, but I was not listening. When she had finished, Daniel stood up and said, "Peter denies the allegations. He has nothing to say and will not answer further questions unless he is charged." He then turned to me and said, "Let's go."

Sergeant Thommeny looked surprised. She looked directly at me and said, "Is that right?"

I too, was surprised and confused by how Daniel was managing the interview. I turned to her and asked, "Can I have a few minutes to talk alone with my barrister, please?"

"Of course, you can, Constable Coffey and I will wait outside and you can let us know if you wish to proceed any further with the interview."

As they both walked out of the room, a constable brought in the coffee and biscuits. "Good timing," I remarked.

After Daniel shut the door, I sculled my coffee, hoping it to have some effect quickly. I then said to Daniel, "If I just explain to the police that this all happened a long time ago and we were both kids, I think I can make this go away. I know he was only twelve years old, but I was only eighteen. I don't understand why his age matters anyway. We were just two kids having fun and experimenting. That was it."

Daniel stood up and started pacing the room before he said to me, "Peter, you know if you confess to these allegations, even if your interpretation is that it was about two kids experimenting, then I can't defend you. Although in your eyes, you were only eighteen years old, you were still an adult having sexual relations with a child who was too young to consent to it according to the law. All I could do after that is plea bargain for you. You know better than to put us both in this position."

"You don't understand, I can't let this go on any longer Daniel; it's killing me. Sarah will hate me again if this goes to trial, and she will not let me see Chloe. We must make this go away. Now."

Daniel walked to the door and opened it, calling out to Sergeant Thommeny. The constable at reception acknowledged him and said he would go and let the Sergeant know that we were ready. Sergeant Thommeny walked back into the conference room with Constable Coffey. Daniel announced that we were ready to leave and that the interview was over. Sergeant Thommeny looked at me directly as she said, we have no choice then but to go ahead and charge you."

"Now?" Daniel said to her.

"Yes, there is enough evidence to charge him," Sergeant Thommeny replied.

Sergeant Thommeny looked in my direction and said, "Peter Walters, you are under arrest for Aggravated Sexual Assault with a Child aged under 14 years on fourteen occasions. Constable Coffey will escort you to the charge room."

I was compliant and said nothing as Constable Coffey led me out of the room and down the hallway to the charge room. I heard Daniel behind me say to Constable Coffey, "I will make sure that bail is arranged, and then I need to leave. I didn't plan on this."

I heard Sergeant Thommeny talking with Daniel as I was walking away. I stopped to listen to them. She told him that he could wait in the waiting room, but that the process usually took some hours for the charges to be laid and bail granted. Daniel looked up and saw that I had stopped in the hallway and said to me, "No point in me staying while they do the paperwork mate. They are going to grant you bail, it will just take a few hours for the paperwork to get done. Give me a call when you get home."

The charging process seemed to take forever; I felt like I was in a trance whilst sitting in another room with the policeman. Finally, Constable Coffey said to me, "I am just going to make a copy of the Court Attendance Notice and your bail conditions for you." He then left the room.

When he returned, Sergeant Thommeny was with him as he handed me the papers. She said to me, "Hello, Peter. Constable Coffey has given you a copy of everything and I am just going to explain your bail conditions to you." Although I was still shocked, I listened while she explained everything and what would happen next.

When she finished, she said to me, "You are now free to leave."

I replied, "Thank you."

I left the station and got into my car, parked just outside. I sat and tried to process what had happened. The effect of the charges was sinking in slowly. As I reflected on my life, I realised it was a complete mess. My legal practice as a barrister had dwindled to virtually nothing after spending almost six months in and out of the hospital following the attack on me. My ex-wife was so angry with me that I could only see my daughter on a supervised basis and now I was facing serious criminal charges.

I realised that Anthony would succeed in completely ruining my life now, just as he had whispered into my ear at the hospital months ago. I needed to work out what I could do to mitigate the landslide of damage ruining my life.

I started the car and drove to my apartment, arriving home without even recalling the drive. As I sat on the lounge again, I thought to myself that it was Groundhog Day. My life was going in circles. As I poured myself what was left of my scotch, my mobile rang, and I saw that Daniel was calling me. I answered, knowing it would not be good news. He said to me, "Peter, I am too close to you to act for you. The charges against you are serious, and you could lose your liberty if you don't defend yourself as best as you can. I am too close to you to act for you, and no matter what you have to say about that, I saw that today and I cannot be persuaded to change my mind. You should call Rupert Showers tomorrow and get him to act for you ASAP."

I didn't even respond to him. I just cut off the call. After all the favours I had done for Daniel, I couldn't believe he was now bailing out on me. My mobile rang, and again it was Daniel. I let it ring out. I would do as he suggested and call Rupert tomorrow, not because he had told me to, but because I knew Rupert was the best criminal lawyer in town. Daniel also knew he didn't need to tell me that.

Daniel was right, and I had to start thinking like a barrister again if I had any chance of defending myself. Anthony wanted to hurt me because he thought I had abandoned him. I could see now that Anthony was acting like a scorned lover. I needed Anthony to know that he had gotten it wrong and to convince him the revenge he needed was not with me, but with his ex-wife and stepdaughter.

I got up and poured myself another scotch. Now that I knew what I had to do, I needed to find a way to do it. I could not sit back and just let Anthony attack me like this. Maybe I needed to confront him to let his guard down, and then I had a chance to change his direction of attack away from me? My mind was racing, and I knew I had to calm down and think this over.

I sculled my scotch, feeling discombobulated. Sitting back and waiting to see what Anthony would or wouldn't do in the past few months had affected me badly. I realised that I had let myself become a sitting target for him. "You can't get ahead standing still," my mother always said. My mother had made some mistakes in her life but teaching us never to give up was not one of them.

Sarah

Chapter 17

It had been a busy week at the office as usual, with judgements in both of my cases being handed down in my client's favour. A flower delivery had arrived for me, which, to my relief, consisted of only one exceptionally large floral arrangement. I suspected Kate had warned Phil against sending the entire florist shop again, causing another catastrophic hay fever outbreak in the office. The note with the flowers read, *Have a lovely weekend. Phil.*

Reading the card, I was not sure if Phil was indicating a desire to see me over the weekend or if he was just staying in touch. In my usual manner of dealing with anything emotional, I ignored any implied complexity and just sent him a text message thanking him. Taking Hillary's advice, I decided not to think too much about it for now.

Sitting at my desk, I was annoyed that this afternoon, instead of joining my staff in the boardroom for Friday night drinks, I had an appointment to see my psychiatrist. Unfortunately, as it had been such a hectic week, this was the only time I could see him. As I picked up my handbag and walked past the boardroom, I resisted their attempts to lure me in for a glass of wine.

As I sat in Charlie's waiting room, I wondered if I should discuss my concerns about Phil with him, or just keep the session to dealing with issues about Peter and Chloe. Although I had decided after my discussion with Hillary to not take Phil too seriously, part of me knew that I needed to work on my personal life as much as my other issues.

I was far more comfortable discussing other people's problems than my own. My decision to go to dinner with Phil (albeit a charity dinner where I was also taking my staff) was flawed, and it concerned me as to why I had agreed to it. Phil's overwhelming and demonstrative shows of affection towards me had penetrated my usual steely guard, which I did not understand.

Charlie came out to the waiting room to usher me into his office as he asked, "How has your week been?"

"Busy as usual, but I'm really worried about Chloe and how the police investigation with Peter might affect her."

"Has Chloe been upset?" he asked.

"I think Chloe believes we are a normal family. I feel like I am misleading her by taking her to see her father for family lunches and acting like that's normal."

"You are not misleading her. Chloe needs to see her father in this way for now. She is not old enough to understand the complications of her father's situation. Children are adaptable and can accept whatever form their parents come in, as long as they believe their parents love them."

"I feel so guilty that Chloe doesn't have a normal family. When we go to the park, I look around and see all these happy families and beat myself up about how I got it so wrong."

"You may think that they are normal families, Sarah, but is there really such a thing? Look at what you and I both went through. Look at what Hillary went through. There is no such thing as a normal family, really."

"I feel like I failed her. How could I have chosen such a terrible father for her if I were a good mother?"

"You "are" a great mother, Sarah," Charlie replied. "You are doing your best to protect Chloe, and at the same time trying to keep her life as stable as possible."

"Sorry, I seem to worry about everything these days."

"That's what I'm here for Sarah. So you can discuss anything that is worrying you with me."

"A client invited me and my staff to a charity dinner. I am not sure why I accepted the invitation. I know he is interested in me romantically, and that I am not ready for anything like that, so I should have just said no. I don't know if I am over analysing things. Hillary thinks I should just have a good time, but I know this guy is not right for me."

"When you say a former client, how long was the period between him being a client and him sending flowers to you?"

I felt embarrassed when I replied, "He has been a repeat client. Meaning, I had acted for him a couple of times. I finished acting in the last matter couple of months before he sent me flowers."

"Was that him that sent you the truckload of flowers I saw in your office a couple of weeks ago? I recall going to your office to drop off a report and Kate explaining in between sneezing, why it looked like a florist shop."

"Yes, they were from him. It was quite a scene."

"How did it make you feel when he did that?"

"What do you mean?"

"It was clearly meant to get your attention."

"I had not thought of it like that." As I saw the look on Charlie's face, I instantly regretted telling him about Phil. I thought he may have looked amused or even a little annoyed like Kate, but instead, I saw a concerned look appear on his face as he frowned and prodded further.

"Do you think he believed such an extravagant display of wealth would impress you?" Charlie pressed on.

I had not been ready for this line of questioning and responded curtly, "I shouldn't have brought the issue of Phil up with you." I looked at my mobile for a distraction and said, "I have an urgent message from Kate. I really need to head back to the office for an appointment."

As she got up to leave, Charlie said, "Please don't go just because we are touching upon an area that makes you feel uncomfortable. This is something we should finish talking about. You are warranted with your concerns about Phil. Always trust your gut instincts."

I stood up and walked towards the door. I turned and said, "He sent me another bunch of flowers this morning. They were large, but just one bunch and the card wished me a nice weekend. I think Kate told him not to be so ridiculous again, and he obviously listened to her. I'm sorry that I can't deal with this now, but I can't. Sorry."

"I understand, Sarah," Charlie replied.

Charlie

Chapter 18

After Sarah left my office, I sat pondering how I had handled things so badly with her today. I felt as though I had let her down as a therapist. She had reached out to me timidly like a child holding out a toy they couldn't make work, and I had not done the best job trying to help her. She had recoiled instantly and disappeared into herself again. I should have been gentler with my line of questioning. If I had been honest with myself, the fact that Sarah had indicated an interest in Phil, the type of person who could sense and take advantage of her vulnerability, had thrown me.

Sarah had been to see me for over six months now, and in each session, she blamed herself for not seeing the side of Peter that he had hidden from her. She was unable to accept that Peter had become an expert in hiding part of himself, and it was not her fault - but blaming herself for not being perfect was something she had mastered. Sarah beat herself up for any mistake she made, or believed she could have stopped others from making. She refused to allow herself to accept that sometimes, even she could not see every outcome of a situation.

It was her imperfections that I admired in Sarah. As I got to know her, I knew that loving a partner was something she may never cope with. But what I also knew was why. That made me one of the only people who could see that her aloofness was in fact shyness, which some people misread as snobbish. When everyone else saw the self-confident, strong, and sometimes even fierce Sarah – I saw her vulnerable side. The scared, shy, proud girl who instinctively knew that she needed to hide her fear of the world, to survive. It would not be an easy adjustment for her to learn how to allow herself to be vulnerable, but until she did, she would never be able to have a successful relationship.

Looking at my afternoon schedule, I saw that I had two more patients to see today. After that, I could focus on how I could help Sarah navigate her way through Phil's advances. I couldn't say I liked the sound of him or how he managed to infiltrate Sarah's personal life, but I was relieved to hear that Sarah had said that Kate had been able to influence Phil, at least regarding his floral deliveries to Sarah. Kate was a great protector of Sarah. Phil was clearly smart enough to realise that. I was now seeing why Sarah had reached out to me; she realised she needed my help.

Jim

Chapter 19

I was glad I called Debbie and made up with her on my way to pick up Ashly. Debbie had surprised me by getting home earlier than usual and sounding grumpy even though I was ironing. As soon as I saw her, I realised she had been at lunch with her girlfriends and not at work. It was odd because she usually mentioned she was going to one of her girl's monthly lunches to me the night before. It was not like her to question me, particularly after a few drinks.

I parked the car and walked towards the school, up to my daughter's classroom. Through the window, I saw her waiting to leave. As I walked into the cloakroom and picked up her bag from the hook on the wall, she saw me and ran up to me. I picked her up and kissed on her forehead as I said, "Hello, princess."

As we walked to the car, Ashley prattled incessantly about her day, telling me every little detail of what she had done at school that day. She loved to talk. She continued chattering during the entire drive home. I loved listening to her. She was so excited when she talked about school and her friends. Just the simple task of being the class "Angel," whose job was to go to each table during the day and collect their work at the end of each activity, made her so happy.

I loved Debbie, and I loved my life. But I knew there was a part of me that Debbie would never understand. "It's best if they don't know, and then it doesn't hurt them," my father always said about wives. He gave me this explanation when he would take me to play poker with his mates. He always told my mother that he was taking me to the park, but he never took me to the park during my childhood, and my mother never worked it out. Sometimes, I tried to hint to my mum about dad's lies when I got upset with him: but she never got them or pretended she hadn't.

As we pulled up in the driveway of our home, Ashley saw her mother through the loungeroom window. "Mummy's home," she squealed as she tried to undo her seatbelt. Debbie had walked outside and opened the car door for Ashley as she said to her, "Hello darling, I missed you."

"Mummy, guess what happened today at school?" Ashley said as she hugged Debbie.

"I can't wait to hear all about it, but can we go inside first because I have made you a surprise."

I watched them as they walked into the kitchen and left me behind. They didn't mean to make me feel left out, but they seemed to do it more often as Ashley got older. The two of them would talk or do things together and forget I was even there.

I walked into our bedroom and headed towards our walk-in wardrobe. I noticed that the blue dress I had been ironing when Debbie came home was hanging there. Debbie had hung up all the ironing that I left in the loungeroom when I went to pick up Ashley.

Walking out of the bedroom and towards the kitchen, I could hear Debbie and Ashley talking. I saw Ashley eating a huge pink cupcake while enthusiastically describing her "Angel" duties to Debbie. Interrupting their conversation, I said to them, "Hi girls, in case you are looking for me, I'm going to have a shower and then change to go out tonight."

"This early?" Debbie asked, looking at her watch.

"You girls are busy, so I thought I'd head off now. Don't wait up for me. We've planned a big poker night, and it will run late."

Debbie did not respond. She turned her head and returned to talking to Ashley, not saying a word to me. I might have taken offence at her lack of response if I had not been looking forward to my night out as much as I was. But instead, I walked away to have a shower and get changed.

I walked past the kitchen as I was leaving, waving goodbye to them as they continued to chat away, but this time, they both turned and waved back at me.

Jim

Chapter 20

As I drove out of my driveway at home, I felt a pang of guilt about where I was going. Luckily, that feeling only lasted until I put on the radio and heard my favourite song. Singing along to the words of the song "I will survive", I drifted into my other world and forgot about my troubles.

I arrived on time and parked the car. When I got out of the car, I took my bag out of the boot, and walked into the building. As I was walking down the hall, I heard a door open behind me, and a voice called out to me, "Hello, Jim."

I turned and saw Claudia dressed in a long flowing pink dress. I smiled and said to her, "Hi beautiful, you look fabulous!"

"Thanks, darling, I know it's a little over the top for tonight, but I love long dresses. I was born in the wrong century, I'm sure."

"You always look amazing," I said. "Do you know if Christina is here yet?"

"Of course, come with me. She is getting her hair and makeup done, and you know that takes hours."

I followed Claudia down the hall. Before she walked in, Claudia knocked on the door and said, "Hi everyone. Jim is here."

As soon as she saw me, Christina got up from the makeup chair and ran to me, flinging her arms around me as she said, "I missed you."

Although she was thirty-six years old, she acted just like a child when I was with her. She had a passion for life and a childlike joy in everything she did, which I found intoxicating. She made me feel alive and happy in a way nothing else did, on the one night a week we saw each other.

"You look beautiful," I said to her.

"I have waited for tonight for so long. I wanted to make sure I looked the best I could for the show," Christina said.

"It's going to be the best night ever, I'm sure."

"Take a seat darling, they will do your makeup and hair now too. We have been waiting for you."

Patricia

Chapter 21

As my sister drove me to my appointment with my solicitor for my mediation, I asked her if I could practise my introduction to the mediator, whom I was about to meet. Of course, she said, go ahead. I laughed and then said, "Hello, my name is Patricia and I have become a bitter and twisted divorcee."

"And that's it?" she replied.

"Give me a minute," I said.

"Remember, everyone is charging by the hour, so you had better get on with it and not dally around like this when you are in the mediation."

"Ok, I get it."

"Good, well get on with it then."

"I will, give me a minute. Ok? Here we go, Dear Mediator, I am here to see if you can help us settle our family law case. You see without warning; my life has turned into a circus. My husband has left me for the nanny of our baby, and I have turned into one of those angry, bitter women that I used to stare at in the coffee shop. You know, those women who look angry whilst dressed in expensive activewear and are trying to convince everyone that they are happily divorced and have beautiful daughters or genius sons?"

"Are you practising this for the rehab clinic or for the mediation?" my sister asked.

I had not wanted to do this. My sister had forced me to. She had arranged a lawyer for me, telling me that she was, "the best divorce lawyer in town," which my sister said my husband deserved. She was right, but it had been challenging for me to stand up for myself when

I felt so shattered. I knew I was in denial and that I had to face the reality that my divorce should be finalised. It just seemed that it was all happening too quickly for me to adjust.

It all seemed so crazy. One minute we were deliriously happily married, with a newborn baby and a beautiful home. Then only months later, I found out my husband had been cheating on me with the live-in babysitter. Now, my husband wanted to move on, and I was being an allegedly difficult ex-wife as I hadn't immediately adapted to my new situation overnight as I should have.

My sister had dropped me off at the entrance of the building while she went to park the car. The staff in the office were immaculately dressed and impossibly polite as they greeted me. I had already been offered a beverage and assured that Ms Walters was running on time for my mediation. I was shown into the boardroom.

The only legal offices I had been in before my divorce were the offices of our conveyancing solicitor when we bought our house. Those offices were basic to say the least, the complete opposite to what I was sitting in now. The office was on the top floor of the tallest building in the city. I walked out of the lift into a large open plan reception area with soaring ceilings, floor to ceiling glass windows, marble reception desk, patterned timber floors, chrome and leather furniture and beautiful paintings hanging on the impressively high walls.

Knowing me all too well, my sister had insisted on taking me today to ensure I turned up today. Sarah's secretary, Kate, came to the reception and led me into the boardroom, where the mediation with my ex-husband was to take place. It had taken over 18 months for my case to reach this stage. Apart from the legal costs I would have to spend if it didn't settle today - and then having to be listed for a hearing, I did not want the uncertainty of where my life was heading to consume me any longer. I knew Sarah could guide me to a reasonable settlement today, and I would accept that.

As I waited in the boardroom, I sat staring out the window. It was impossible not to look out of the full-length windows with the view of Sydney Harbour. I only wished I could relax and enjoy it with a glass of wine. I didn't want to see my ex-husband. But the mediation, if successful, would result in us being able to enter a financial settlement, ending our court proceedings and providing for the future support of our son. I had to see him to get this over with.

Initially, my ex-husband and I believed that mediation would be a waste of time and money. My ex-husband's lawyer had told the Judge about our confrontation in the lift when we last attended the Family Court, trying to convince the Judge to allow us to skip the mediation step of the process. The Judge had told us both that the Court had now made mediation compulsory before we could proceed to a hearing. He had been compassionate and acknowledged that he understood how distressing going through a divorce and being in Court was for us. Still, he reiterated the high success rate of mediation even in high conflict matters. He had also taken the opportunity to say that although he was sympathetic to my situation, I needed to refrain from yelling at my ex-husband and his wife, which had been embarrassing.

Sarah had told me in preparation for the mediation that although my ex-husband wanted to move on with his life as quickly as possible, may seem upsetting to me, that I needed to see it as being positive in reaching a settlement with him. I knew my ex-husband desperately wanted to shed me from his life like an unwanted snakeskin, so he could focus on his new wife and life. While not wanting to give him what he wanted; I needed to be free of him.

I had been trying to process everything as quickly as everyone had expected me to. Still, the legal process left me feeling overwhelmed at times. It was a system of no-fault divorce. The Family Law Act said so. No-one seemed to care that my husband had broken my heart, broken his vows and had run off with a person whom I paid, and we trusted to look after our baby.

It apparently didn't matter that I had tried to be a supportive wife to my husband during our marriage and especially during the hard times, like when he had been retrenched shortly before our son was born. I had wanted to get him to see his retrenchment as the perfect opportunity for one of us to spend time with our baby, which he would never have otherwise had. My husband however, had used the opportunity to have an affair with the nanny.

I heard a knock on the boardroom door and voices. The door opened, and Sarah Walters entered with a man I presumed was the Mediator. They were in deep conversation with each other as they walked in. Shortly after, my ex-husband and his lawyer followed them into the boardroom.

Whenever I saw my ex-husband, I felt like bursting into tears or screaming. My counsellor had told me that these feelings were normal and part of the grieving process. He had given me exercises to try and help me cope, and he assured me that as time went by, the pain would ease. It was now 18 months on, and I still couldn't see that it helped. The pain each time I saw him was, in fact, getting worse. My lack of control when I saw him was evident in the lift at the Family Court a couple of months ago, where I had lost control, yelled at him, and froze in the back of the lift. Security had been called by two concerned ladies to help me out of the lift.

I had no control over constantly replaying the moment I discovered the affair in my head. In an instant, I would be back in the moment when I had heard my husband and the babysitter on the baby monitor. I felt like I was standing on quicksand when I held the handset and saw them making love. It was like a nightmare that wouldn't end. What I had seen my husband doing made no sense at all. When I confronted them, I thought he would say sorry and ask her to leave. I thought he would beg for my forgiveness. But instead, he had said to me, "I'm sorry you found out this way. I wanted to do the right thing and wait until Billy had started at day-care. I did not mean for this to happen now."

All I could say in response was, "Ok." I had felt so stupid saying it, but that's all I could think of saying to my husband, who had just told me he was leaving me. The comment had somehow hit a nerve with Kevin, as he walked over to me and said, "Look, I care about you, and I love Billy, but I need to live my life the way I want to, which is not here anymore. My lawyer will send you an email, and I hope we can sort this out between us quickly. I am trying to be fair." I had walked the two steps to the kitchen stool and sat down and when I said, "You already have a lawyer? How long have you been planning this? "

"I have not seen a lawyer yet, but I know I have to and I have a name of one."

"I don't know how you expected me to take this. I am sorry, but I can't make any sense of this right now."

Kevin then said firmly to me, "I am going to pack up my things now. Call me when you feel up to talking, and I will come back, and we we'll discuss it." He then kissed me on the top of my head like he would a child as he walked out of the room.

I heard Sarah say my name, jolting me out of my thoughts. She said to me, "Patricia, this is Scott Wilkinson, the lawyer acting for Kevin."

Scott introduced Kevin to the Mediator, Jamie Smythe, and we all sat at the boardroom table. Kevin looked great. The best he had in years. He seemed relaxed, tanned, and appeared very happy. In complete contrast, I had put on twenty-three kilos since we had separated, was miserable, and on antidepressants.

Sarah sat beside me. She touched my arm gently and reassuringly whispered to me, "You don't need to say a word if you don't want to. I can do all the talking. I just need you to be in the room during this period."

The Mediator started with his opening statement, which went just as Sarah had explained it would, and then he told Kevin that he would speak with our lawyers first and bring us back into the room after that. We stood up, and Sarah guided me into a conference room. My ex-husband and his lawyer were shown into another conference room.

Once seated in our allocated rooms, Sarah said, "Kate will come in shortly and bring you a coffee, tea or water and make sure you are ok. After my quick chat with your husband's lawyer, I am confident we can resolve this today on the basis that we had discussed. I am returning to the room with the Mediator now, and I will be back shortly." Sarah put her arm on my shoulder and said, "I'm sorry, Patricia, I know you hate every minute of this, but after today you will be able to move on with your life and concentrate on your future, not your history."

I said her, "I know, and I am trying to be strong."

"I know you are," Sarah said. As she started to walk away, I began to feel emotional again and blurted out to her, "I know my marriage is over, and my husband is the happiest I have ever seen him, but I am just not coping with it." I then leaned against the wall, thinking it would stabilise me, but as if in slow motion, I started sliding down the chair until I slumped onto the floor.

As if on cue, Sarah's secretary Kate had walked into the room with a tray and knew exactly what to do. She put the tray of glasses on the table, picked up the box of tissues and sat on the floor next to me. She handed me some tissues to wipe my eyes before giving the box to me. I stammered, "I am so sorry."

Kate said to me with her arm around me, "Breathe slowly and deeply. You will be ok. Try and drink some water slowly. It will help."

Sarah crouched down and said to me, "I will leave you with Kate while I go and speak to your husband's lawyer. I am sorry I can't help with your pain now, but I can try and finalise this for you. Kate will look after you while I am gone."

About an hour passed, and then Sarah came back into the room. By this time, my sister, Maria, had arrived and was sitting with me. Sarah seemed pleased that I was sitting at the table and looking composed again. Sarah said to me, "I have good news. We have reached a settlement, and he has agreed to everything we asked for. He didn't want to at first, but he eventually relented, and we have the deal that we discussed was your best position on the table now. I have the terms in writing here for you to read."

My sister asked Sarah, "Why are you giving him what he wants?" Of course, he has agreed to what Patricia wants. He'll agree to anything to get out of this marriage and set himself free. Patricia should take him to Court and make him pay. The Judge should hear about his affair with the babysitter and his retrenchment from his job that forced Patricia to go back to work earlier than she had planned. It's outrageous that you are letting him get away with this. What was fair about what he has done to Patricia and Billy?"

I was stunned by my sister's outburst. I immediately apologised to Sarah. Sarah sat down and touched Maria's hand. Maria pulled it away quickly but didn't say anything. Sarah said to her, "I am sorry that you are upset, and I understand it must be awful seeing your sister so utterly distressed. But if she can resolve her family law issues today, that will end her stress, which is in her and her son's best interests."

Maria stood up, her anger apparent as she said to Sarah, "Upset? That prick has destroyed her. Look at her; she has put on so much weight and is on antidepressants because she is so depressed. If I hadn't heard you on the radio and dragged her in to see you, he would have walked all over her, kicked her out of the house, and left her with nothing. You need to make an example of him, not let him off the hook like this."

Sarah stood up and, facing Maria, said to her, "The only way Patricia will be able to move on and recover from this is for her to get on with her life and detach from Kevin. Staying connected to him will keep her in pain and make it impossible for her to heal. I know it seems to you he is getting off lightly, but a moral penalty for what he has done is, unfortunately, not something the Family Court can give you. All we can get for Patricia is financial security to enable her stability. Delaying this settlement will only cause her more pain and incur more legal fees. I do not believe that she would get a better result in Court if she went to a hearing of her matter."

My sister replied, "If Patricia settles today, that prick will be so happy because he can move on with his life. The only way to make him suffer is to keep this court case going. I know it is causing stress to him and his new wife, and they deserve it."

"I am sorry you feel that way, Maria," Sarah said. "You also need to consider its terrible effect on Patricia."

Sarah then walked over to me and said, "Patricia, his lawyer told me today that he got your ex-husband to agree to our proposed settlement. He said Kevin feels guilty and regrets how things ended between you, but he wants to and will move on with his life. He will let you keep the house if he can keep his redundancy payout and superannuation. His lawyer pointed out that the offer was off the table if we didn't settle today. If the matter went to a hearing, his view was that his client's guilt would have dissipated by then, and the offer would be at least thirty per cent less than they are offering today. That would mean you would not get to keep the house, which is the main thing you wanted in this settlement."

I stood up, walked over to my sister, and said, "I can't cope with this going on any longer. This must end. I need to know that I can keep the house to stabilise Billy and me. Up until now, he had been demanding that it be sold. Sarah is right. Kevin will change his mind if this goes on. I need to sign the papers now and end my marriage which Kevin did 18 months ago. If I don't finish this now, there may not be anything left of me to fight on with."

When I sat down, I felt like I was in control for the first time in a long time. I suddenly felt like chains were being lifted off me and that I could breathe. Sarah saw it and smiled at me, relieved that I was obviously feeling some relief from the imminent settlement.

I said to Sarah, "Let's do this. Let's sign the papers. You are right, and I should have listened to you earlier. I don't have to like him, and I don't have to forgive him, but I do need him out of my life to end this torture."

Sarah placed the legal documents on the table in the room, and we reviewed the terms on each page before I signed them. By this time,

Maria had calmed down and was listening intently to the terms of the settlement. After signing the documents, I lifted my head and smiled at Sarah before saying, "Well, that was the end of my marriage and the start of my new life. It feels good."

"I'm sorry that you have had to complete all this paperwork, Patricia. I know it's been exhausting, but it's done now, and I'm happy for you."

"Thank you, Sarah. I'm going to take my sister and son out to dinner and have a lovely bottle of wine to celebrate. Thank you for your support and your patience with us today. This would not have happened without you. I know Maria was difficult today, but she did lead me to you, knowing you would help me find the best way forward."

"It's been my pleasure being able to help, and you know where I am if you need anything. Kate will be back in a few minutes with the copies of all the signed documents for you to keep," Sarah replied.

Maria stood up quickly and said to Sarah, "Thank you. I am sorry for my outburst."

"It's times like these I wish I had the love and support of a sister like you, Maria. It was lovely to meet you, and I hope you all have a lovely dinner tonight."

Peter

Chapter 22

I know that a 49-year-old man should not sit in his loungeroom drinking scotch and feeling sorry for himself; but I was. Not only had the police charged me with historical child sexual assault offences from 30 years ago by a man who was in jail for being a paedophile, but my ex-wife had called me to tell me that I now couldn't see my daughter until I sorted out the pending charges.

My ex-wife, a lawyer herself, should presume I was innocent before punishing me for being guilty. She had just called me and said, "Peter, after speaking to my psychiatrist, we think it would be best for Chloe to have a break from seeing you until there has been a resolution of the situation with Anthony."

I told her I thought it was unfair, and that I was devastated by her decision. I should have been invited to participate in the psychiatrist's conversation when they had discussed this. But after talking to her, it was clear she would not change her mind. Now, the two people whom I thought would have me supported against Anthony, were running from me. First my friend Daniel and now Sarah. It was not like Sarah to avoid helping me, or anyone for that matter. We may be divorced, but she had never stopped being my friend; until now.

As angry as I was when I spoke to Sarah, I knew I had no choice but to give in to her. I had to use all my energy to solve one problem at a time. I agreed to stop seeing Chloe, so I could concentrate on trying to work out what to do with Anthony. If I didn't fix this situation, it would clearly ruin my life and land me in jail with him.

After reading Anthony's statement, I knew I needed to see him. The only chance I would have of changing his mind was to talk to him face-to-face. That would be the only way to determine why he was doing this to me. His sudden actions in making a criminal complaint against me, over 30 years after the alleged events and whilst he was in jail, clearly smacked of the act of a desperate man. Why no one else could see that, especially Sarah, was beyond me. Why he was attacking me and not his ex-wife and stepdaughter, whose allegations put him in jail, was something else I needed to know.

I desperately wanted to go to jail to see him, but I didn't want to do that unless I knew he would agree to see me. Otherwise, the police may accuse me of trying to interfere with a witness. My only avenue would be to send Anthony a letter to the jail and ask permission to visit him. My gut feeling was that he would agree to see me, even if it was just to see my reaction to his statement.

I knew that once I saw Anthony, I could work out what driving his attack on me. Did he really believe that I was the cause of his problems, or was there another reason that he was making the complaints against me decades later? I needed to know which one it was to work out if I could resolve this with him.

I understand that Anthony was angry. I would be angry, too, if my wife and stepdaughter had caused me to go to jail with what Anthony said were false allegations. I regretted not paying attention to Anthony's trial because I had not realised the connection with Sarah at the time. It wasn't until Anthony visited me in the hospital after the attack on me at my chambers that I had any idea that Sarah had been acting for his ex-wife. I was shocked that after the verdict, he had arranged the delivery of an envelope to Sarah's office, a letter detailing our friendship as kids and even included photographs of us together.

I didn't understand why Anthony had brought up our friendship then to Sarah or now to the police. It had been over 30 years since we had been friends. We were both just kids experimenting and having fun as kids do. He had now turned it around in his statement to the police as me being a predator and groomer.

I sat at my desk and started working on my letter to Anthony. I would keep it simple and ask if he would give me permission to come to the jail and see him. He would know why I was asking to see him. Then I would have to wait for his response.

Mark

Chapter 23

I know I was not the only person who had gone through a family law court case, but every time I came into the court room, I still found it difficult to believe I was here. I felt like I was watching a movie on Netflix; except I was in it.

I sat watching it all, like I was having an out of body experience. I listened to the opening submissions by my barrister, and he seemed to sum up my case quite accurately. But my ex-wife's barrister seemed to be talking about someone else other than me. He was trying to make me look like a terrible husband. He said that I was never at home, and because of the long hours I had to work, that my wife had to be both parents to our children. I wanted to ask her barrister how I was supposed to somehow have jumped straight from university, into our marriage and juggle the extraordinary time demands of my Medical Degree, Internship and Specialist training whilst driving kids to school, cooking dinner, and helping them with their homework.

My ex-wife's barrister conveniently made no mention in his opening submissions of the housekeepers, nannies, pool cleaners, ironing ladies and gardeners that I paid to assist my ex-wife because of my working hours, nor the fact that she had said to me from the moment that we were married, "I want to be a stay at home mum, so that you can save lives."

I was grateful when the Judge announced he was adjourning for morning tea. As I stood with my legal team outside the courtroom waiting for our coffees, I felt my mobile vibrate and when I pulled out my phone, I saw that the call was from the hospital. I walked away from the others as I spoke to the Registrar from the hospital. When I finished the call and walked back to the others, Sarah asked me, "Is everything ok?"

"The Registrar at the hospital called. I have an extremely ill patient undergoing chemotherapy and who is not responding well. It didn't help her when he had to give her the news that I was not able to see her this week."

"That's tough for her. I'm sorry. I can see you are concerned."

"It's not just her. Other patients are coming into emergency, and the interns and Registrars are nervous, because I am not checking their diagnoses. Being away this week is turning out to be more of a nightmare for them than me because they usually have my support with the patients. I feel terrible about it. I should be making other people's lives my priority, not mine."

"I feel awful too, but unfortunately your proceedings must be finalised, and this is the only way we can do it. Your wife has refused every offer you have made in relation to your property and your children. Unfortunately, unrealistic expectations can cause so much financial and emotional damage for people and everyone else who is affected, like your patients."

"Do you think this is about unrealistic expectations created by greedy lawyers?" Mark asked. 'I heard from the kids last night that her lawyer told her she would get 80-90 per cent of everything because I earn a good income and because she is fifty-three years old and did not work throughout our marriage. That is why she thinks she will get it. If her lawyer had told her, she would get 50 to 60 % per cent, then maybe she would have taken one of my offers. I don't understand why she is so angry at me when I did nothing wrong except work hard for our family. She had an affair with my best friend, and I lost both of them." I inadvertently started laughing. Sarah asked, "What's so funny?'

"As I said, "I lost both of them," I realised I sounded like I was singing a country and western song. They are always about losing your dog, wife, or best friend."

"I'm glad you can still laugh at the situation you are in. It's hard to know where the rationale comes from for people to continue legal cases that should have been settled. Sometimes I believe bad legal advice can drag legal cases on longer than they should. I was in a case once where the husband was determined he would only give his wife 30 %

of the assets of the marriage. As the case went on and it became clear to both sides that she would get about 50 % from a judge, his lawyer tried to get him to increase his offer, but the husband refused. He just kept saying out loudly in negotiations to his lawyer, "But you told me when this started that she would only get 30 %." The result was, even when his lawyer told him he had been wrong with his initial estimate, the husband would not accept it, and in the end, the Judge awarded the wife fifty-two and a half per cent. The judgement was a disaster for him. He had to pay another 22.5% than he expected to his wife, and the judge ordered him to pay both his and his wife's legal fees because we had made an offer of settlement for 50%."

"That would have hurt," Mark said. He did sound very stubborn though.

"He was stubborn Mark. I have also heard of people who have gone from lawyer to lawyer, until one of the lawyers gives them the advice they want to hear, so there are always two sides to every story. People who really want to settle, decide what they think is a fair thing and then get advice on whether it would work out for them legally. Who knows what happened with your wife and why she is so angry with you? Maybe her anger deflects her feelings of guilt? At least we are now closer than ever to the end of this litigation, and we can't wind back time."

"I know Sarah. I just want to get this hearing over with and have a decision by the Judge; whatever it is. I need to get back to my patients and the hospital where I am needed and wanted."

"We will get that Mark. I promise you this hearing will be over this week."

The court officer came over to us and said, "The Judge is ready to come back now, are you ready?"

"Yes, we are," Tim replied.

As we sat in the courtroom, I looked across at my ex-wife. I could not help but notice how relaxed she looked. She really looked as though she was enjoying herself. I looked to the back of the courtroom and saw her boyfriend Sam, who had been my former best friend, sitting there. I remembered like it was yesterday when Sam had separated from his wife and had asked me, "Could I stay with you for a few weeks, Mark? I have a place sorted out, but it won't be available for three weeks, and I could really do with the company?"

I had not hesitated to help him, although my ex-wife had seemed annoyed at first, feeling as though we were taking sides in his divorce.

I had reminded her how we had her girlfriend stay with us last year, when her girlfriend was going through a divorce. I was the one who had pressed her to agree to Mark staying with us.

How could I predict that three weeks later when Sam said we needed to talk, that it would be me, not Sam moving out of our house? I would remember that day for the rest of my life. The day my best friend told me that he had fallen in love with my wife, while we were sitting on the veranda of my home having a beer after work.

The court officer announced the arrival of the Judge, and everyone stood up as the he walked into the courtroom and sat down. Before the Judge could say good morning, my ex-wife's barrister stood up and addressed the Court, "Before we continue, Your Honour, we have a problem we need to bring to Your Honour's attention. We are sorry it's such late notice, but we have only just received the documents under subpoena from the bank, and it shows that Dr Paul has not declared a bank account with a major sum of money deposited in it. Unless Dr Paul is prepared to admit attempting to hide this account and give us access to all the bank statements, we may need an adjournment. We need to establish the quantum, source and history of the funds that have been in and out of this frequently used account. Currently, there is a substantial sum of over $1 million deposited in it, Your Honour."

The Judge looked directly at my barrister, "Mr Bartlett, what do you know about this?"

Tim replied, "My learned friends have not given me the professional courtesy of informing me of this information before bringing this to your attention Your Honour. In relation to my instructions, my client has given full financial disclosure. If my learned friend provides me with this subpoenaed material, I can seek instructions."

The Judge clearly looked annoyed and said, "We will have a short adjournment for you to obtain instructions from your client. He needs to explain to me how he has a bank account with over $1 million in it about which he apparently doesn't know."

After leaving the courtroom, Tim and Sarah directed me into a meeting room and Sarah said to me, "Mark, I just don't believe this. I went through everything with your accountant and PA. I thought I had the details of all your accounts."

I replied, "Sarah, this is not my bank account. I don't know how this has happened. I do not have millions of dollars in bank accounts that I am hiding. I am a specialist doctor, and I make $350,000 a year. I know what I have, and that is not my money. I wish it were because I'd happily give her half of it. I had to borrow the money from my father for your legal fees. I wouldn't have to do that if I had money hidden."

Tim responded this time, saying to me, "Well, we will have to work out what has happened. Has the bank stuffed up here? Is there another Mark Paul? There must be an explanation to this."

Tim said to Sarah, "Please get all the subpoenaed material from the other side and then you need to call the bank. We will also need to get Mark's accountant and his PA here, and they may have to go on Affidavit. This is serious."

"Of course, but Tim, can you ask the Judge for some time please. We will need at least until after lunchtime to give me time to get a hold of Mark's staff. It's wicked for the other side to bomb us with this like that."

"I'll speak to the Judge and the other side, who think they have us on toast now. You'll have to work miracles here, Sarah and quickly."

After Tim left the room, I said to Sarah, "I promise you I am telling the truth. My secretary and accountant have worked for me for fifteen years and know everything about my finances."

"I trust you, but the perception is winning over reality here, and we need to fix that quickly."

Bruce

Chapter 24

I woke up, and as I opened my eyes, the night before slowly came back like a bad dream. I had drunk too much, called my girlfriend Marci, and forgotten about my wife Emma coming on the boat for dinner with me.

I looked beside me and was relieved to see Emma asleep next to me. With great relief, I realised I was in bed at home. I looked at my watch and saw that I had slept through my 5am alarm. I had not done that for at least ten years. I couldn't remember what I had drunk or taken last night on the boat, but I had never felt this bad before in my life.

I got out of bed and walked to the bathroom. As I walked past the mirror, I stared at my reflection and realised I looked as bad as I felt. How I got home and into bed was something I didn't remember but was very thankful for. I headed straight for the bathroom and turned on the shower. As I stood under the warm water, I was already feeling better.

When I walked back into the bedroom, I saw that Emma was awake, sitting in bed and texting on her phone. She looked up at me and smiled as she continued to text. I said to her, "Everything ok?"

"Of course, why wouldn't it be?" she replied.

"You are texting, and it's early, that's all."

"I was texting Sofia to tell her I would be late for breakfast. I didn't want to leave before you woke up, and you have not slept in this late since our honeymoon."

"I know honey. I slept through my alarm, but it's fine. My board meeting isn't until 10 am today."

"That's lucky," Emma replied while texting on her phone.

As I finished getting dressed into my suit, Emma got out of bed. "Have a nice day, darling," she said as she headed towards the kitchen.

Feeling like I had dodged a bullet, with Emma not bringing up anything about last night, I almost ran to my car to get out of the house and head to work. After my board meeting, I would make some calls to work out what happened last night.

Kate

Chapter 25

I loved my job. I had worked with Sarah as her secretary for over ten years. We had both had personal ups and down's during this time, and although I knew she was my boss, I also knew that we were friends. When she married Peter, I thought they were the perfect couple. He was charming and funny, and although he was not as successful as Sarah was in his career, I thought that would be a plus for them. Peter was very supportive of Sarah's drive and work ethic, and when Chloe came along, he was happy to be the stay-at-home parent for a while, so that Sarah didn't have to.

However, it didn't work out. When Peter stopped working, he and Sarah had nothing in common. As Sarah worked her usual long hours and weekends, Peter became demanding and difficult, constantly complaining that she was putting her work before her family. He seemed to ignore the fact that is what they had agreed to do when they had planned to have Chloe.

Perhaps I was biased, but I admired Sarah and how she handled her divorce from Peter.

I was becoming concerned about her lately. I did not think Phil would be positive in her life. It appeared that he was gaining her attention, which was unusual for Sarah. I knew it was not part of my job, but I felt I needed to protect her from this man. At times she was just too nice for her own good.

After showing Con Habib into the conference room to meet with Sarah, I went back into my office. I called the psychiatrist whom I knew Sarah had been seeing. I knew it was a naughty of me, but I thought I would chase up a report he was doing in one of our cases and see if I could get him to talk to me about Sarah. I had been dying to speak to him since Sarah told me that she had brought up Phil with him. I was relieved when he answered the phone. I said to him, "Sorry to be demanding, but I am just chasing up the family report in the Lee matter."

"I am just finishing that now, Kate. I can email it to you in about thirty minutes."

"Thanks, Charlie. Once we get that, we can book the mediation the Judge ordered."

"No problem, Kate. I was hoping to tell Sarah I had nearly finished the report when she had her appointment today, but as you would know, she cancelled it," Charlie said.

"Sarah told me about it. I know she got grumpy with you after what you said when she told you about Phil. I can't believe she discussed Phil with you. I didn't know she felt anything for him but bringing him up with you means that she obviously does."

"I wasn't expecting it either. I had no idea that Phil was a former client and that he had sent that overwhelming flower delivery which turned your office into an instant florist. It clearly had affected Sarah in a way she was not expecting," he said.

"I can't believe he managed to impress her with that stunt. For a woman who is so intelligent, how can she be so naive when it comes to men."

"It's easy to see how the attention of a man sending you flowers is touching. The way he did it is the cause for concern," Charlie replied.

"I agree. The guy sends a florist shop full of flowers like a lunatic, invading and overwhelming our whole office and causing a couple of the other girls and me to have sinus, asthma and allergy attacks, and Sarah falls for that."

"That is what Phil does; he shocks people. He can see if his angle is working when he gets them off guard. Sarah interpreted the flower delivery as a man desperately trying to get her attention and show how much he cared about her. But because she has had an emotional void from losing her parents and then being taken away from her grandmother and brother, she is vulnerable to a manipulative vulture like Phil."

"I feel awful judging her now you have explained it to me like that. Poor Sarah."

"All we see is the confident, outgoing Sarah who would normally laugh off such an absurd gesture of wealth and ego. People like Phil work out the weaknesses in people and then play on it to their advantage."

"I see what you are saying, but why does he want to do this if he really doesn't care about her? Kate said.

"Oh, he does care about her, but not in a genuine way. Sarah is a trophy to him. She is a beautiful and impressive woman; that's clearly a notch he wants on his belt. He is a selfish narcissist."

"Well, that's one description of him," Kate said. "I would prefer to summarise him as a serial womaniser, a conceited but successful and rich misogynist who preys on emotionally vulnerable woman like Sarah to satisfy his ego. I bet once he got Sarah, after using her as a handbag for as long as it suited him, he would become bored with her, cheat on her and then dump her like all the other women in his life."

"That is his pattern. But let's see it as a positive start that Sarah has brought up Phil with me because it obviously means that she is questioning her feelings about him. If nothing else, Sarah still believes I am a good judge of character and bringing him up with me means she is doubting her own judgement about him."

"Yes, you are right. That is a good sign then that she is talking to you about him."

"Did she tell you that she was annoyed with me?" Charlie asked.

"Oh, yes. You are in trouble, but not so deep that she didn't ask me to call you and chase you about the report. She will come around – you know that."

"I think I will pay the price for a little while yet. While that is the case, you will need to watch Phil and what he bombards Sarah with next. If I am right, his next move will be to show he is sincere," Charlie replied.

Kate laughed before she blurted out loudly to Charlie, "The Children's Hospital Ball. He invited Sarah and all of us to a ball. I thought he was kind and grateful, but this is all just part of his plan to blindside Sarah."

"Kate, I have no doubt that he will put on the show of all shows at the charity ball, trying to impress Sarah with his kindness and generosity. Phil is clearly trying very hard."

"It's too late to pull out of it. The staff are so excited about it. But don't worry, Charlie. I will ensure Sarah does not fall into Phil's lap because of this stunt."

"Always keep an eye on her. Never underestimate this man Kate," Charlie replied.

"I won't," I said. "He may have thought he had worked out how to win Sarah over, but he has forgotten he has to get past me to get to her."

"Sarah is fortunate to have you, Kate."

"Thanks, Charlie and I will be in touch. Together we can keep Phil under control."

Peter

Chapter 26

I had only posted the letter to Anthony three days ago, so I was shocked when I received a call from an unknown number, and it was from Anthony responding to my letter so quickly. He said he had called me as soon as he could after receiving it.

Anthony had excitedly told me that he was lodging an appeal to his conviction, and if that was successful, he might be out on bail soon. He said his lawyer told him it could happen within the next few weeks.

When I asked Anthony if I could visit him in jail, he responded enthusiastically, "Of course." I believed that if I could just meet and speak to him, I would have a chance to find a way to get him to retract his allegations against me.

When I told Anthony that I would visit him on Saturday, I heard an audible gasp from him over the phone before he replied, "That's only three days away."

When I asked, "Is that too soon?"

He replied, "No, I look forward to it."

I was relieved that Anthony still sounded like a naive and excitable twelve-year-old boy. My recollections of our time together were of good times, fun and laughter. I hoped to remind him of that and find out how he had rewritten history to demonise it, as it was portrayed in his statement to the police.

After thinking about what Anthony had said to me, I wondered if Anthony's lawyers had suggested that he make the allegations against me as an avenue for him to appeal his conviction. Perhaps I was merely being used as the sacrifice for Anthony's freedom? If that was the case,

I needed to find a way where Anthony could still have his appeal, get out on bail, but later drop the charges against me? Maybe that was the solution to this nightmare.

It was all starting to make sense to me now. I had found it hard to believe that Anthony had instigated the allegations the police were investigating. Although I knew Anthony had been angry when he found out that I was Sarah's husband, I thought the letter he had sent to her had been sent to hurt and embarrass her rather than to hurt me, as Sarah and I were already divorced.

Now the reason Anthony was directing his anger towards me and not towards his ex-wife and stepdaughter made sense.

I picked up Anthony's statement and read it through again, this time in another light. I tried to read it through the eyes of a judge who would have to decide whether there was a reasonable basis upon which Anthony's mental state had been impaired at the time of the charges, and whether that evidence had not been placed before the Court at the time of the hearing. I was impressed. It really was a genius angle, but it did require him to throw me under the bus to get himself out of jail.

Mark

Chapter 27

After pacing up and down the corridor of the third floor of the Family Court for what seemed like an eternity, I watched as the lift doors opened and my accountant finally stepped out. He walked toward us, carrying a bundle of documents. He looked concerned, which worried me. I walked over to him to direct him into the meeting room. As we walked into the room, Brian asked, "Mark, what is going on? The account details you gave me are for a St George Bank account we closed twelve years ago when we moved offices. After that, we moved banks to NAB, remember?"

Sarah introduced herself to Brian and said, "Hi Brian, we have spoken on the phone a few times over the last couple of years. Nice to meet you."

"Pleasure to meet you, Sarah," he replied.

"Brian, please come into our room and have a seat so that we can explain to you what the problem is and what we need your help with."

"Brian walked into the room and sat down. He said, "I really don't understand. I closed all the accounts for Mark with St George Bank and changed banks for him when he moved offices, and that was twelve years ago."

Sarah asked Brian, "Are you telling us that you believed that this account was closed? Because it appears it is still in Mark's name and operating with over $1 million in it? Could it be possible that this account was not closed?"

Brian frowned as he responded and said, "I suppose it is possible that the bank may not have closed the account as we had instructed. But I know it is impossible that the $1 million that it is in the account is Mark's money. I withdrew all his funds from all his accounts to zero balances. I know that and have the statements from the time since I did it. I had to do that, as it is an essential part of the process to close an account." Brian then handed the copies of the bank statements he was referring to, to Sarah.

Sarah took the statements from Brian and looked through them. She then spread out the bank statements she had received from the solicitors for Mark's wife on the table. She then said to Brian, "You can see from these bank statements that there have been deposits into the account regularly over the last few years, and the current balance is just over $1 million? How do we explain this?"

"I can guarantee that Mark has not deposited these funds. I run all his financial affairs, and this is not his money. Why someone else would deposit funds into the account I cannot answer."

Sarah responded, "That is the missing piece of the puzzle, isn't it? Why would money be deposited into an account that was apparently closed and not theirs?"

"I have never heard of something like this in 30 years of accounting," Brian replied.

Sarah picked up the bank statement and said to me, "The mailing address is a PO Box in Mosman. There is also a letter from the bank confirming that the account address was the office address, but the mailing address was the Post Office Box. Do you know who leased your offices after you moved out of them Mark?"

"No, I don't know, Sarah, that was twelve years ago. I have rarely been in the area since."

Brian said to Sarah, "I was there the other day. It's an upmarket chocolate shop now. My daughter noticed it as we drove by and asked if we could go in and look. They have a chocolate mixing machine and hand-make all their products. It's quite impressive."

Sarah said to Brian, "It must be the new tenant using the bank account. Brian, who is your contact at St George Bank? You need to get onto them and find out why the account was not closed as per your instructions. If it is still being used, and if so, by whom. That will be the answer to this riddle."

Brian stood up and said, "I will go and call them now. I can't believe a stupid error like not processing the paperwork to close off the bank account has resulted in this mess."

Sarah paced the room and said to Tim, "Why would someone else use this account if it wasn't in their name and why? Who puts $1 million in an account in someone else's name? It must be money laundering?"

It suddenly dawned on me. I said to Sarah, "I think I know what happened. After I moved out of the office, I remember that I got a call a couple of weeks later from the new tenant to let me know that they had some mail from the bank that had arrived for me. I thanked him and asked if he could forward it onto me. The guy asked me what I thought of St George as a bank, and I told him my accountant and PA managed everything and had no idea except that I had now moved my accounts to NAB. He did forward the letters to me, and they arrived at my new office. They were just bank statements with zero balances, so I threw them all in the bin, thinking nothing of it."

Brian walked back into the room and said, "I've just got off the phone with St George. As I recall, the account was drawn down to zero by my transferring the balance into a new account at NAB. They have a record of us requesting that the account be closed, but for some reason, it wasn't. Someone has been using it since, regularly depositing and withdrawing large sums of money. I told the bank that it was not Mark that has been using the account, and they have now called the fraud squad, who they said would want to speak to Mark. It seems we have been unwittingly caught up in a messy and possibly criminal situation."

"Brian, can we get written confirmation of this to show the judge what has gone on and that this is not Mark's money."

"They are working on that now. It isn't Mark's money," Brian replied.

"I can't believe we are having to try so hard to show these million dollars are not Mark's. This could only happen to me," Mark said as he paced the room. "The complete reverse of stealing. I am trying to prove money isn't mine; that is in my name."

"I don't know if this makes you feel better, but this has not happened to me before in a case," Sarah replied."

"Don't you love this process, Brian?" Mark said. "Your wife leaves you for your best mate. Then her lawyer's find $1 million in a bank account you stopped using 12 years ago. As a result of that, of course your ex-wife's lawyer thinks you're lying and hiding money. To prove yourself innocent, you must find out whose $1 million dollars is in the bank account in your name to give it back to them."

"I'm sorry Mark," Brian responded.

Sarah said to Brian, "Sorry for the pressure Brian, but we must urgently get copies of these bank statements and account details to the Judge."

"I'm onto it,' Brian said. "I will talk to the bank again now and get it all and confirmation in writing."

Con

Chapter 28

The hardest part of my wife leaving me, was the pain it was causing my daughters. I know they were trying to support me, but they also loved their mother, even though she was ending our marriage and our lives as we knew it. It was not fair that their lives would now have to change and they would lose their home, which they had lived in since they were born.

I know that my girls had tried to talk their mother into changing her mind, or at least to consider going to counselling, but it had not worked. I know they felt conflicted and hurt in their feelings toward her and pity for me. I fluctuated between feeling angry at my wife and sad for daughters. What I had worked so hard to achieve in my life was financial security for my family. I never thought that my wife would rip this away from our daughters, with her concern only being for herself.

At the request of my daughters, I had agreed to meet with my wife to discuss what she wanted. Although I knew it would be a waste of time, my daughters had pleaded with me to see if I could reach an agreement with her without involving lawyers. The main thing they said they wanted, was for everything to be sorted out amicably. They said that they just wanted peace between their parents, whom they both loved.

I was devastated when my daughters told me they would be fine if the house was sold; if that was what their mother wanted. I couldn't help but feel angry at my wife for doing this to them. If she wanted to leave the family to be with another man and his children, why didn't she go? Why did she need to disrupt our daughters lives by forcing us to sell our home?

When I had called her to arrange the meeting, my wife had requested that we meet at our local coffee shop. She didn't want us to meet at home, as I had suggested. She had clearly given the practicalities of our meeting some thought. It appeared that she had been planning ending our marriage for a while and that I had been the last person to know how she felt.

I arrived early for our meeting. I chose to sit at a table near the entrance looking out to the street. I had to admit, if I was to be honest, that I still hoped I could talk sense into my wife about what she was doing. As I looked towards the street, I saw my wife walking towards the coffee shop, holding a man's hand. They stopped about twenty metres away, and the man let her hand go before kissing her. They both then walked in different directions. She smiled at him before he walked away. She was still smiling as she walked into the coffee shop and saw me.

I stood up as she walked towards me. She leaned to kiss me on the cheek before I pulled away and sat down. Sensing my unhappiness, she said to me, "Thanks for meeting me. The girls would really like us to try and sort things out. They don't want us to have lawyers writing to each other or to go to Court, and neither do I."

"You started the involvement with lawyers, Eva, not me," I replied as I sat down.

"Con, please. Just be reasonable. I had to get the lawyer to write to you because you refused to talk to me about it. Selling the house is the right thing to do now. I don't want to take any of your superannuation, as that is what you live on, and I know that you will continue to support our girls. It's fair we both get half of the house. That will let us both move on with our lives and allow me to support myself. I am not asking for more than half of the house and our girls think that is fair."

"Why don't you stop this, Eva? That would be the fairest thing to do for the girls. To stop this nonsense and let us be a family again."

"Con, I am not staying married to you, and you must accept that. I thought this meeting was about us trying to reach a settlement, not a reconciliation or I would not have agreed to it."

"I thought I could talk you out of your insanity, but I was wrong. Goodbye, Eva," I said as I got up and walked out of the coffee shop.

I walked briskly around the corner but stayed close enough to see Eva. I watched as she remained seated and then took her mobile phone out of her handbag and started to make a call. Her boyfriend walked in and sat across from her before she could dial his number. I watched as he reached out for her hand.

I walked to my car and called my cousin. "It's over," I said to him.

"There is no hope?" He asked.

"No. None. Her boyfriend brought her to the meeting but stayed outside. Then after I left, he joined her again. She is not coming home."

"I understand," he said. "It's honourable you tried. It's a pity she did this. I liked Eva."

Emma

Chapter 29

It was a relief when Bruce left for work. When he had got out of bed, it had taken all my self-control not to burst out laughing when I saw the back of his head as he walked to the bathroom. That feeling disappeared quickly though and was replaced by anger when I recalled who Marci was and how she had appeared wrapped around his neck last night when he came home.

To control myself, I sent a text message to Sophia. I knew she would be waiting to hear from me. Instantly upon texting her, *OMG he is up and I just saw what we did to the back of his head*, Sophia text back, *Don't say anything to Bruce about last night just yet. Text me after he leaves for work.*

I could not believe that Bruce had just got out of bed and pretended as if nothing had happened. He was extraordinary. Either he had been acting or had no memory of the night before; either scenario was terrible. I had promised Sophia last night not to raise anything with him and to let him go to work and meet her at the coffee shop as soon as he left. I sent her a text message to let her know he had left and that I would meet her in thirty minutes.

During the drive to the coffee shop, I had been worried that Bruce would call me and ask me about last night, but there had been no calls from him yet. Although I knew he deserved it, I also knew he would be angry at me if he knew what we had done to him. The night had been surreal, and I was still trying to process it all while at the same time trying to block it out so that I didn't burst out crying whilst I was driving.

I arrived at the coffee shop at 9 am, but as usual, Sophia was early. I saw her sitting at our regular table. Sophia smiled at me as I walked up to the table. No matter how I felt, I knew I would be all right when she smiled. Sophia got up, put her arms around, and said, "Are you alright, honey?"

"I am now," I said as I sat down. "I am starving. I don't know if being pregnant or stressed makes me hungry lately, but I'm always starving."

"A bit of both, Sophia smiled as she replied. "I am just relieved to see you are all right. It was a tough night."

"It was horrific," I said.

Sophia could see that I was stressed. She said reassuringly, "He will never know you were involved. He will think Marci did it and accuse her of it. Marci will deny it, and then it will all blow up between them. I wish I were a fly on the wall when she got the call. It's no longer our problem. Let's order and enjoy our breakfast while he tries to figure out what happened."

"I hope you are right," I said.

"I know last night shocked and upset you, but for now, you need to try and put it out of your head. You need to concentrate on the baby, which means not being stressed. Trust me, Bruce won't mention last night if you don't. Let it go."

"I'm really trying to, but the fact that my husband brought home another woman after forgetting to pick me up for dinner is not easy."

Sophia just burst out laughing. Everyone in the coffee shop turned to look at her. When she noticed the attention, she had garnered she stopped laughing and said to me, "I am so sorry Emma. I really did not mean for that to happen, but the way you just put what Bruce did last night just made me see how nuts it all was."

I smiled at her and said, "Honestly, I can't believe what I just said. It was nuts, is still nuts and I think all we can do is laugh or otherwise I will cry."

"Let's change the topic then," Sophia replied. "I think he has taken up enough of our morning."

After having a couple of cups of tea and changing the topic to the baby with Sophia, I started to relax. As soon as our breakfast arrived, I practically inhaled my scrambled eggs. I ate them so quickly and realised how hungry I had been. Watching me, Sophia asked, "Same again?"

"I can't believe I just did that."

"One for you and one for the baby," Sophia said as she waved to the waitress for the same again.

"Thank you for looking after me. You are my rock. My mother always told me that husbands may come and go, but girlfriends are forever."

"Your mother is such a wise woman. I remember she told me that the only thing she loved more than getting married, all six times, were the breaks she had in between being single."

Mark

Chapter 30

The scene was chaotic, which was not what I had expected during a Family Court hearing. The mystery of the undisclosed bank account had caused so much excitement for my ex-wife's lawyers. Unfortunately, it would lead to nothing for my ex-wife and me, except more hours of legal fees for us to pay to solve a money laundering scheme for the police.

Brian had been onto the bank, and my secretary had called to say she was on her way to the Court with the documents. As instructed by Sarah, I stood waiting at the lift for my secretary to arrive. Finally the lift stopped at our floor and she got a shock as the lift doors opened and she saw me standing in front of them. She was holding a large bundle of documents which she immediately handed me.

I said to her, "I am so sorry you had to rush over here with this. My apologies."

"I enjoyed the walk and I wanted to help," she replied.

Brian walked over to us and immediately took the documents out of my arms as he said to me, "I will take those." He walked into the conference room, and we followed him as he sat down and quickly flicked through them.

After a few minutes, he said to me, "We need to show this to Sarah and Tim. It explains what and how this happened. Where are they?"

"In the room next door, they were going through some of the other subpoenaed bank statements," I said.

Brian picked up the statements, and we walked into the conference room, where Sarah and Tim were seated. Brian said, "I have good news. We have the bank statements showing that someone else has been operating the account. The account was empty when they started using it, and there has been a trail of deposits over the last twelve years. The fraud squad from the bank are now investigating this. I have two emails from them to show the Court that the monies were not from Mark or any of Mark's companies or trusts. The fraud team will provide more information as it comes to hand."

"Great work Brian. Tim and I can now give this information to the lawyers for the other side at the same time as letting the Judge know we are ready to resume," Sarah said.

"I am sure this was not what they were expecting," Tim said as he and Sarah headed off looking very pleased.

When Sarah returned to the room, I said to her, "I just got a call from the hospital. The patient I spoke to you about earlier today is deteriorating badly."

"I am sorry to hear that," Sarah replied.

"Sarah, I really need to go and see her and the team of specialists who are working on her case. Would it be possible for me to come to Court a little later tomorrow so I can attend the hospital for a couple of hours in the morning? The mornings are when the teams do their rounds for the patients."

"I'm so sorry to hear that, Mark. Let me see what we can do. You are supposed to be in Court the whole time of the hearing, but I will ask Tim to seek to leave for you from the Judge to come a little later. Once this issue is sorted out, we will only be going through objections to affidavits for the afternoon. So, today is the best day for you to be excused in the circumstances."

"While I am at the hospital, I would like to be able to see any other patients that need me as well. I know the Registrars are struggling with my absence at court this week."

Sarah approached Tim, who had just walked back to them. She explained Mark's request to him. Tim replied, "Of course, I will put it to the Judge. The Court will resume, and I will ask him from the bar table for his consent."

The court officer informed us that the Judge was ready to resume in Court in five minutes. We all headed back to the courtroom. When the Judge entered the courtroom, I impressed myself with a reflex action of standing and bowing to him before he sat down.

Everyone else in the room sat down except for Tim, who immediately addressed the Judge saying, "Your Honour, we have unravelled the mystery of the undisclosed $1 million bank account. The account had been a St George Bank account in our client's name. Our client's accountant had requested the account be closed about the same time our client moved offices some twelve years ago. Due to a bank error, the account was not closed and was subsequently used by the occupants of my client's former rented premises. Those persons have been using the account for the last 12 years. We have bank statements that we seek to hand up, copies of which have been provided to my learned friends to examine. We wish to confirm that the police and bank fraud squad are now investigating the matter."

The Judge examined bank statements, slowly flicking through several pages. He then looked towards the barrister for Mark's ex-wife, "Do you accept the evidence and explanation that has been provided?"

"Yes, your honour."

"Good. Then we can then recommence the proceedings," the Judge responded.

"There is only one other thing, Your Honour,' Tim said. "As my client is the Director of Oncology at the Royal Hospital, his attendance in Court is causing difficulties for the staff and his patients, particularly one of his gravely ill patients. Our client seeks your leave to be excused from attending court tomorrow morning, so that he may be able to be present at a morning round with this patient and the rest of his medical team tomorrow morning. This will mean that he will be present in Court after lunch. I note your Honour, that we are only making objections to affidavits during the rest of today and tomorrow morning, so I believe it would not prejudice any part of the hearing if he were absent during that period."

His Honour looked directly at me and said, "Dr Paul, your attendance is required throughout your hearing unless you are excused. To be fair to Mrs Paul, can you please tell me how imperative it is that you attend the hospital tomorrow morning?"

I replied, "Your Honour, I would not be exaggerating if I said I am concerned that my patients' lives are being compromised by my inability to check on them and their treatment in the mornings. One of my clients is responding badly to treatment, and they cannot determine why. I am her treating specialist, and her condition is deteriorating rapidly. I will, of course, attend the hospital after Court today. However, I would like to check on her and my other patients in the morning, being crucial times in their chemotherapy treatment."

The Judge had listened intently with direct eye contact with me while I spoke. He replied, "Dr Paul, you are excused from attending court tomorrow morning until lunchtime, and if this difficulty again arises at any other time during this hearing, I assure you I will try to assist you as much as possible. I implore my learned friends at the bar table to do the same."

My ex-wife suddenly shouted out loudly, "No." She then stood up and briskly walked over to the bar table next to her barrister who had already turned towards her. He stood up and whispered something to her, but she was demonstrably upset as she waved her hands in the air and then pushed him aside to speak into his microphone.

My ex-wife then proceeded to speak to the Judge directly and said, "No, Judge, you can't let him do this. Throughout my marriage, I have had to put up with him not being around and saying, "Sorry, but I must go to the hospital. They really need me there. What about me? Why don't I matter, and why do people always regard him as so wonderful? All I got was during my whole marriage were people saying to me, "Your husband is amazing. He saved my life." Your honour, my husband was never home, not on my birthday or our anniversary. Every special occasion he seemed to be needed by the hospital and he would go running. He should have to be a normal person now and sit in this Court during this court case like all other ex-husbands must."

The room was silent and everyone was staring at my ex-wife. Now that she had stopped speaking, she looked around, and as she saw the look on everyone's faces, especially the Judge's, she walked back to her seat and sat down.

The courtroom was silent. Her legal team looked like they wanted to crawl under the bar table. The Judge inadvertently had his mouth open. My ex-wife had slumped down into her chair and had now started crying.

I walked over to my ex-wife and put my arm around her. I could see everyone in the room watching in suspense for her reaction. I whispered to her, and she nodded. I looked up and motioned to her partner, sitting in the back of the room, to take over from me.

The Judge observed us from the bench and said to me, "Dr Paul, is Mrs Paul, ok?"

"Yes, Your Honour. She will be fine, but she could do it with a break and a cup of tea. I just apologised to her for needing to seeking leave to see my patients. I honestly did not expect it to be so upsetting to her."

The Judge announced, "We will now adjourn for Mrs Paul to have a break. During this time, I implore both legal teams to consider negotiations to try and reach a settlement in this matter. Now that the issue of the mystery bank account is solved, I cannot see any real reasons why two such experienced legal teams, as are in my Court today, cannot properly guide the parties to a settlement that would be a reasonable outcome in the circumstances of this matter. To assist, I refer you both to my recent judgements from last week, and I will have my associate provide you both with copies. I will resume when you both notify the court officer that you are ready. If a settlement is not reached, Dr Paul is excused from attending Court when we resume this afternoon and until 2 pm tomorrow afternoon."

Tim whispered to Sarah, "I was in the case he has referred us to. He is letting us know how he will decide this matter if he has to make orders."

"You will need to explain that to the other side, Tim. They have not been on their game so far," Sarah replied.

"Let's hope they get it after I point out the Judge's key findings in that case. If they do, we will have this case settled this afternoon, and Mark can get back to his patients and start his new life with the remaining half of his assets."

"Good luck explaining it to them. I would go so far as to underline the pertinent points. In the interim I want to take a walk and I will go and get us all a coffee," Sarah replied.

"I have a feeling this will settle. By the time you are back, I will have a draft set of settlement terms done," Tim said as he walked off to negotiate with the other barrister.

I asked Tim as he walked past me, "Did the Judge say that if we weren't going to settle, I could leave early?"

"Can you give me half an hour? Tim said. "I will know by then if we will settle or not."

"Of course." I will sit in the conference room, call the hospital and see how I can help over the phone until you let me know."

"And I will go and get us all a coffee," Sarah said. "If Tim is right, we will be doing some intensive drafting in the next hour."

Con

Chapter 31

Walking back to my car, I was angry at myself for not following my instinct. Eva knew that I would do anything to make my girls happy. She used them to lure me to a meeting where she thought she could convince me to do what she wanted. She was clearly besotted with her new man. She had forgotten about her marriage vows and her duty to her family, which should mean far more to her than fulfilling her own selfish desires. We had often discussed that marriage was about a commitment to not only each other, but more importantly to our children. It was about creating a legacy for them to continue living in this country that we had struggled to become a part of. Building a stable foundation for them and for their children to grow from.

After I saw Eva with her boyfriend, holding his hand and walking to our meeting, I knew it was over. I knew she was gone, and there was no turning back. I had heard enough now that sorting this out legally meant that I would lose my house and my daughters would lose their home.

I had seen four different lawyers to get advice about my divorce. They had all told me the same thing, but their advice ranged between Eva getting between 35 to 55 % of all of my assets. I decided to retain the two lawyers I liked the most, one male and one female. They had very different styles, but they were both highly respected.

Apart from Sarah, I also retained Neil Berkus. He had a reputation for being ruthless, mean and a woman hater. He tactfully advised me how to cause my wife as much stress as possible by dragging out the proceedings and cutting her off financially. He said to let the house look run down so that if I wanted to pay her out of her share of it, the valuation would be as low as it could be. I knew I would find that difficult to do if this process took years; as he said it might, as I prided myself on my home. Having the lawn un-mowed and the garden untidy was something I could not do.

I had told Neil that I had also retained Sarah Walters. I had agreed with him and my accountant that Sarah would be the lawyer I would keep officially on record with the Court. I wanted my daughters, friends, and family to believe that I was trying to do the right thing by my wife. Sarah Walters had a reputation for being a hard but fair lawyer.

I had thought about it and agreed with Neil that I should make the court proceedings go for as long as possible, so it was as stressful as possible. This would cause pressure on my wife, and I knew that would inevitably affect her and her new relationship. If her boyfriend was after her money, he would have to be patient. I was not going to hand over half my house just because Eva wanted to be free to be happy with him.

I had been surprised at how brave Eva had been acting, and I now knew it was because he was putting her up to it. I knew that Eva would never leave me to live a life on her own. She needed a partner because she had no life skills. She had never had a job in her life. She had never had to pay a bill, rent or mortgage payment in her life.

As financial stress was not something she had ever had to deal, the best chance of getting her to settle would be to drag her through protracted, intrusive, and expensive litigation. I also thought that her attractiveness to her boyfriend may fade when she became stressed and a financial liability rather than an asset to him.

The advice Neil had given me was to denigrate Eva's contributions as a mother and homemaker to Sarah. He said these allegations would really upset Eva, and, in his experience, more times than not, the constant denigration resulted in a wife agreeing to a settlement. Neil said the usual allegations he used were that the wife had psychological issues and/or consumed alcohol and/or prescription medication regularly and, as a result, had not contributed to the family or the marital assets and was an unfit mother.

I told Neil I did not want to say that Eva had been a bad mother throughout our marriage. Up until recently, Eva had been a wonderful mother and wife. The change from her being a devoted mother and loving wife to the woman she now seemed to have become had happened over the last few months. Until then, I could not fault what a wonderful wife and mother she had been. I thought her change in attitude in the previous few months may have been caused by menopause or the medication she was taking for menopause. Still, now it was too late, even if that was the case.

My brother had said I could go back to work with him and that if I did that, I could get a loan to buy Eva's share of the house, so I didn't have to sell it. I didn't like my options, but I had to be grateful I had one at least.

Neil had told me that once I had accepted the divorce, I would be able to move on quickly. In his experience, most men quickly got new partners these days. He advised me if I got into a new relationship that I needed to get a financial agreement done to avoid this happening again. I had said to him that there would never be another relationship. Still, he had told me that every man he had acted for re-partnered in months, primarily via social media. "Your daughters will probably set you up on dating sites, Con. No one wants a lonely, sad parent. Never forget, when one door closes, another one opens," he said.

I really didn't like Neil. I wondered what life had become when it seemed that a process had now developed where wives were replaced via the internet quickly and expediently, like getting a new car. It concerned me that this may one day happen to my daughters.

I found myself constantly worrying about the future of my daughters. I understood that marriage was difficult, but at no time during my marriage had I ever thought of leaving Eva or putting anything before her or my children. From what I was hearing from everyone now, especially my lawyers, divorce was considered not only acceptable but almost inevitable these days instead of once being frowned upon. The example for our children must come from us as parents, as Eva and I had always discussed.

How I wish I could remind Eva of this.

Sarah

Chapter 32

After seeing Mark's ex-wife's outburst in Court, I was relieved that I could excuse myself from the others. At the same time as being surprised by her outburst, I understood it. Mark was clearly treated differently in his role as a specialist. To her, he was her husband, and she should have always been his priority. For him, saving lives was his life's commitment, and he did not see the cost to his wife and family until it was too late.

When I arrived back at the Family Court with coffee for everyone, I saw Tim speaking to an older man. Mark was walking out of the conference room after making his calls and he also saw them. Mark said to me, "That's my father," as he walked towards them and hugged his dad. Mark introduced then introduced us to each other, "Dad, this is my lawyer, Sarah Walters. Sarah, this is my father, Ted."

Mark's father was a distinguished-looking gentleman. Immaculately dressed, wearing a suit with a matching tie and pocket handkerchief. I noticed that he had an Order of Australia on his lapel. Ted said to me, "I was in town for a meeting this morning and thought I would quickly visit and see how Mark was doing in Court. I had loaned him a lot of money to pay for your services, Ms Walters, and I was interested to see how it was all going."

"Sorry, that's my father's sense of humour, Sarah," Mark said, looking embarrassed.

"It's a pleasure to meet you, Mr Paul," I said.

"Why were you talking to Tim, Dad?"

"I introduced myself to him," Tim interjected and said as he heard Mark ask the question to his father. "I noticed him outside the courtroom door and recognised him from the photo you showed me."

"Do you carry around a photo of me Mark? I didn't know you loved me so much," his father said with a smirk on his face.

"Dad, stop it. Not everyone gets your sense of humour. I have photos of you, mum, and the kids on my mobile phone."

"He loves getting cross at me," Ted said to Sarah.

"Anyway, which photo did you show Tim, Mark?" Ted asked.

"It was the photo of you in the army Dad, because Tim had a photo of his father in his office, who also served. I can't imagine how Tim recognised you from that."

Tim said, "My father served, and we lost him. I don't believe you have aged a day since that photo Mr Paul. Thank you for your service."

I could see that both Mark and his father were touched by Tim's acknowledgement of Ted's service.

"Tim told me that it looks like you have settled the case," Ted said.

Mark looked up at Tim and asked, "Is that right? They have accepted our offer?"

Tim looked very pleased with himself as he replied, "Yes, they have and they have signed. All I need is for you to sign the settlement terms and we are done. I was coming to find you in the conference room when I spotted your father."

"What are we doing talking then. Let's do this before she changes her mind," Mark said.

"Let's all go into the conference room to review the terms so you can sign them, I said.

"Should I wait out here?" Ted asked Mark.

"No, Dad, please come in," Mark replied.

I then said, "Please come in with us, Ted. The settlement terms include the loan repayment terms for monies Mark owes you for his legal fees."

After going through the terms of the settlement, Mark had just signed the last page when there was a knock on the door by the Judge's associate. He opened the door, peeked in, and asked, "Are you ready to hand up the terms to His Honour?"

"Perfect timing," Sarah said as she handed the signed terms to the associate. "Great work. I will get two copies done for you. His Honour will see you all in the courtroom in fifteen minutes."

As we walked out of the conference room, Mark saw his ex-wife and her partner, his former best friend, step out of another conference room and walk towards the courtroom. He turned and said to me, "Sarah, it's amazing. I no longer felt sadness or anger, just relief." His father, Ted, patted Mark on his back. I was touched by Ted's support of his son.

I said to Ted, "You are welcome to come into the courtroom. You will see the show live and get some idea of how your money was spent."

"See, she does get my sense of humour," Ted said to Mark.

"I am so glad this is over now. You two would drive me crazy," Mark replied.

As we walked into the courtroom, Mark asked his father to sit beside him, just behind Tim and me. The Judge proceeded to finalise the matter. He addressed Mark and his ex-wife directly, saying, "I congratulate you both on coming to the agreement contained in terms of settlement before me, which will now become Court Orders. I know this has been a long and difficult case for both of you, and I wish you both well."

Mark stood up and said, "Thank you, Your Honour."

His Honour asked Mark, "Is that your father with you?"

"Yes, Your Honour," Mark replied.

The Judge said to Ted, "I was happy to read that one of the first loans to be repaid in the settlement terms will be to you, Sir. Your loan to your son will be repaid directly to you from the sale of the family home, which is being placed on the market for sale immediately."

Ted had stood up when the Judge had addressed him. He replied, "I never doubted that Mark would repay me. Never at all."

His Honour took off his glasses as he said to Ted, "There had been some discussion in the evidence that the loan was a gift and non-repayable, but your affidavit was clear on your view. I am glad that issue was settled amicably."

"Your Honour, I helped Mark because the financial stress of his legal fees was distracting him from his work. His work is too important for him to have been distracted by something I could easily help with. I knew he would repay me before I needed the money again."

Deep in thought, his Honour said, "I am sure I have met you before, Ted. I thought I recognised you when you walked in, but your voice rings a bell with me."

Ted replied, "Your Honour when I saw your name outside on the courtroom door, I remembered your father telling me proudly when you were appointed a judge. Your father and I served together in the army.

I met you several years ago at your mother's funeral. After your father remarried, I have not seen much of him. Please give him my regards."

"I remember now. How nice to see you again, Captain. I have not seen much of my father since he remarried either. You must also be very proud of your son for becoming a doctor and doing his magnificent work."

"I am a very proud father, but I would have liked to see you at work too. I am being selfish when I say I am sorry the matter settled."

The Judge smiled and then said, "If the matter had not been settled, and you had been called to give evidence about the affidavit you filed relating to your loan to your son, I would have had to excuse myself from the case, Ted. It could have been a disaster for everyone."

"Why would you have had to do that?" Ted asked.

"Because there is no way I could view your evidence as being unreliable. You not only served this country, but you did so with my father. I am required to be impartial, and I would have been biased in my opinion of you. Now, as the parties have reached an agreement, this is not an issue, and I hereby make the orders in accordance with the terms of the settlement before me."

"Glad we dodged that bullet," Ted responded.

"I'm glad I could see you again, Ted, with such a wonderful result for everyone here. I will ask my associate to give you my contact details, and if you wish to come and watch one of my cases, or just come in and have morning tea with me, you are most welcome."

"I would enjoy that," Ted replied.

As Mark walked out of the courtroom with his father, he said, "I can't believe you knew the Judge. Thank goodness we avoided that complication. I don't think I could have coped with another drama today."

"Yes, that would have caused us great problems," I said.

"May I buy you all a drink?" Ted asked.

Mark looked relaxed and even happy as he said, "By the way, when dad asks you for a drink, it's not just one. Just beware."

"There is a great bar across the road called "Love Bites," it's our local. Will that do?" Tim replied.

"Perfect, but do you think we could ask the Judge to come too?" Ted said.

"You just got his number from his associate. Dad, you can call him and ask him."

Bruce

Chapter 33

As I got into my car, I wondered for a moment if I should be driving. My recollection of the night before was vague at best, with the only clear thing I could remember was forgetting to pick up my wife for dinner. It was a miracle that she was not cross with me this morning.

I started the car and decided to take the risk of driving to the office. I hoped that my luck would continue for the day. I felt fine, which was a miracle, and I had an important meeting I had to make. I put my mobile on the car charger as it had died overnight. I knew that I had to start getting in the right head space. It was an important pitch to an important new client, and I needed to be impressive. I knew exactly what I needed to do and how to present it.

My mobile beeped with messages as soon as it had started charging. I played the messages. There had been five messages from Emma asking what time the driver would pick her up for dinner from last night. *Why hadn't Emma said anything this morning? Did I eventually speak to her?* I asked myself but remembering nothing.

I punched the air whilst driving, annoyed that I had allowed myself to get into such a state that I had stuffed up badly. After my meeting, I would need to deal with finding out what I had taken that had made me lose all memory of the night. It just wasn't normal for me.

I could not believe how stupidly I had let Renae talk me into going on his boat yesterday. When Renae said that Emma could come on board for dinner, I should have known that it was just his ruse to get me there mid-week. Things always got out of control when I was with him and ended in chaos.

My mobile rang, and I could see the call was from Marci. I let the call ring out so it diverted to my message bank, and then I started to remember bits and pieces of the day before. I remembered Marci was there, but I needed to remember how Marci got on the boat.

Pulling into the car park at my office, I looked at the time and was relieved to see that I was half an hour early. Luckily, the traffic had been light this morning, so I would have time for a coffee and a rundown of the agenda with my PA before the meeting. After parking my car, I walked to the lift and, as usual, sent my PA a text so she could have my coffee ready for me.

The lift doors opened, and as I walked out, my PA, Tina, promptly greeted me with the agenda for the meeting. She handed it to me, saying, "I will bring your coffee into your office in a minute and go through it with you."

"Thanks. I need coffee urgently."

"I hope you weren't too late picking up Emma last night. She called me, but I told her you had already left by then. I tried calling you, but you didn't answer, and then your phone seemed to be off."

"I stuffed up."

"What's that mean?" Tina asked.

"I don't have time for this now. I will tell you about it later. I need to get into the right head space for the pitch and talking about last night won't help me do that."

"Ok, got it," Tina replied.

As I walked towards my office, Tina called out, "Mark, what on earth is on the back of your head?"

"What?"

Tina then leapt towards me and told me to turn back around as she stared closely at the back of my head. She touched the back of my head as she said, "It's ink. Why were you with Marci yesterday? I can't believe she did that. What were you thinking?"

I was stunned. I had no idea how Tina had just found out about me being with Marci.

"What is wrong, Tina?"

"Are you serious? You have no idea?"

"Yes, why are you touching my head and bringing up Marci now? I am about to go into a meeting and don't have time for these hysterics?"

"You want to go into the meeting with that on the back of your head?" "What are you talking about, Tina? What do you mean something is on the back of my head?"

She put my hand on the back of my head. I knew something was wrong. Tina suddenly realised I had no idea Marci had drawn on my head without me knowing.

"I didn't know Marci was that smart! You don't even know, do you? She has written "I love Marci" in the middle of a heart on the back of your head, you idiot."

I had no recollection of this, and I didn't think Tina was making it up, but it was hard to believe. "I need to see it. How can I see it?" I said to Tina as I tried feeling the back of my head with my hand. Tina thought for a minute and then ran to her desk. "Where are you going?"

"To get my mobile. I'll take a photo, and then you can see it." Tina grabbed her mobile phone, took a photo of the back of my head, and then showed me her phone.

"How did she do that? We need to get this off now, Tina. I have a meeting in 30 minutes."

"Let's go into your office ensuite and try scrubbing it off. It looks like she has used a really thick ink, though. I hope it's not one of those waterproof ones, or you are in trouble."

"What do we do if we can't get it off?"

Tina frowned, took a deep breath, and then said, "If we can't get it off, we get you into the boardroom; first, seat you closest to the end wall at the table, and you do not leave until everyone else has left."

I realised how much I owed Tina. She was remarkably calm while I was completely rattled. "I'm sorry, Tina," I said.

"We had better see if we can get this off," Tina said.

I followed her into the ensuite of my office. She took a packet of wipes out of her handbag and tried those first. I moaned as she rubbed the back of my head firmly. Tina then said, "These wipes remove waterproof mascara, but I am not getting anywhere here except maybe causing your head to go bright red."

"It feels like you are trying to rip the skin off my head."

"It's not coming off this way. We need to work out what else to do. Maybe I could cover it with foundation?"

"We need to get me through this meeting. I promise I will sort things out with Marci after that."

"Sure, you will. You said that years ago,' Tina replied as she tried applying foundation to cover the back of my head. "This isn't working either."

"What now?" I asked.

"Bruce, I am not a magician. I'm just your PA. Removing graffiti off the back of your head is not in my job description," Tina said. Looking at each other, we realised the situation's ridiculousness, and both burst out laughing.

Tina said, "We must go back to plan B. You walk into the boardroom now and sit with your back to the far wall. You cannot leave until everyone else does."

"Let's go," I said.

Sarah

Chapter 34

It had been a fantastic way to finish a long day in Court and end a three-year court case. Having celebratory drinks with Ted, Mark's father, and Tim at the Love Bites Café was such a great idea by Mark's father. We even had a guest appearance by Judge Stevens.

It was now 6.30 pm, and as I strolled back to the office, I knew that all my staff would have left for the day. I walked into my office, opened my bar fridge, and poured myself a glass of wine. I relaxed in my leather chair, leaned back, threw my shoes off and put my feet on the desk.

I enjoyed this part of my day. Wine in hand, being alone and enjoying the view from my office. The sun was setting, and the boats and yachts were scattered across the harbour. My law lecturer at university had said to me to explain to me why he was not taking a break from lecturing to grieve after his mother died, "Sarah, no matter what drama is going on in your life, the lives of others continue to go on, and as such, so must we." I wondered why that saying always came to me and, as always, if it was comforting or disturbing.

Kate unexpectedly walked into my office and saw that I looked tired. "Are you ok? I thought your case settled today?"

"Hi, I thought you had gone home. We settled but had drama during the day, so it was a long day. Would you like a glass of wine?" "No thanks. I must go. I had left, but I forgot something, and when I came back, I noticed you in your office. How did you get Mrs Paul to settle?" she asked.

"The Judge told us all to go out and settle, which was the best thing he could have done for them. It's been three years for Mark, and it's finally over. There could have been no better result for him, and he deserved it."

"I'm relieved for Mark. He is nice, and the case was hell for him."

While sitting at my desk, my mobile rang. Kate answered it, put it on hold and then told me it was Phil. I said to her, "Please tell him I will call him when I'm in the car. I need to get home soon to have dinner with Chloe."

"No problem," Kate replied.

After giving Phil the message, Kate said goodbye and left the office.

I was confused about why I was even bothering myself with Phil. I had avoided Phil's attempts to flirt with me over the years until now, and I had even successfully brushed off many of his offers for lunch to celebrate finalising one of his matters.

I knew his disastrous personal life history, having acted for him in his last three relationship breakdowns. I had listened to the lawyers for his ex-wives and partners recount how he had vigorously pursued their clients, at times relentlessly. I even knew that to add salt to the wound of his ex-partners, Phil always had a new love interest in the wings as he ended his last relationship.

If I was honest with myself, if nothing else, the fact I was feeling something made me feel better. Since breaking up with Peter, I had not dated anyone, and the recent revelation about Peter's sexual history as a teenager had totally destabilised me. I had found Phil's advances flattering rather than annoying. I had not realised, until he sent me flowers, unfortunately in the form of a florist shop, how much I had missed someone finding me attractive.

I felt guilty when I recalled the image of Kate, becoming increasingly enraged as the couriers went up and down the lift several times to deliver the multiple flower arrangements sent by Phil. It still made me laugh. I can still see how annoyed Kate was as arrangement after arrangement arrived, each one causing her allergy to flare up increasingly until her sneezing was uncontrollable. The scene was so ridiculous it was hilarious.

Looking at the time, I finished checking the messages on my desk and picked up my jacket and handbag to go home. When I got into my car, I was about to return Phil's call when Kate rang. She had been checking her emails on the train. The Family Court had notified her that two judgements we were waiting for had been listed to be handed down in the morning at the same time. I had just hung up on the call with Kate when Phil called me. I answered the call and said to Phil, "Hi, that was good timing. I was just about to call you back."

"Kate said you would call as soon as you got in your car, so I was worried." "Sorry, I just got a call from Kate while she was on the train about a couple of my matters. We were just notified by email from the Family Court they have been listed in Court tomorrow morning at the same time."

"Do you get cut in half to appear at both?" he replied.

"Wish it was that easy. We had to move three conferences around for one of the associates to appear in one of the cases."

"How can the Family Court give you such late notice, the night before and two cases at the same time? It seems a little unreasonable?"

"I am sure the Court thinks I should be appreciative."

"I always found it a strange place. Anyway, how was your day?"

"I was in Court all day, but we settled, which was great for both parties. It had been set down for hearing all week, so it also lightens my workload for the next couple of days."

"Maybe we could have lunch?' he asked.

"Maybe. Can I get back to you in the morning?"

"I thought your week would be freed up a little now your two cases have settled?" "It should be, but I just wanted to check in with Kate first that there is nothing urgent that had come up which she has slipped in already to my appointments."

"Or check that you don't have a better offer?"

"Not at all. I rarely go to lunches, so my staff are not used to working around it. My time could already have been filled in as soon as they knew my case had been settled. That's all I mean."

"I understand now," he said.

"I am just about to pull into my garage, so I may lose you now. If I do, I will call you tomorrow, Phil."

I had wound down the window in my car to press the intercom to my garage. I suddenly felt completely flustered by the pressure from Phil's advances.

"Kate said you would call me as soon as you got into the car, so I waited for nearly an hour before I tried calling you again. Now you are cutting me off before letting me know if we can have lunch this week. All a little rude, isn't it?"

"I am sorry, but the phone cuts out in my garage. I can barely hear you," I said.

"Should I call you back later tonight?"

"My daughter is waiting for me to have dinner with her. I will call you in the morning."

"I would love to have dinner with you too. She is a lucky girl. But soon, right? We will have dinner."

"Sure. I will call you tomorrow," I said before I realised, I had just agreed to have dinner with Phil.

As much as I hated to admit it, his bombastic tactics worked. I quickly ended the call as I parked my car.

Anthony

Chapter 35

When my psychiatrist suggested to my lawyers that I used the fact that Peter had sexually abused me as a child as grounds to appeal my sentence, I thought it was a genius idea. At the time, I had been angry about what my ex-wife and stepdaughter had done to me with their allegations and that Peter's ex-wife had helped them do it. Peter had not been the subject of my anger at the time. Still, unfortunately for him, the psychiatrist believed what we had done together had caused boundary issues in my relationship with my stepdaughter, which he said, had caused my behaviour which had led to my conviction.

I had not predicted that Peter would try to contact me, let alone write me a letter and send it to me at the jail. When I called him, he sounded not only calm but friendly. This surprised me, and I must admit, I was looking forward to seeing him again. I wanted to know why he had just cut me off in his life and never contacted me again. The person I had spoken to on the phone did not seem like the ruthless person who had left me when I was only 12 years old. I didn't know what to expect when I saw him, but I knew that I had been excited for the last three days about his visit.

It was the longest hour of my life while I was sitting in the waiting room for Peter to arrive. I was nervous about seeing him, but at the same time, I wanted to see how I felt about him. I was intrigued about what he thought he could achieve by visiting me. *What did he want from me? What was his angle?* I asked myself.

When I told my lawyer that Peter was visiting me today, he advised me against it. He felt that if anyone found out from the prosecution that I had accepted a visit from Peter, that it could risk my chances in my Appeal. I knew there may be that risk, but I needed to see him. One way or another, we both needed other each now. Whether we could come to an agreement on that, we would see today.

As the door opened and Peter walked into the room, I realised how much I had missed him. It was as if time had stood still, and I was transported back to being twelve years old again and staring at my hero. I looked into Peter's eyes, hoping that he wasn't angry with me.

The table separated us, but I wished I could have leapt across it to hug him. Instead, I proceeded with a polite but strained conversation about how we were, before Peter said to me, "Anthony, can we please discuss what we both want to know today. I don't care what you said in your statement to the police. I know you don't believe what you said about me, and you wouldn't be able to stand up in court and say those things. So, what are you trying to achieve by making these allegations against me? If it's to get an apology, please tell me what I did wrong, as I thought we were both having a good time when we did what we did as kids."

I was so surprised at what Peter had said that I replied meekly and said to him, "Really? You are not mad at me for what I said in my statement?"

"No. I just want to understand why you did it. I do not believe that you think that I was hurting you. I thought we were having fun," Peter replied.

"Don't you understand that I was hurt and angry with you for going away and leaving me without saying goodbye, the way you did? I stayed angry for a long time."

"When was this?" Peter asked.

"When we were kids. When I first came to jail, I started seeing a psychiatrist. He asked him to talk about my childhood, and when I told him about us, he asked me about our ages when we were friends. He then told me that he believed our relationship may be the reason for my issues with my emotional boundaries. When we discussed it further, he thought he should tell my lawyer about it. Together they developed the idea of making the allegations in my statement to seek to have you charged as the reason for me to appeal my sentence. It was new evidence that the court could consider, they said."

"So that's what happened," Peter said. "Now I understand."

"Do you? Are you angry with me?" I asked.

"No, I am not. I understand you trying to get out of jail."

"Peter, why did you leave without saying goodbye? What did I do wrong?"

"You were never told?" Peter said, clearly shocked at my question.

"No, I asked Madeline, and she said she hadn't heard from you. Then you never came back again to our house again."

"I thought Madeline would have told you, but maybe your father didn't tell her what had happened," Peter replied.

"What happened? Something happened with you and my dad?" I asked.

"Your father went into your room one day and found the stuff I had hidden in that secret drawer. He came to my house and told my parents that I had brought Marijuana to your house and had smoked it with you and told them that you were only 12 years old. He wanted to call the police until my parents explained that I had not bought it illegally. My father had cancer and had it legally for medicinal purposes for his pain, and I had obviously taken some without them knowing. Your father agreed that if I stayed away from you and Madeline, he would not report me to the police."

"And you couldn't come and say goodbye to me?"

"Anthony, my father was dying from cancer, and I had already caused him all this trouble. I was not going to risk going to your house and your father calling the police on me. I felt bad about it, but I thought he would have told you and Madeline to stay away from me."

"Dad said nothing to me about it. I am so sorry that I got so mad at you about that. Are you sure you are not angry about my statement to get my Appeal?"

"No, it was a genius idea by your lawyer. I wish it wasn't me that you needed to have charged to be able to appeal. But now that it is, I want you to do what you need to get bail and then we can work out what to do next to fix this."

"Really? Will you go along with this to help me get out of jail? I asked.

"Anthony, I understand how you are feeling. You were deceived by your wife and stepdaughter, which landed you in jail, and you are trying to do whatever you can to get out. Ideally, I would like to work with you on how to get you out of here and for the police to back off me. Once we get you out, we can work that out together."

"I had to make the statement to get an appeal. I worked on it for months with my psychiatrist to get it right and include all the facts he and my lawyer thought I needed."

"Peter, I am so happy that you are not angry at me, but I feel guilty about my psychiatrist now. Sam had helped me so much, and he genuinely likes me – I know that. I hope I am not letting him down by telling you what we have done."

"Sam seems like a good guy and has helped you a lot. I'm sure, just like me, he wants to help get you out of jail. Do whatever Sam and your lawyer tell you that you need to do to get out on bail pending your Appeal. After that, we can work out the rest."

"I can't believe you are willing to help me. We expect to be in court soon. Sam said I should get bail if that is the case. If I do get out on bail, can I see you?"

"That's great news. The sooner you get out on bail, the sooner we can start a new plan. I really don't want to go to jail for you to get you out of jail," Peter said.

"Can you come to the appeal hearing? You could listen at the back of the courtroom, and if I am granted bail, we could go and celebrate straight away," I asked.

"Anthony, I can't be anywhere near that court. I am the reason you have an appeal, remember? I am the monster who did terrible things to you as a child, so you didn't know what you were doing with Jessica was wrong. If they see me in that courtroom, it will look like a set-up by us."

"Yes, you are right," I said. "I get that."

Peter gently touched my hand and said, "Once you get bail for the Appeal, we will have plenty of time to see each other again. We need to be patient. We have no choice but to be patient and work together on this. We can't do anything stupid."

The prison guard entered the room, and as he stood with the door open, he said, "Your visiting time is up. You will need to leave now."

Peter then stood up and said to me, "Stay strong and I'll see you soon." Now that I understand your case, I can try to work out a solution for us. Hopefully, one where I don't end up in jail so you can get out."

Peter then gently touched me on the shoulder as he walked out of the room. For the first time in a long time I felt hope that I could get my life back.

Sarah

Chapter 36

I felt relieved after I walked into my apartment and shut the front door. Locked away safely in my home, I could leave the stress of Phil's phone call behind me as I looked forward to the evening with my daughter.

When I walked into the kitchen, I saw Chloe helping Maria with dinner. She immediately ran over and hugged me. I was so relieved by the change of pace at home. It was my sanctuary away from the madness of the rest of the outside.

After dinner, Chloe was excited to surprise me with the cupcakes she had made for dessert. The joy on her face as she watched me eat one of them in anticipation of my reaction was hilarious. We both washed up, and then Chloe went to her room to work on her homework.

I walked into my study as I usually did after dinner. Although dinner with Chloe was lovely, I was feeling flat. My successful day in court with Mark today seemed a world away. The realisation that Peter may be charged in relation to his inappropriate relationship with Anthony was overwhelming. I sat, ruminating on how I had gotten it so wrong and how Peter had kept his sordid past a secret. My thoughts were interrupted when I heard my mobile beep. I picked it up and saw that I had received a text message from Phil which read, "How is your night?"

I felt that Phil was now invading my personal space. I'd told him on the phone that I would call him back tomorrow. I did not understand his message and I was now feeling too discombobulated to figure it out. As though he was reading my mind, my mobile rang, and it was him. I said to him, "Hi, my night has been lovely."

"Are you sure?" he replied.

"Yes, why?"

"You don't sound nearly as happy as you did on Monday when you were in Bowral, that's all."

"I've had a busy week, and I've just started on some work."

"It's a beautiful night, way too nice to be working. Why don't you come for a helicopter ride with me?"

"A what?" I said.

"A helicopter ride around the city. It's such a beautiful night to go flying. Want to come?"

"Now you have a helicopter?"

"Yes, it's a new toy. I love it, and I am addicted to night flying. Please come? You'll love it."

"Thanks, Phil, maybe another night. It sounds wonderful, but I need to get some work out of the way."

"It is wonderful," Phil said. "Look, I know I have a bad reputation, and I know that I have not been the most faithful of men, but Sarah, no one has ever accused me of not being fun and entertaining, have they? What's the worst that could happen? That you have an exciting night?"

"You make a good case, Phil. Maybe you should have been a lawyer," I said. I couldn't believe Phil made me laugh even when I felt so stressed.

"Far too grown up a career for me. Anyway, call me when you want to have fun. I'm going to head off and go flying now."

I realised that Phil had turned the call from him from being stressful, to pleasantly distracting. I could now see how he was so successful with women. His view on life and his financial ability to enjoy the best life had to offer, was so crazy it was alluring.

I still could not lift the anxiety I had felt about Peter. It didn't help even when Peter was cooperating with me. When I called him and suggested that we stop our lunches with Chloe on Sundays until he had resolved his issues with the police, he agreed with me.

I felt awful about stopping him from seeing Chloe. I didn't want to prevent him from having any contact with her. I suggested that he continue to call and facetime her. I was shocked when he responded positively, saying, "As much as I will miss seeing Chloe, I understand that this has been hard on you. I will do whatever it takes to show you that I am sorry this has happened and try to make it easier for you to cope. If that means that things change for now, I agree to it all."

I recalled Peter's favourite saying, "Nothing changes if nothing changes." He was obviously changing his angle to alter the dynamic of the situation. I intuitively felt that Peter's conversation with me was not as transparent as it seemed. He was planning something and I was worried as far as Chloe was concerned.

I closed the door to my study as I called Rupert. I said to him, "Hi Rupert, can I run something by you?"

"Sure, Sarah."

"I called Peter and told him that I thought we should stop his visits with Chloe until he sorted out the situation with the police and Anthony."

"How did he take it?" Rupert asked.

"Far too well. He was a different Peter. He spoke to me as he had never done before. He would usually lose it and then lecture me about his parental rights. There is something wrong, Rupert. I can feel it," I said.

"You would know if there was a change in his behaviour Sarah, and I trust your judgement. Either way, the fact that he has agreed to stop seeing Chloe for now must be a relief for you. It will give you a break from seeing him and give me some time to look into the charges against him."

"Thanks, but I don't want you to get into an awkward situation with what you can and can't tell me. I want to know; do I need to do anything to protect Chloe because I haven't seen something coming that I should have."

"I understand. Leave it with me. I will call you on a need-to-know basis. If you don't hear from me about Peter, it's ok for now."

"Thanks, Rupert. I don't know how I would cope without you and Hillary."

"You don't have to deal with this on your own. I'm not only your lawyer Sarah, more importantly I'm your friend."

"I am so blessed to have you both. I really am." I said.

"We're all lucky to have each other. I do not call many people loyal and honourable, but you are one of the few. Together we will work out a solution to this situation with Peter and Anthony that protects Chloe and you from any fallout."

"That is so kind of you, I don't know what to say."

"Goodnight, will do," Rupert replied.

"Goodnight and thank you," I said.

Debbie

Chapter 37

I walked out of the kitchen and over to the loungeroom window to watch Jim pull out of the driveway. I could see that he was on his mobile phone as soon as he got in the car. Ashely ran over to me. I said to her, "Honey, I've arranged a play date for you tonight because I need to go out too. Sandy is coming over to get you in a minute."

I knew Jim had lied to me about where he was going tonight. I could see it in his eyes. I could stand anything, but not that. I had to know the truth, or I would go mad. I planned to follow him when I left the house tonight, arranging with my neighbour to babysit Ashley. My neighbour had been waiting for my text message, and she came over right away.

I'd managed to catch up to Jim's car quickly and had stayed at least 20 metres behind him. I could see that he was chatting away on his mobile phone. Jim was oblivious to me following him. He continued to drive for about 15 minutes until he reached an industrial estate. He drove up to a large warehouse, where he stopped and parked. I watched him get out of his car and walk into the building. I followed him. There were no signs or a directory at the entrance. As I was looking about, I heard a voice and I turned around. "Hi, can I help you?" a lady said to me who was pulling along two large suitcases.

"Hi," I said.

She walked towards me and asked me, "Are you here for the show?"

"Yes," I replied.

"Are you one of the stage volunteers?" she asked.

"No, I just came to watch the show," I replied.

"You're here early. It doesn't start until 8 pm."

"Oh, that's ok," I said, feeling nervous. "I'll come back then."

"Have you got tickets yet?"

"No, where do I buy them?"

"I've got a couple of complimentary tickets. I usually give them to my friends, but they are both working tonight. Here, you can have them; everyone needs a lucky day."

"Thanks, that's very kind of you," I replied.

I walked back to my car. I stared at the two tickets in my hand and thought I should ask my brother Max to come with me for support. I called him and asked, "Max, are you busy tonight?"

"No I'm not, but what's up, Debbie? You sound stressed."

"I think Jim is having an affair. I followed him to a building and watched him walk inside. I just found out there is a show there tonight. Can I pick you up to come with me to it?"

"Debbie, this sounds a weird."

"Max, I need you. I know Jim is in there and the show that at 8 pm. Can you bring your new video camera?"

"I will do anything you want; you know that. But if you think there is someone else, do you really want to torture yourself with seeing it, let alone taking videos of them?"

"Max, there has been something going on for a while, and he keeps telling me it's just my imagination. Even today, he came home early from work and told me he was trying to help me out with doing the ironing. I need evidence to make sure I can convince myself, not anyone else, so that I can accept things and move on. This has been killing me for months."

"Ok, if you put it that way, come and pick me up and we'll go together," he replied.

I drove straight to Max's place. He opened the door and as soon as he saw me, he hugged me and said, "I made you a toasted sandwich and poured you a glass of wine. We'll need this because I suspect it will be a long night."

"Thanks, I'd love a drink but feel too sick to eat."

"Please try to eat something, Debbie. It could be a long night."

"You're right. It could be. Or it could be my imagination again. Maybe he is playing poker in a back room with the boys, and I'm just a nut case like he says I am. I am dreading this, but at the same time, I must do it. I have to know."

"I get it Debbie. Let's eat and we'll go and deal with this together."

After finishing our wine and toasted sandwiches, we got in the car to go to the show. I pulled up in the parking lot, which was now nearly full. I was surprised at how different the building looked at night. Two groups of girls were walking in, and as they got closer, Max stopped and stared at them. He turned and looked at me and said, "Everyone seems so dressed up. Are you sure we'll get in?"

"We are going in no matter what."

"Ok," Max said.

I handed over our tickets at the door and we walked in and sat right in our allocated seats which were luckily in the middle row of the theatre. The room was so dark that we could barely see the seats. I looked around the room to see if I could see Jim in the room. "I can't see anything," I said to Max.

"Sit down, Debbie. When the show starts, you might see more."

Just as he spoke, the lights came on and a woman walked onto the stage with a microphone, singing.

The lights flashed across the room, and I could now see faces in the audience. The first face I recognised was Alan. He was sitting in between two women. I touched Max on the arm and whispered to him, "Max, that's Alan. His daughter goes to school with Ashley. Jim and Alan are supposed to be playing poker together tonight. Take a photo of him, or film him, or both."

"Debbie, what he does is none of our business?"

"Max, do it. What I do with it, if anything, I'll work out later."

"Right," Max replied.

Just as Max got his camera out and started to zoom in, the music stopped, and the lights suddenly went out. The lights then came back on, and another woman started singing on the stage. Two more women walked onto the stage, one dressed in blue and the other in a red dress, both wearing wide brimmed, elegant hats. The show started with both the women singing and dancing together in a well-choreographed routine.

The scene started to change dramatically when one of the women began to unzip the back of the other's dress. As she bent over to unzip the dress, the girl in the blue dress lost her hat, and at that moment, I realised it was a man. I turned to Max and said, "Max, this is a drag show."

"You're right. *It is.*"

I then asked Max, "Is that Jim in the blue dress? Can you recognise him?"

"I honestly can't tell from here."

"Use your video, zoom in, and look."

"Good idea," he said as Max took the video camera, focused, and zoomed in. I could see by the look on his face that it was Jim.

I asked him, "It's Jim, isn't it?"

"Yes, my brother-in-law is dancing on the stage in a blue dress."

"Film it, Max, don't lose it. We need proof," I said.

"Got it," Max replied.

The show continued with the other woman stripping off her dress to reveal a red bikini. She then assisted Jim in unzipping his dress to reveal him wearing a one-piece swimsuit. Max couldn't look at me. He just kept filming. To my relief, the music finally ended, and they both left the stage. Max turned to me and said, "Let's go, Debbie. I'm going to get us both a drink."

Anthony

Chapter 38

Today was the day of my court appeal. It had been six months since I'd been convicted and sent to jail. I knew I was one of the lucky ones to get an appeal within a year. Many others had been waiting for much longer than I had.

I stood outside the courtroom with my lawyer and barrister. They told me that they were sure that my leave to appeal would be successful as my allegations against Peter provided new legal grounds. The prosecution had confirmed that if the Judge granted my leave to appeal, they would not oppose my bail application; which meant I would get out of jail today.

My lawyer motioned for us to walk into the courtroom, and I felt confident my life was about to change. I sat in my usual spot in the courtroom – alone and in the dock. I was used to it now. I'd decided that it was an advantageous position in the courtroom, as I could see everyone in the room.

The courtroom was relatively empty this time. It had been full of people during my trial. Today it was just my legal team, the Prosecutor, the Court Officers, and the Judge. My sister and psychiatrist were outside the courtroom waiting to be called to give evidence. My barrister stood up and addressed the Judge with the impressive list of reasons that my Appeal was based on, why it should be heard and why I should be given bail pending the Appeal.

The Judge appeared interested in the submissions by my lawyer, which was a good sign. Sam, my psychiatrist, was called to give evidence. He explained how my relationship with Peter, when I was only 12 years old, would have caused me to develop psychological and boundary issues. He said that those issues would have impaired my mental capacity relating to the conduct I had been found guilty of. Sam was impressive in his evidence, describing in detail how my experiences had distorted my emotional development and caused me to develop borderline personality issues.

My sister Madeleine also gave evidence. She reaffirmed the historical facts and dates when Peter was her boyfriend, how he had befriended me and had stayed overnight on multiple occasions at our house, in my bedroom. She broke down and cried in the witness box, expressing her guilt for not realising what was happening to me at the time, with Peter.

The prosecution acted very differently during this court hearing. It was nothing like the trial I had been through with Jessica when I had been found guilty in a jury trial. The Judge had even commented as such, at one stage enquiring about the lack of evidence in response, this time by the prosecution.

It only took a few hours before the hearing was over. After the summations by both sides, the Judge announced that he was ready to hand down his judgement. In his judgement, he granted me leave to appeal and bail, on the conditions that I reside in my sister's care at her home, and that she provide a bond of $100,000 secured on her home.

After my legal team had finalised the bail terms and the paperwork was finalised, my lawyer escorted me down the stairs to the exit. I saw Madeline sitting with Sam on a bench at the front of the court. As soon as I walked out, she ran over to me to hug me. As I embraced her, Sam had walked over to me to and shook my hand. I said to him, "Thank you, it's because of you that I won today. I am eternally grateful."

I noticed a man in the distance who appeared to be staring at me. I was unsure if he was a reporter, but just as he started walking closer, a lady who had her back to us appeared. She spoke to him briefly before she put her arms on his shoulders, gently steering him away. As they both walked away, the lady turned around briefly, and I was sure when I saw her face that I knew her, but I couldn't recall who she was.

I'd called Peter twice from jail since he had come to see me. I wanted to make sure that he was not angry with me. He reassured me that he wasn't and that we could deal with everything once my Appeal and bail were finalised. He told me to call him and let him know as soon as I got the verdict.

Tina

Chapter 39

I could not believe what Bruce had done. Firstly, he had caused chaos the night before, by forgetting to pick up his wife for dinner, then he had turned up to work with writing on the back of his head. The artwork, a childish love heart with Marci's name in texture on the back of his head. It might have been funny if he had not had an important board meeting this morning. Still, Marci would have known that was a possibility, having been his former secretary.

I watched Bruce through the boardroom's glass walls directly across from my desk. He sat with the back of his head to the wall throughout the meeting, which had clearly ended as everyone, including Bruce, was now standing up and getting ready to leave. I could see that Bruce had made it through the meeting without turning his head around.

I should have known something was wrong when Emma called me about Bruce last night not answering his calls. I had a suspicion that Marci had gotten hold of him again. He'd assured me that it was over with Marci a year ago, but he had promised that before. I thought Emma becoming pregnant would have motivated him to clean up his act and stop him fooling around like he had been doing over the past few years. It continued to astound me that a man who was so intelligent could be so easily distracted and seduced by women.

The boardroom door opened and as people started leaving, I knew the cue. I would have to walk in so Bruce could remain in the room until they had all left. As I walked in, I said goodbye to everyone and closed the boardroom door before walking up to Bruce at the end of the boardroom table. He sat back down at the table while I spoke to him, so it looked like I was taking notes for all intents and purposes. I said to him, "You are so lucky you got away with this today. This can't go on, Bruce. I will resign rather than facilitate this kind of behaviour. You are hurting Emma and ruining your career."

Bruce stood up and said curtly, "Don't lecture me. It's not your place to tell me how to live my life."

"Covering up for your affairs is not part of my job description Bruce. Good luck with Marci, particularly getting her name off the back of your head," I replied.

Bruce sat down and looked defeated. "Look, I'm sorry. I'm really stressed, and that was a tough meeting. Please give me a break Tina. I need your help right now, not a lecture."

"I am not lecturing you. You might have forgotten that Marci had written her name across your head, and if I had not told you, you would have been thrown out of the meeting before it had even started. I know the other partners only put up with you because they have to. I was the one who reminded you that sleeping with your staff constitutes a valid reason for getting rid of you, so Marci had to resign. Don't you see what Marci is doing now? She is sending a message to Emma, so you get divorced. Are you so stupid that you can't see that? If that is the case, I will have to resign because I thought you were one of the most intelligent people I had ever worked for until now."

Bruce's face suddenly changed. Clearly, what I had said to him had finally sunk in. "You're right. Marci would only have done this to me to get a message to Emma. How did I not see that?"

"Finally, you understand what I've been trying to tell you for months."

"I do. I'm really sorry I've been so stupid."

"Now we have the problem of getting the writing off your head before anyone sees it, especially Emma. I did some googling while you were in the meeting, and everything I read said it could take a bit of time. It may take a couple of days. I am unsure what the solution is, except that you don't go home until it comes off."

"I know that I am already in trouble with Emma. I am still trying to work out how I ended up at home last night, but I know I forgot to send a car to pick her up for dinner. I saw the missed calls when I finally put my phone on the charger when I was driving to work this morning. Emma said nothing about it, which means she is upset with me."

"Poor Emma, she was so stressed when she called me yesterday asking to speak to you," I said.

"Tina, if I can't go home, I need you to help me by calling Emma and telling her I have to go to Melbourne for a couple of days for urgent meetings," Bruce said.

"On the condition you let me buy her a present from you," I replied.

"What?"

"You need to buy her a present. Give me your Amex, because I'm going to Tiffany's to buy her the diamond necklace she wants from you."

"I don't know anything about a diamond necklace?"

"At the Christmas party, she told me she loved my diamond Tiffany cross necklace, so you are buying her one. I will have it delivered to her from you, with flowers, while you are in Melbourne. Got it?"

Bruce stood up to leave the boardroom, looking carefully to see that no one was around as he did. He said, "I suppose it's cheaper than a divorce."

"Yes, it is. I'll book you a flight to Melbourne to leave around noon and a suite at Crown Towers." Then I stood up, handing him a company cap.

"What's this for?" Bruce asked.

"Before you walk out of this room, you may want to cover the back of your head."

"I can't believe that I totally forgot about that."

"I'm sure you can make it look like you are wearing it for team bonding purposes – don't you think?"

"Thanks Tina. Glad you think this is all so funny," he said as I smirked when he put the cap on.

Peter

Chapter 40

Anthony had called me twice since I had visited him in jail. Each time he called, he seemed more relaxed. During the phone calls, Anthony told me about the appeal books, and I was highly impressed with his work with his lawyers. I was also impressed with him for doing a law degree while in jail. Clearly, all this planning by him was why he would win his court case and be out on bail today.

Anthony had already told me that the first thing he wanted to do when he was out of jail, was to see me. This was even though it was obvious that we should wait at least a few days before meeting up. We needed to be cautious about who knew about us talking to or seeing each other so that it didn't destroy his Appeal case which was based on me allegedly sexually abusing him as a child.

Anthony's lawyers had told him that his bail conditions must include him residing at his sister's home and reporting into the police station at the end of each day.

It was obvious to me now, that to solve this situation that he had created by having me charged, I needed to rekindle our friendship again. I knew he felt guilty about making the accusations against me to enable him to get his freedom. I would play whatever game I had to, if it resulted in Anthony dropping the charges against me and me being able to move on with my life again.

I was still unsure of the solution of how we could achieve us both getting off the hook, but I believed if we worked together utilising our legal skills, we had to be able to come up with an answer.

I knew that Anthony would contact me as soon as he had won the Appeal and was out on bail. I was getting myself ready for the call. I also sensed that he would be impatient about getting together to see me and that we needed to be careful where we met, so I was organised.

Anthony

Chapter 41

After my bail was finalised, I knew it was stupid, but the first call I desperately wanted to make was to Peter. I knew I couldn't tell anyone that we had agreed to meet. My lawyers had warned me not to speak to Peter if he tried to contact me again. But I ignored them.

I had lied to Madeline. I told her that I needed to meet immediately with my lawyers to discuss the next steps for my Appeal hearing. She asked me, "Would you like me to come with you or wait for you? I am happy to."

I lied and said to her, "No, it may take hours. You go home to the kids, and I will get a cab to your house as soon as we finish."

Although Madeline looked disappointed, she knew that I had already made other plans. Despondently she handed me the new mobile phone I had asked her to arrange for me. Sam walked over to me and said, "Madeline told me she is happy to drive you to my practice for you to continue your therapy. Call me to arrange it whenever you are ready."

"Thanks, Sam. I will call you next week," I said.

I kissed Madeline before walking away briskly. I briefly looked back and saw that Madeline and Sam were still speaking as I walked around the corner. I felt a pang of guilt about lying to her about where I was going now.

I walked further down the street away from the court out of their sight. My hands shook as I sent Peter a text message, but I knew he would expect it. The simple freedom I felt from using a mobile phone again was wonderful. Peter was the first person I wanted to see, and I would never take my liberty for granted again.

I needed a face-to-face meeting with Peter to go through my recollections of what I had said had happened in my statement and work out how we could help each other get out of the mess I had placed us in with my allegations against him. I heard my phone ping and saw a text from Peter. He had text me the details of where I should meet him.

I hailed a cab and finally relaxed after telling the driver the address.

Looking out the window as we drove towards Peter's home, I realised how much I had missed my freedom. I had passed my time in jail by planning this moment, researching the law, finding the names of cases, and drafting the statements I knew I needed to win my Appeal.

The taxi pulled up at Peter's apartment and I saw Peter standing at the front of the building. As I got out of the taxi, he said, "Welcome to my home. We can relax and talk here without worrying about being seen by anyone."

Peter led me into his apartment building. We walked into the lobby and got into a lift to go up to his apartment. As we walked into his unit, I saw an an ice bucket with champagne in it and two glasses beside it. "Have a seat," he said whilst he popped the cork and filled up our glasses.

"Thank you for doing all of this," I said.

"I'm trying to understand why coming to see *me* was the first thing you wanted to do when you got out on bail," Peter said.

"I felt I needed to explain what I did to you, and for you to understand my motives. I also needed to understand what happened all those years ago."

"What do you mean by that," Peter asked.

"When you just vanished all those years, we never got to say goodbye to each other. You were my closest friend, and I thought we loved each other. For years I stopped making friends, just in case they just disappeared like you did."

Peter replied, "I'm sorry I didn't understand that. I'm sure your father thought he was doing the right thing. He threatened to call the police if I ever came to your house again to see you, or Madeline. I was scared because I had done the wrong thing by bringing weed to your house and letting you smoke a joint when you were so young. It was stupid of me, but I was just an ignorant adolescent. Still, I didn't realise how much my inability to explain this all to you had hurt you so much."

I said, "We were just silly kids, doing what kids did. I suppose my father was doing what he thought was right. I just wished someone had told me about it."

"Me too," Peter said.

"Really, it was just a misunderstanding that, unfortunately, caused me great pain for many years. But we now have the chance to make it right, and then I think I can move on."

"The problem now is, you're out of jail and have come to terms with our childhood drama, but how do I get out of the firing line now that you have used me as your excuse?"

"That's why I'm here. That's what we need to work out. I thought, between us, we could sort out a way that this can turn out well for both of us."

Peter looked relieved. He said, "I'm relieved to hear that, but it won't be easy. I've thought about it, and for your Appeal to succeed, I need to be found guilty. I'm not sure how we can make that work for both of us."

"I know it seems that way, but I am working on an angle, Peter. I haven't solved it yet, but I need to be able to prove my case and do it so that the police may not be able to win a prosecution against you. I came here to tell you what I am thinking."

"I can't wait to hear it," Peter said.

Sarah

Chapter 42

Today was one of the rare days that I had been embarrassed by my clients' conduct. All of us who worked in Family Law were used to working with our clients in highly stressful conditions. Still, I rarely had a client who behaved rudely to the barristers I took them to see; or to me.

I had just finished a long and challenging conference with one of my clients and a senior barrister at his chambers. It had been a difficult conference, with my client simply refusing to accept the advice we were giving her. At one stage, my client's demeanour changed from being a pleasant and polite lady to an almost deranged person who I thought would leap across the barrister's table to slap him.

It was a relief when the conference was over. I walked my client and her new partner out of the building and onto the street. Then I walked back inside to apologise to the barrister.

As I entered his chambers, he said to me, "Seriously, your client was lovely until I told her that she wouldn't get what she wanted. Then it was like the wind had changed direction, and she became another person. I suppose that's what happens when you are a famous beauty queen and used to getting your own way for most of your life."

I replied, "I am so sorry. I never expected her to act that way. I had given her my opinion on what I thought was a reasonable settlement. But now, seeing how she acted today, I honestly believed she thought she would get a different viewpoint from you."

"Your advice had been correct, and I said that to her. Why would she think she was entitled to anything more from her husband after a short marriage? That didn't make sense," he said.

"We did our best. I wish her luck getting 50% of her husband's assets after a four-year marriage where her only contribution to the marriage, on her own evidence, was basically being photographed with him."

"It was very funny when she said that. Did you also notice how her voice changed when she got really angry? She sounded so different. It was like she had another personality popping out there. She went from an elegant, aged beauty queen to a street fighter."

"I did notice that. She told me once that when she won her first beauty competition that she was sent to elocution lessons by the officials to try to get rid of her country accent."

"Well that explains that" he said. "At least we finished early today. I'll be home in time to have dinner with the kids, which my wife will be happy about."

"Give my love to Catherine and the kids," I said as I picked up my handbag to head back to my office.

As I walked out of the building onto the street, I noticed that it seemed unusually busy. Then it dawned on me it was Thursday night shopping. As I looked around, people watching as I liked to do, everyone tonight seemed happy. They were either chatting on their mobiles or with each other.

Turning the corner, I stopped to quickly look in the window of my friend's jewellery store. As my eyes immediately focused on a beautiful necklace, I saw my friend's face appear on the other side of the window. He smiled and motioned for me to enter the store.

I always felt wonderful in Nick's store. "Ciao Bella," he said as he hugged me. He then leaned into the window, took the necklace I was looking at, and put it around my neck. Nick smiled and said, "stunning." He took my hand and said, "Let's have coffee," as he led me to the coffee shop next door.

As soon as we sat down, Nick immediately asked me, "What happened? Why do you look sad?"

I smiled knowing that I could never hide anything from him, and said, "I am having trouble with my ex-husband. I tried to get some help with it, and now I'm also having trouble with my psychiatrist because he keeps wanting me to talk about my childhood. I don't want to do that because it makes me sad, but he insists I need to. It's just all confusing me now."

"I agree with you, Bella. My father and I used to talk about this. When he came back from the war, his way of dealing with the terrible things he experienced, was to never talk about or think about it again. My father was never sad. He was always grateful to be in a peaceful country here in Australia. We think that is a better way than going over and over a past that hurts you. I know that not everyone agrees, but we are not everyone, Sarah."

"I'm so glad that you can see what I mean. I hate it when my psychiatrist takes me back to a place where I can't control or fix anything. There is no upside to it. I want to know how to do my best now and in the future as a mother, friend, and human being. I can't do my best living in my past."

"Good idea. Let's forget the past and think of wonderful things. Wear that necklace until you feel happy again. When you feel sad, touch it, and think of my father's favourite saying, "Yesterday is history, and tomorrow is a mystery." Life is about enjoying today and doing what we love with those we love. The rest does not matter."

Rhonda, who was the owner of the coffee shop, saw us and waved. She then approached us, smiling. As she got closer, her eyes were immediately drawn to the necklace I was wearing and she said, "That is just stunning Sarah. Are they Argyle Pinks? she turned towards Nick to ask. I already knew where this was going, so I stood up and took off the necklace and handed it to Rhonda, who inadvertently squealed as she took it.

"I need to show Jeff," she said as she ran towards her husband at the back of the coffee shop.

"At least I got to wear it first,'" I said to Nick.

Nick replied, "Rhonda saw that necklace in the shop this morning in the window, but it was not until she saw it on you that she fell in love with it. That is the magic you have, Sarah." We both looked over and saw Jeff walking over to with Rhonda.

"Well, thanks Nick. Rhonda has told me she is not taking the necklace off, so we had better go over to your shop and pay for it," he said, trying to sound annoyed.

Rhonda, who had been standing behind her husband, wearing the necklace with her right hand gently patting it. She threw her arms around her husband, demonstratively kissing him. He said to her, "I said you could have it, darling. Now let Nick and Sarah have some peace." He then took her hand and walked her away towards Nick's store.

I said to Nick, "I love the joy you bring to people. Look how happy they are. I have never had clients who looked that happy in twenty years, but yours do every day."

Nick had a smile beaming across his face. "That is what I love seeing, passion, love, and joy. I am so lucky my job lets me do what I love and bring happiness to people. I watched my father and grandfather bring this joy to people, and I knew that's what I wanted to do in my life."

"Do you ever feel bad about how much money women like Rhonda get their husbands like Jeff to spend on them? I don't even want to ask how much that necklace costs, but I know it is substantial, and he didn't even ask the price before he said yes to buying it."

Nick smiled as he replied, "Sarah, Jeff was the grumpiest old man in town before he met Rhonda. He does spoil her, and she does cost him a fortune, but he man of substance. He owns more coffee shops than I have diamonds in my store. Look at him smiling. He is actually happy now, and what is life if you are rich and not happy? He enjoys life and will live at least ten years longer because of her. If that is not value for your dollar, then what is?"

"You are so wise Nick. I'm glad I stopped to look in your window. I should let you go and sort out payment for the necklace, and I'd better head back to my office."

"Want to get another necklace for you to wear, Sarah? I feel bad now," Nick said.

"Don't be silly. I had fun wearing it first, and now you have a sale. That was the best result we could have had tonight," I said as I hugged him goodbye.

As I walked back into Nick's store with him, I noticed a brochure on the counter for the children's hospital dinner and asked, "Are you going to that function?"

"No, we are not. Rhonda invited us to her table, but we couldn't make it. We have donated a diamond necklace for the charity auction, though."

"I'm going. I wish you were going. A client invited me."

Rhonda and Jeff caught our conversation. "Who are you going with?" Rhonda asked. "It's a sell-out, you know. Like I said to Nick, anyone who is anyone will be there!"

"A client invited me," I replied.

"What's their name? I'm on the committee and I know who has the best tables."

"I'm just happy to be going," I said.

"You have to tell me who it is now I know you're going," she said.

"Phil Thompson," I replied.

Rhonda looked me up and down with renewed interest. "So, you are his next target? Lucky girl. Have you been in his new helicopter yet?"

"What do you mean by that?" Nick asked, sounding concerned.

"Phil buys a table every year, but rarely comes himself but usually sends his staff. He said he was coming this year and requested a good table. We are happy because we need big money to donate and buy at the auction. I knew if he was turning up himself, that he was trying to impress a new woman."

"So, he's single?" Nick asked.

"He is single at the moment," Rhonda said as she laughed.

"At the moment? What do you mean by that?" Nick asked.

"He has a habit of not being single for long, but frequently. He's in and out of relationships and marriages quickly. Following his love life is better than any Netflix show."

"What does that mean? Not good, I think?" Nick asked again.

"When I first met Phil over twenty years ago, I thought he was a handsome and successful young man on his way up. He married a beautiful girl, and because the media have always loved him, the romance was well covered. We all read about him sending not only a dozen red roses, but a dozen *bunches* of a *dozen* red roses. Then he bought her all the clothes of the entire window of a Valentino boutique one day, and the whole collection of an art gallery exhibition they went to. It appeared that he was head over heels in love with the woman."

"He sounds very romantic," Nick replied.

"Yes, he is very romantic. But he falls out of love as quickly as he falls in love. Then he repeats the same courting ritual again."

"No?" Nick exclaimed.

"And that's not the worse part."

"Really? It gets worse?" Nick said, frowning now.

"He falls all over a woman until they fall in love with him, and then as soon as they commit to him, he starts flirting with other women.

I have seen it as early as on his honeymoon. It just leaves the woman so confused and everyone else embarrassed."

"But how does he keep getting new women if everyone knows what he does?" Nick asked.

"I used to wonder about that Nick, but until you meet the man, you cannot understand. He is just the world's best salesman. He could charm anyone and usually does. I mean, look at the trail of bad behaviour he has left behind already, and he is still the most entertaining man in the room. Everyone can't wait to see what he does next."

"Maybe he just hasn't met the right woman? This is just not something I understand. Marriage is about family, not playing games," Nick replied.

"You are such a romantic, Nick. And that very lure that you suggested; that he just hasn't found the right woman, is what keeps them trying," Rhonda replied.

"I have met men like this, non-committal until they meet the right partner, and then they fall deeply and madly in love forever."

"He does commit, just not for long! He told me that his greatest motivation to become rich was to be able to do whatever he liked, including getting divorced if he wasn't happy. He said that each time he falls in love with a woman, that he "hopes" it will last forever, but his main priority in life is to have a good time at any cost."

Nick said, "But Rhonda, for relationships to last forever, you need to work at them. Has anyone told this man that? Please tell me that he doesn't have any children."

"I think that at least half of Sydney has tried to give him some advice on what he is doing wrong. The problem is that he is happy with how things are. He likes the rollover in women and the constant emotional rollercoaster in his life. I think he finds it entertaining and interesting. He said to me recently, "Rhonda, the day you stop is the day you die, and I'm not ready to die yet."

"These women must get so confused by him making them feel like a princess one day and then leaving them the next," Nick said.

"I thought that his exes would hate him, but a couple of them I have spoken to don't. One of them said that no man had ever made her feel as special as Phil did, and she is grateful she got to feel that passion in her life. Another one is convinced that she is the love of his life, and that he will marry her again," Rhonda replied.

Nick threw his hands up in the air as only an Italian could do and, shaking his head said, "She thinks they are Elizabeth Taylor and Richard Burton?"

"He's a very clever man who is also passionate and romantic. He uses his money to create experiences for these women to make them feel special. Whether the ride is worth the fall is a risk that is theirs. Personally, he is mean because he tells each of these women that they are the love of his life.'"

"Why do you invite him to go to the ball Rhonda?" I asked.

"Why do you have him as a client Sarah? Because we are all happy to take his money, aren't we? That's our job. Besides that, he is always publicly generous, looks good, so it suits us. We will feed his publicity-driven ego if it helps worthy causes."

Nick put his arm around me and said, "Go to the ball with him Sarah and have some fun. Enjoy his company for the night because he sounds entertaining. But I want you to find a man who knows that a woman, who loves him, is the most important thing in his life."

Emma

Chapter 43

Meeting Sophia for breakfast was the best thing I could have done. She had such a calming effect on me. I knew that if I had not had her support, I would not have been able to have acted calmly with Bruce this morning. Particularly when he had woken up without apologising to me. Her advice was always right when it came to men, and I knew that although she knew that Bruce had behaved terribly last night, not fighting with him whilst I was pregnant was the best advice, she could have given me.

I was surprised when shortly after I arrived home, a courier arrived with a bunch of flowers and a parcel. I called Sophia as soon as I opened the parcel and saw the Tiffany box. Although I knew Bruce realised that he was in trouble for not meeting up with me last night, I thought the most I would get from him was an apology – not flowers and jewellery from Tiffany's.

Bruce knew I loved Tiffany's jewellery, but not being a jewellery person it made me wonder if I should be even more concerned about last night. He must have felt awfully guilty to have gone to this much trouble to appease me.

I opened the box and saw the beautiful Tiffany cross necklace that I had always wanted. The note with the box said, *"Emma, thank you for everything. When you wear this necklace, I hope you remember how much I love you and our baby. Bruce x*

I tried to call Bruce on his mobile, but it went straight to message bank. Just as I was about to call him at the office, his PA Tina called me and said, "Hi Emma, I just rang to let you know that Bruce had to go to Melbourne for an urgent meeting. Hopefully, he will be back in a couple of days. He had to race off quickly and catch the first flight we could get him on, but he will call you as soon as possible."

"Thanks, Tina. I tried to call him on his mobile, but it went straight to message bank, so he must be flying now."

"He was booked on the noon flight, so I would say so."

"I just received a present by courier from Bruce with a beautiful bunch of flowers. Did you arrange that for him?" I asked.

"No, he did it himself, with a little help from me," Tina replied.

"It's a Tiffany necklace, Tina. I have always wanted one, but I didn't know he knew that."

"I have a small one, Tina. Bruce asked me where I got it from, so he could get one for you. Your cross is much bigger than mine."

"Thank you for helping him. I wondered how he did it by himself."

"My pleasure," Tina said.

I heard a knock on the door and answered it. As soon as I opened the door, Sophia noticed my necklace. "That's beautiful," she said. "I'm glad Bruce is trying to be a better husband today. Did he send a note with it?"

"Yes, he did," I said while grabbing the note for her to read.

I saw the look on Sophia's face as she read the note. I said, "It's lovely, isn't it?"

"Of course, it is. I'm relieved Bruce is being nice to you. He has obviously realised he stuffed up now."

I smiled at Sophia. I knew it was hard for her when Bruce was awful to me. She seemed genuinely pleased for me, which made me feel better. "Have you got time to go to lunch?" I asked.

"Of course. I didn't come all this way not to eat."

"My treat, I am so happy today that I want to take us somewhere nice. Where do you want to go?"

Sophia picked up her handbag and said, "Let's drive and pick somewhere on the way. If you are ready, let's go."

"I hope Bruce calls me back soon. I would love to talk to him," I said as I got into the car.

"I would love to talk to him, too," Sophia said, making us laugh.

"Seriously, with the surprise of my new necklace, I completely forgot about what we drew on Bruce's head. I wonder how he got it off," I said.

"I forgot about that too. But since he sent you flowers and bought you a present, he doesn't suspect you did it."

"Bruce must think it was Marci who did it," I said. "I do feel a bit mean about that."

"Do you think he's gone to Melbourne on business, Emma?" Sophia asked.

"That's what his secretary told me."

"Maybe he went away because he couldn't be seen with the writing on the back of his head?"

"So you think that he's actually in hiding?"

"Yes, I think that's it. He's in hiding from everyone at work and from you. He thinks you didn't see it, so he's gone to ground until he can get it off his head."

"That makes me feel terrible," I said. "Should I say something?"

"Absolutely not. I was hoping you wouldn't remind me what he did that made us to put it on his head. He deserved it and more."

"What if he brings it up when he calls?"

"You know nothing. This is our secret, and it must remain so now and forever."

"Ok, if I must," I said, laughing as I caressed my new necklace.

Peter

Chapter 44

I had thought about nothing else over the past two days except where it was safe for me to meet up with Anthony when he got out on bail. I knew that it had to be somewhere private, where no one saw us or could overhear our conversation. It was not ideal, but my apartment was the only place I could think of where we could have some privacy. When Anthony agreed to it, it was just as significant a risk for him as it was for me. So, I made the place as welcoming as possible for his visit.

Anthony shocked me with what he said to me when he arrived at my home. I thought I would spend the best of the afternoon trying to convince him that what had happened between us was not as he had recalled in his complaint against me. The fact that he had now admitted that he knew that to be true, and that he had worked out a plan so that we would both be able to get on with our lives was such a relief.

We'd only been chatting for a short time, and it seemed to come out of the blue when Anthony said to me, "I think I've got it. I've worked out a plan."

"I can't wait to hear how you think we can sort this mess out," I said as I poured him a glass of champagne.

"I'm so sorry I had to do that to you," he replied.

"You do understand this has almost ruined my life. The letter and photographs you delivered to Sarah's office after your trial, resulted in me only being able to see my daughter on supervised visits. Then when these allegations were made, Sarah stopped me seeing Chloe at all."

"I'm sorry, and I know you are finding it hard to trust me, but I have this worked out. If we work together, we can eliminate all of this mess."

"Well, I have nothing to lose by listening to you. So, tell me, how do we do this together?" I asked.

"Well, my lawyers told me that my Appeal hearing will be soon: within six months. But the hearing for your case won't be for at least twelve to eighteen months. So that gives us time to find a solution," Anthony said.

"That's great, so you will be free and have your conviction quashed, and I will face criminal charges after that? What's in this for me again?" I asked.

"Peter, all I did during the last few months was research legal cases for a precedent. Once my Appeal is granted, then my case is over. The likelihood of me being retried is almost nil, particularly regarding the time I have already served and my mental condition."

"I get that, Anthony, but that won't stop the case against me."

"It will if I don't give evidence against you. The police have no case against you without me, and then they will have to drop the charges against you."

I realised that Anthony had given this a great deal of thought, and he had produced a brilliant solution. But I was still hesitant to trust him, and he could see that."

"I know you aren't sure if you can trust me, but even if you didn't trust me, why would I want to go through another trial once I was free? Think of that?"

"But how will you justify to the court and the police that you don't want to give evidence against me? Why wouldn't you want me convicted of what I allegedly did to you if it was so bad that it caused you significant psychological damage? They won't buy it."

"I've read up on this too in recent cases. Many victims find it too traumatising to relive the events that caused them trauma, to testify. You know they can't force a witness to testify, and they will look like absolute gooses if they turn around and say I made it all up, and they fell for it."

I realised that Anthony's idea was brilliant and viable. Rupert couldn't have devised anything as good as this plan. I picked up the bottle of champagne, topped up our glasses, and said to Anthony, "I think that's the most brilliant plan I have heard of in my legal career. You should finish your law degree and become a criminal lawyer. This may be the start of a brilliant career path for you."

Anthony looked pleased that I was happy. He took the glass of champagne from me and I led him out to my balcony, where we sat down. "Here's to us," I said.

Anthony said, "You know, if I had listened to my lawyers to not talk to you, I would never have known the truth about why I didn't hear from you when I was a child; and we wouldn't be here together again today. I don't know how I produced the plan, but once I did and I researched it, I knew it would work."

"I'm relieved you took the chance and met with me so I could clear that up with you. And you should know the truth. But we can't risk being seen together before your Appeal. That is an essential part of this plan if it's going to work. No one can know about this except us."

"I know, don't worry. I've told no one," Anthony said.

"You need to play this carefully with Madeline as well. She will be your star witness and needs to support you."

"I know. I wasn't going to stay here long today. I want to reconnect with Madeline and get to know my nephews. My father ruined not only my relationship with you but with her too, because I blamed her for you not coming back to our house again. I just wanted you to know my plan, so that you didn't turn against me. Once we finish our champagne, I will go home to her house, and we don't need to see each other until my Appeal is over. I found out in jail that there is an App that we can use called "Telegraph." We can download it on your phone now, and there is no way to trace the calls or text messages we make between us."

"Are you sure? No way to trace it?"

"I'm sure. It's encrypted, and I've used it by helping a couple of guys with their Appeals while I was in jail."

As we were standing on the balcony, a tram went past. Anthony watched as it stopped below my unit and people boarded the tram. He asked, "How long have you lived here and how long have we had trams in Sydney? I thought we only had them in Melbourne."

"It was only finished a month ago, and it's great. I get to the city in ten minutes from here."

Anthony stood up, looked around my apartment, and said, "I can't wait until the Appeal is over and I can get myself a place. Before I go, do you want me to install the App on your phone so we can test if it works?"

"Good idea," I said.

I handed my mobile to Anthony, and he installed the App on my mobile. To test it we sent a couple of messages to each other and then he said, "It's all good to go. Now I should go back to Madeline's before she gets upset with me."

I walked Peter to the door and said, "Are you getting an uber or a taxi back to Madeline's? There are usually a lot of taxi's that drive by," I said.

"A cab is fine, but I can get one on my own. I do remember how to do that."

I went down the lift with Anthony and walked him outside. We hugged goodbye. I now felt much more confident that we could sort everything out because he was genuinely sorry for the trouble he had caused in my life.

We saw three taxis' go past, but they were on the other side of the road. Anthony said to me, "I'll walk over to the other side to get a taxi. I am heading that direction anyway to Madeline's."

"That makes sense," I said, as I watched Anthony walk to the tram stop in the middle of the road before turning to wave goodbye to me. It was then, that I noticed her on the other side of the road. It was Jessica. She stood staring at Anthony before she called out his name. I saw Anthony look up at her. I'm sure he recognised her. They both stared at each other before she turned and walked away. Jessica looked angry. I hadn't even thought about how she must feel about this man, who had been her step-father and who was now out on bail whilst appealing the conviction he had received for multiple acts of child sexual abuse upon her.

Anthony looked back at me and saw that I had seen them both. He then looked back across the road. I saw a taxi approaching on the other side of the road, and Anthony had also seen it. He raised his hand, waving at the taxi as he ran to cross the road to the side that the taxi was approaching on. At the same time, a car had just turned the corner and it hit Anthony. I saw Anthony flung into the air by the impact and land at the side of the road. Several people rushed to his aid.

I stood frozen. I didn't know if I should go to him or walk back into my unit. I realised that first thing I should do was to delete the App he had just installed on my phone.

After deleting the App, I looked up, and by this time, I saw a woman performing CPR on Anthony. A crowd had gathered around them, and I heard an ambulance approaching. I decided there was nothing further I could do and walked back into my apartment.

When I got back inside, I watched the scene from the safety of my balcony. The ambulance had arrived, and Anthony was being treated by them. Seeing the champagne bottle on the table, I picked it up, together with the glasses and carried them to the glass recycling shoot outside my unit and disposed of them. The fact that Anthony had been at my unit did not look good for me, and if I could help it, I was not volunteering any knowledge of what just happened. I thought I had seen Jessica; but maybe it wasn't her. I poured myself a scotch, turned on my television, and collapsed on my lounge.

Bruce

Chapter 45

I saw Tina laughing at me when I walked out of the office. I'm sure she enjoyed the stress I had gone through this morning. Getting through the meeting without anyone seeing the writing on the back of my head was not the easiest thing I had ever had to do. Now I had to leave the office wearing an office cap to cover up my head.

As I walked to my car, I recalled with relief that I had an overnight bag in the boot of my car. At least I could change into jeans at the airport, so I didn't look as ridiculous as I did now, wearing a cap with my suit.

As I drove to the airport, the phone kept ringing to the point of driving me crazy. Emma, Tina, and Marci were calling and texting me. I just needed to get away and have some peace to work out how to get my life back in order. I changed at the airport lounge, ordered a scotch and sat down on a lounge just as I received another text from Marci, telling me she needed to speak to me urgently.

I was so annoyed, I stupidly called her. I told her that what she had done had nearly cost me my career and marriage. She said she had no recollection of the night before and apologised profusely, but promised she would never have done anything as ridiculous as draw on my head. I hung up with her mid-conversation, furious at her denial and obvious lies.

Luckily, my flight was called, and walked out of the lounge to board the plane. I couldn't wait to get away. The stress was getting to me, and I was not coping well with it. I found my seat and ordered a scotch to calm myself down. The conversation I had with Marci had been infuriating. How she thought she would get away with it was beyond my comprehension. Tina was right; Marci had written on my head with the intent to jeopardise my marriage and my job.

As the plane landed in Melbourne, I had just started to relax. I had many regrets and having sex with Tina had been one of my biggest. We regretted it as soon as it happened. She was married at the time, and I was engaged. Apart from being a mistake, it was the most unsatisfactory sexual experience I had ever had. Until then, I had thought that any sex was better than no sex, but the incident with Tina left me confused. We had been drunk and working back late when it happened. She had been sitting on the back of the lounge when she lost her balance and fell backwards. I grabbed her, resulting in us falling onto the lounge with me on top of her. Kissing and fumbling whilst removing our clothes, sex seemed to happen; but then it got complicated. Things were inexplicably awkward, and it was all over before it started. We both seemed to sober up instantly afterwards. We were both so embarrassed that we just dressed hastily without speaking, and then left the office expeditiously in silence.

Neither of us had ever alluded to or brought up the incident again. Still, when Tina had caught me with Marci one-night last year in the office kissing on the same lounge, I thought I detected a look of jealousy in her eyes. Being the professional she was, Tina didn't show it, or mention anything about. She just closed the door softly before leaving, so Marci didn't know she'd seen us.

Turning on my mobile now we'd landed, I was not surprised by the series of text messages from Marci. My mobile just kept buzzing with alerts until I counted six of them. "Please, you need to call me. It's serious," was the last voice message from her.

I had already anticipated this behaviour from her, and I had earlier called my lawyer to deal with it. I was not going to talk to her again. She was crazy if she thought she could play these games and still live in my unit and continue to get the allowance from me that I transferred to her each week. That was now going to end. She had to leave my life, and my lawyer should have already called by now, to give her the news.

A text message came up on my mobile from my lawyer, Clint. The message read; *You need to call me asap.* I wondered if Marci had threatened him with something, so I called. Clint answered immediately, "Mate, are you alone? Can you talk?"

"I'm on a plane just landing in Melbourne. I don't care what Marci says. Just get rid of her."

Clint replied, "It's not that simple, mate. Yes, she does not want to move out of the unit, but more importantly, she's just told me that she's been diagnosed with hepatitis B."

"What? Is this a joke?"

"She pricked herself with a needle about three months ago helping a lady at the gym. The lady had diabetes and was trying to give herself an insulin shot in the changing room. When Marci tried to help her, the needle slipped and pricked her. Then last week, the lady had called the gym owner to tell him that she had been diagnosed with hepatitis B and that she needed to find the kind lady who pricked her finger trying to help her."

"Has Marci had a blood test?" I asked.

"Yes, and it was positive. That's why she's been trying to call you. She said you spoke to her briefly today, but it was to yell at her about something ridiculous, then you hung up on her before she could tell you."

"What the hell does Marci having hepatitis B mean to me? And is there any chance that I would get it from her" Bruce asked.

"Look, apparently there is a minimal risk that you can get it from her. But if you did, Emma is at risk as she's pregnant, which is very dangerous to her and the baby. Apparently, you can have it and have absolutely no symptoms at all."

I was now unable to speak. I heard Clint saying his name, but I just hung up and sat back in my chair, trying to comprehend what had just happened to my life. My mobile buzzed again, and it was a message from Emma thanking me for the necklace and asking me to call her. My mobile rang again. It was Clint, "Mate, don't hang up on me. You can get a doctor in Melbourne to do a blood test at the hotel. In the meantime, let's leave things with Marci until we sort out whether we have a bigger problem than evicting her."

The flight attendant came over to me and asked, "Sir, are you ok." I suddenly noticed that all the other passengers had left the plane except me.

"Thanks, I'm fine. Sorry, I was distracted by a call," I said as I got up to walk out of the plane.

"You sure? You look grey," the hostess replied.

"That's the least of my problems," I said as I stood up and walked up the aisle to the exit.

Sarah

Chapter 46

As I walked into my office reception area, my receptionist nodded with a sign of approval. "Love your new suit," she said. I walked past the reception area towards my office. Seeing Kate on the phone, I waved hello and continued to my office. I'd just sat down at my desk when Kate walked in with my diary and list of clients for the day.

"That was a great segment you did this morning on the "Today Show." I loved your responses to her questions about the new legislation changes. But most importantly, that suit looked fantastic on TV and your shoes are amazing. Tell me, do you swing your legs like that on purpose to show them off?" she said, giggling.

"Thanks, Kate. I don't know about the swinging leg thing, but I love these shoes, and so did the host, Kerrie-Anne."

"Well, you aced it today. Anyway, back to the real world; this week's new client summary list is on your desk. The two clients that Adam referred are there," Kate said.

Juggling my weekly intake of new clients was Kate's biggest challenge. The diversity of people that came to see me never stopped surprising me. She often asked why a man would prefer to use a woman in his family law case, especially those who were male chauvinists. I thought it was because they thought a woman lawyer acting for them would annoy their wife more than anything; more times than not, they were right.

As I sat at my desk, I got a text from Peter, which read, "Call me ASAP. Anthony has been in an accident, and he is in critical condition. I've texted Howard and waiting to hear if he has heard anything? I'm not sure what to do."

I sent a text back, "I will call Howard and get back to you."

When I called Howard, he answered on the first ring, and I told him about Peter's text message. Howard immediately asked me, "How did Peter know that?"

"I don't know. I just received a text message from him. I presume someone told him," I replied.

"But who would tell Peter, Sarah? Anthony was taken to the hospital unconscious an hour ago and is now dead. I only found out via my police connections because the hospital had contacted his sister to advise her that he was in a critical condition. She had asked them to also contact the police immediately due to his bail conditions."

"How awful for her," I said.

"The driver has tested nil for alcohol or drugs, so he has not been charged. Witnesses have said that Anthony had crossed the street trying to flag a cab and did not see the car coming around the corner. He had run straight in front of it trying to catch the cab."

"I don't know how Peter found out about it." I said.

"It may have something to do with the fact that it happened across the road from Peter's apartment. Anthony was at Peter's apartment visiting him as soon as he was out on bail. His lawyers had advised Anthony against it."

"If Anthony had gone to see Peter, and if he was hit by a car running across the street to get a cab, Peter hasn't done anything wrong, has he?"

"That's an excellent question, Sarah. I have no doubt the police will try to ask Peter, but he will not answer and will no doubt call me instead."

"Have you spoken to Peter?"

"Not yet. I got his text message a few minutes after finding out about the accident. The police have so far put together the facts that a car hit Anthony, and that Peter lives in the apartment block across the road."

"At this point, the connection to Peter is only circumstantial. No one can allege that Peter had anything directly to do with the accident. However, without Anthony's evidence, the police will have to drop the charges against Peter. Without Anthony giving evidence against Peter, they would never be able to prove their case beyond a reasonable doubt."

"I see. So that may raise suspicions that it wasn't an accident?" Sarah asked.

"Not that I have heard yet. A witness said they saw a young lady standing across the street, calling to Anthony, just before he started to cross the road. They said he was running across the road trying to hail the taxi but looking in her direction."

"So it was clearly an accident? The car that hit him was not at fault?"

"Yes, that's right. The driver had just turned the corner, and Anthony had run right in front of him. The driver stopped immediately and has been cooperative with the police. He even had a video camera on his dashboard, which filmed what happened."

"I know this is very sad for Anthony's family, but it was an accident."

"It will not go unnoticed by the police that Anthony happened to be leaving Peter's unit, just before running across a road to hail a cab to get home in time to comply with his bail conditions. And then he was distracted by a mystery woman, causing him to lose concentration, so he ran in front of a car, which cost him his life."

"When you put it like that, it sounds awful."

"It does, but it's all circumstantial evidence, and they can't convict him. If Peter does what I tell him, this will all be over very soon."

"I hope so. There's has already been enough pain and suffering. Nothing that can happen now will help Anthony, but the charges being dropped against Peter will enable us to get on with our lives."

"I hope for you and Chloe that this is finally the end of this mess. I will do my best to sort it out. I'll call Peter now and make sure he doesn't speak to the police without me."

"Thank you, Rupert. Please keep me updated."

"Will do," Rupert replied.

Bruce

Chapter 47

I did not even remember getting into the taxi from the airport to the hotel. I arrived at the hotel, checked in at reception, and went straight to my suite. As soon as I walked in, I took off the cap I had to wear to cover the artwork on my head and called my doctor.

I was surprised at how calm my doctor was about my call. He didn't seem to think there was much chance of me having contracted hepatitis B. But he had agreed that having me tested was essential due to Emma's pregnancy. He said his secretary would immediately arrange with the hotel to get a doctor to my room for a blood test.

Unlike my lawyer, my doctor thought, mainly as I was interstate, that there was no point in upsetting Emma by telling her about the situation until my results were back. He said that as Emma was pregnant, he would be surprised if she had not had regular blood tests in the last few weeks, and if they had not shown any issues, this was a good sign. I asked if one of the regular tests would have been for hepatitis B for pregnant women. My doctor told me it was one of their main tests, as precautions were necessary if it was an issue. Particularly as it could be transferred in vitro to the baby.

The call with my doctor made me so much calmer. My mobile rang, and I saw that it was Emma calling me. I had to let it go to message bank. I knew she would tell from my voice that something was wrong, and I didn't want to upset her more than I already had.

I poured myself a scotch from the minibar. Now that I had calmed down, I felt sorry for Marci. As awful as it felt, I needed to leave this problem with my lawyer to resolve. I had enough on my plate right now to deal with.

The hotel phone rang, and I answered it. The receptionist said the doctor would arrive at my room within an hour. Feeling relieved that things were in motion, I poured myself another scotch as I stared at the text messages on my mobile. Message after message from Marci, then a message from Emma, and then Tina which read, *you need to call me, please*. They could all wait.

I thought about Emma, and I knew how much she loved me. I knew that Emma was not the love of my life, but my mother had told me that the woman you marry is not necessarily the love of your life. She had convinced me that Emma was the perfect wife for me. My mother had pointed out that Emma was madly in love with me, devoted, intelligent, financially independent, and attractive - which was in stark contrast to other women I had dated. They had been mostly busty blondes who liked to have fun and were financially and academically challenged. "If you must, you can have your fun girls on the side, but darling, you cannot breed with them," my mother had said to me.

My marriage to Emma, I believed, was a happy one. Emma was pregnant, and I was doing well at work. We had a lovely home and were both happy enough when I was home. I had no intention of leaving Emma. As far as I knew, Emma was happy too. She was excited about her pregnancy, and I knew she would be a wonderful mother. The thought of being a father had excited me too, and my mother was thrilled about finally becoming a grandmother.

Reminiscing about Marci, it was as though it was yesterday when I fell for her. Two years ago, I became addicted to her body after the first time we were together. It wasn't love; it was just sheer lust. She made me feel like no woman had ever done before. She did not demand any other commitment from me except my financial support. Up until now, the arrangement was perfect.

I knew that Marci had targeted me, and that didn't even bother me. In hindsight, I enjoyed it. After starting as a new receptionist at my office, she approached me one afternoon. She asked if I wanted a drink after work. She didn't flinch when I said I was engaged and living with my fiancé.' She smiled at me and said, "It's just a drink."

Marci suggested we get to a bar just around the corner from the office. After we finished a bottle of wine, I politely asked her to a restaurant for dinner. In response, she placed a hand on my thigh and said to me, "I made something at home for us just in case we got hungry." Standing up, she picked up her overcoat and handbag and led me out of the bar.

As she walked into her apartment, her intentions were clear. She led me through the lounge room and onto the balcony, with a dinner table set for two, a champagne bucket filled with ice, and a bottle of champagne. I thought to myself that she must have been confident she would get her man tonight. Marci had then said to me, "You open the champagne while I check on our dinner."

I obediently followed her instructions, popped the cork of the champagne bottle chilling in the ice bucket, and poured us a glass. I could hear Marci's movements in the kitchen, and I couldn't help but wonder if she had done this regularly. She came out of the kitchen and said, "Dinner won't be long now. Enjoy the champagne and the view," as she headed down the hallway. I sat on the lounge on the balcony, looking over the city lights.

As I refilled my glass, I heard Marci walking towards me on the timber floorboards in her stilettos. As she put the plates down on the table, she leaned forward to kiss me, and her overcoat gapped open, revealing that she was naked. I was instantly mesmerized.

Our physical attraction was so intense that it did not go unnoticed at the office. I was surprised when I explained to Marci that our relationship had become a problem with my partners in the office, and she had offered to resign immediately. She said that my job was far more important than hers. She then suggested that if I were willing to give her an allowance until she found another job, our times together could be whenever it suited us. Marci resigned that day and had not had a job since.

Marci had been patient and discreet over the last two years, but I knew she never wanted another job. The fact that she was available at any time of the day for me was becoming a luxury that I was not prepared to give up. When the landlord sold the place, she had been renting, Marci moved into one of my rental units, which made things even easier for us.

As I sat staring reflectively into my scotch, I could not believe that such a strange run of events had so instantly shattered our perfect arrangement. Firstly, Marci had tried to sabotage me with Emma by writing on the back of my head. Now, Marci had found out that she was hepatitis B positive. I knew the relationship could not continue indefinitely without Marci wanting more from me. Still, I had not predicted it to end this way.

Sarah

Chapter 48

I had just come back from court when Kate walked into my office. She said, "I need to fill you in about a lady that Gary has referred to you."

"Is it a patient of Gary's," I asked.

"Yes, she is. He is worried about her. Her partner's lawyer is demanding that she vacate the apartment she is living in."

"Were they living together?"

"No. She has been in a relationship with a married man for over two years who is not only married to someone else, but whose wife is also pregnant."

"She is living in a unit he owns then?"

"Yes, has been for the last two years. He told her last year that he was transferring the apartment into her name. Yesterday, his lawyer told her that he never intended to give it to her, that she needed to move out immediately and their relationship was over."

"Had her partner told her that their relationship was over and why?"

"I was confused when she started to explain it to me, but from the gist of it, he accused her of something, and she completely denied it. He is convinced she is trying to sabotage his marriage and wants nothing more to do with her. He has told her to communicate with him via his lawyer from now on."

"Sounds like a mess," I said.

"It gets worse. Gary said she got some blood test results today that confirmed that she was hepatitis B positive. When she told him that her boyfriend was also kicking her out of her apartment, he thought we could help her."

"What a terrible time she is having. Does she know how she contracted hepatitis B? Do they realise that this could be a serious problem for his pregnant wife if it's passed onto her?"

"She said that a couple of months ago at the gym she goes to, that she was helping a lady give herself an insulin injection, and she accidentally jabbed her finger. She said the lady had been having an episode at the time, and she was trying to help. The gym manager came to find her this week as the lady had called him to try and identify who had helped her, to let her know to get tested."

"That was really bad luck."

"She is coming in next week on Tuesday to see you. She told her former partner's lawyer that she is retaining you."

"Let Gary know that I will look after her."

"Of course. Excuse me, Sarah. That's my line ringing," Kate said as she walked out of my office to take the call.

Kate put the call on hold and walked back into my office and said, "Sarah, it's Con Habib on the phone. He said he is calling from the police station where he has been taken for questioning by the police."

"Did he say why have police have taken him to the station?"

"No, but I just saw the story flash up on the news feed on my computer that they just found a woman's body in the Parramatta River. They said the police had taken the estranged husband in for questioning. I hope that isn't him."

Kate walked back to her desk and put the call through.

I answered, "Hi Con, it's Sarah. What has happened?"

"Sarah, the police came to my house and told me that I they need to ask me some questions about the death of my wife. I do not know what has happened. They are telling me she died. They asked if I wanted to call my lawyer, so I told them that I wanted to call you."

"Con, I am not a criminal lawyer, and that is who you need right now, but I am going to arrange one for you."

"My wife, Sarah. They told me she is dead."

"I am so sorry, Con. Unfortunately, the first person they will question is the spouse? Are you ok?"

"I am ok. My daughters were crying when I left the house, and I am worried about them. I'm calling you because they are telling me my rights, but I know they think I am guilty."

"I can call a lawyer for you who specialises in criminal law to come to the police station for you now. Would you like me to arrange that for you?"

"You know what happened with my wife, and I don't want to explain that to another lawyer Sarah. Do I have to do that? Tell another person how she left the children and me and wanted me to sell my house for her and her boyfriend?"

Sarah quickly interrupted Con, please do not discuss anything else with me on the phone. I have not suggested another lawyer because I am upset with you. I don't do this area of law, and you need an experienced lawyer in criminal law as the police are interviewing you in relation to a murder. I am trying to do the best thing for you. You must not talk to anyone else about your wife or your family situation except your criminal lawyer when he arrives at the police station."

"Ok, yes, Sarah. I will wait for the lawyer you get me. What is his name?"

"I will call a lawyer I know called Rupert Showers. Con, please put me back on the phone to the police officer, so I can let them know that I am arranging him to come to the police station to represent you and that they must not question you without him."

Con did as Sarah directed and handed the phone to the police officer. Sarah informed him that Rupert would be arriving at the police station shortly. The police officer replied sarcastically, "Great, can't wait to see the infamous criminal lawyer, Mr Showers."

I hung up and dialled Rupert on his mobile. In the interim Kate walked into my office and told me that the police had called and said that the body found in the Parramatta River was the body of Mrs Habib. "I can't believe that Mr Habib had been in our office yesterday, and I felt sad and sorry for him. I think he killed his wife," she said.

Howard answered the phone and I said, "Did you hear about the woman who was found dead in Parramatta River?"

"Yes, of course, why?" he said.

"The man they have taken in for questioning is one of my clients. He is at Parramatta police station now, and he just called me. I told him I would contact you to act for him. His name is Con Habib, and he can afford you. Can you go now to help him?"

"Sure, I will do that for you. But are you ok? You sound upset, Sarah."

"I'm in shock, but I can't say any more. Thanks for looking after him."

"I'll call the police station now."

"Thanks, Rupert."

I slumped into my chair. I said, "I think the world has just gone mad. I have not had two such cases ever in my career, let alone back-to-back."

Kate agreed as she handed me a piece of paper. "This is the name of Marci's boyfriend and his lawyer, Clint Sanders, just in case he calls you."

"That's a blast from the past, Clint Sanders," I said. "I haven't heard of him in years. Last I heard, he went corporate and had moved out of litigation."

"Is he a reasonable guy – Clint?" Kate asked.

"He was. You never know though; he may have changed."

"That may be the trifecta for poor Marci," Kate said.

"It's a rather tangled web. But we have been in worse positions."

"We certainly have," Kate replied.

Bruce

Chapter 49

The concierge called to let me know that the doctor was on his way to my room. I heard the doorbell ring shortly after, and I opened the door to a doctor dressed in blue medical scrubs. He followed me into the lounge area, and as I turned around, I saw the bemused look on his face. He asked me, "Is that a tattoo on your head?"

I had completely forgotten about Marci's artwork on the back of my head and I was embarrassed. I said to him, "No, it's not a tattoo, it was drawn on my head."

"That's funny. Who is Marci, your daughter?"

"It's a long story, sort of a bad joke, one which I did not find funny."

"Sorry I asked, he said. "Let's get started then." He proceeded to set up his medical equipment on the coffee table. When he had finished, he asked, "Have you been feeling unwell lately?"

"I've been fine, I said.

"I will check your blood pressure first, then take a blood sample."

"I think my blood pressure is the least of my worries right now," I replied.

"I will be able to confirm that in just a minute, Bruce," he said as he placed the armband on my arm for the high blood pressure machine. "You know high blood pressure can lead to a stroke or heart attack, so it can be serious," he said.

"Great," I replied.

"Your blood pressure is fine," he said. Then he moved onto taking several vials of my blood. "Just put your finger on that for a minute," he said as he removed the needle.

"How long will it take for the results to come back?"

"About twenty-four hours."

"That long?" I asked. "Is there a way I can pay for urgent results?"

"This is an urgent service."

"It will be the longest twenty-four hours of my life."

"At least you are in a nice hotel. I can think of worse places to be," the doctor replied.

"How do I get the results?"

"Your GP will call you. I assume you haven't told your wife about this yet?"

"Not yet."

The doctor shrugged his shoulders and said, "It's not going to make a difference unless she is sleeping with someone else, too, I suppose."

I said, "She is pregnant."

"Being pregnant doesn't stop you from having sex with someone else necessarily."

"That's not funny," I said.

"Sorry, couldn't resist it," he said smiling, while packing up his medical bag and walking to the door. "It's only my opinion, but I don't think you present as though you have hepatitis B."

"Thanks," I said.

"My pleasure," he replied as walked out of my suite.

Kate

Chapter 50

As I walked into Sarah's office, I knew by her face that it had been a tough day for her. Sarah looked tired, and she rarely looked tired. I respected how she could manage all the complexities and drama of her client's cases and always remained calm and composed. I knew she would appreciate a change in the pace at times like this, so I decided to bring up the ball, especially since Phil had called me only a few minutes ago to discuss it.

I put the printout of the email from Phil on Sarah's desk in front of her as I brought it up with her. "Phil has called me a few times about the ball to get the names for our table. I printed out the invitation for you. It's only a week away now."

"Have you given him all the details he needs from our end, Kate?"

"Yes, of course. But I still need to figure out what I will wear. Do you know what you are going to wear?"

"No, I have not even thought about it. I should call Mel and see what he has at his boutique? He said he was working on a new evening collection the last time I saw him. We could go together and get something."

"Seriously, Sarah, that's a lovely thought, but I can only afford to buy a dress from Mel after I win lotto. I can't afford what he charges for a dress."

"Remember, Mel said he would give you a huge discount on one of his samples. I know he wants you to have one of his dresses Kate. He loves you."

"I know he offered that to me, but I couldn't take him up on it. It wouldn't be fair for him to sell something cheaper to me than if he sold it to one of his socialite or celebrity clients."

"He doesn't usually sell his samples. But let's go and look this weekend. It will be fun, and Chloe loves going there."

"Ok, let's do that. At least the next time Phil calls asking if I have shown you the invitation, I can say yes and that you have even started dress shopping."

"Has Phil really rung you several times about the ball?"

"Of course, he has. He is panic-stricken that you will pull out, last minute. I am starting to feel sorry for him."

Sarah started laughing. "You are starting to feel sorry for Phil? The man is a genius."

"I said, starting to feel sorry for him, not like him. He has a lot of work to do, but he does show some care and concern for you, which I did not know he had in him."

"What do you mean that he is showing care and concern? What has he said now?" Sarah asked.

"He has been asking if you are excited about the ball, if you are worried about what to wear and whether he could help in any way, like booking a hire car for us to get there."

"I hadn't thought of that yet, and it's next week. You could book a stretch hummer to take us all to the ball.

"Phil has already booked us cars, Sarah. He said he has booked one for the staff, and I will give his secretary the addresses to collect them. He has also arranged for one to collect you and me."

"Has he? How nice of him."

I was not brave enough to tell Sarah that Phil had hinted to me about helping her find a dress for the ball. Although I knew I would be blown away, when he told me what he had in mind, I was not sure how it would go down with Sarah. Phil had sworn me to secrecy, so that was my out. I should have told Charlie and asked his opinion, but it seemed harmless. I looked up to see Sarah walking out of the office as I asked her, "Where are you going?"

"I'm going to Howard's office to talk to him about Con. He called me and said he needed to know what happened in his family law case. The Police are alleging that they believe he killed his wife to avoid paying her out in the family law settlement."

"That sounds serious," I said, wondering if Con had killed his wife.

"Do you think he did it, Sarah," I asked?

"I don't want to think that way about my client Kate, and I can't ask him that direct question."

"Why? Because then I would have to tell the police he told me that. In his interests, I shouldn't ask him."

"I'm glad I'm not a lawyer," I replied.

Bruce

Chapter 51

It had only been eight hours since I had the blood test, but it seemed an eternity. I felt frustrated, angry, and lonely. I could not believe I was alone, sitting in a hotel suite, waiting for blood results. I had been an idiot, and although I could accept that I may get sick from my mistake, Emma and the baby did not deserve it.

The doctor had been right. If I had to wait it out somewhere, this hotel was as good as it got. Lying on the semi-circle-shaped lounge that looked over the Yarra River with a scotch in my hand wasn't something I had any right to complain about. The butler had delivered a complimentary bottle of champagne with canapes. I had devoured the canapes, realising that I hadn't eaten all day.

I stared at the bottle of champagne, and it just didn't seem right to drink it alone. It was unreasonable of me, but it made me think of Marci. I now realised what a mess I had made of her life too. She was ill through no fault of her own, and I should be helping her, not throwing her out of her home. I had behaved like a monster. I was a monster.

As I looked at my phone, I saw another text message from Emma. I had sent her text messages in response to hers, to let her know that I was busy in meetings. The thought of speaking to her and lying was just beyond me, although I knew it was cruel not to call her. Text messages were so easy and unemotional – luckily. I knew that she loved me enough to put up with any form of communication.

Marci was never as easily pleased, but she stopped contacting me after I had told her to move out of the flat. I wished I could change my mind and let her stay, but I just couldn't cope with dealing with her right now. I would have to leave it to my lawyer Clint to do that.

I saw my reflection in the mirrored lounge room wall, and I realised what a sad fool I looked. Usually, women everywhere loved me. It was ironic and sad, at the same time. Would any of these women still love me if I was hepatitis B positive? Would any of them want to nurse and care for me? I knew that Emma would. She would look after me even if I gave it to her. Why had I been such an idiot to jeopardise her and our baby?

I was looking at the clock. Time was going slower and slower. My only comfort was hoping that if I drank enough, I would fall asleep so that some of the time would pass while I was unconscious. Once I had the results, I could decide what to do. That was if I lived through this waiting period of the longest 24 hours I had known.

My mobile rang, and I saw that it was my doctor calling. I answered immediately, and said, "Your test is back, and you are negative for Hepatitis B."

"Thank you," I said.

"Just as I thought," he replied, before hanging up.

I walked to the window and stared out at the Yarra River. I was so overwhelmed that I started to cry with relief. My life was not ruined, and my wife and unborn baby were not in danger. I picked up my mobile and called Emma. She was so excited to hear from me and thanked me profusely for her new necklace and flowers. I listened to her talk about the baby moving and how she had gone shopping with Sophia. I had never felt more in love with her than I did now. I told her I would be coming home the next day before I remembered that I would find a way to remove the ink from the back of my head before I saw her.

After speaking to Emma, I thought about Marci. I wanted to ensure that I sorted something out with her so that she was ok and happy for me to move on from our complicated arrangement. I decided that if I needed to give her my unit, I would. I decided to call my lawyer to let him know.

When I called Clint to tell him that my blood results were negative, he seemed as relieved as me. "Thank God," he said. "I was so worried about Emma and the baby."

I said to him, "This has been the biggest wake-up call for me. I don't want anything more to do with Marci. Please do what you need to do to finalise everything with her. Give her the unit, if that is what it takes to make her go away."

"I don't think I will have to go that far, Bruce, but I am glad you have decided to end that relationship for both your sakes."

"Thanks, Mate. I will be back in Sydney in a day or two. Let me know what I need to do."

"Got it. Leave sorting out Marci with me. You look after Emma."

Sarah

Chapter 52

After getting him up to speed on the facts regarding Con's family law matter, I left Howard's office. Howard explained to me that Con had been his own biggest problem. The police had started to think that Con may be a suspect, mainly because all Con talked about was his divorce. When they asked him if that was why he killed her, he became confused that they did not understand what he had been telling them. Howard said what Con was really trying to explain to the police, was why he had not been with his wife when she had disappeared. He was trying to explain to them, that because of the divorce, she had moved out and that is why they were not living together.

After leaving my file with Howard, I walked back to my office. I saw Kate as soon as I walked back in, and she asked me, "What's happening with Con? Are they going to charge him with murder?"

"They are trying to put together a motive, and the divorce was the most obvious. Howard is confident that they don't have enough to charge him though. Poor Con, he is quite confused and in shock. His daughters had arrived to be with him, so I left them all and my file with Howard."

"Do you know who found her body?" Kate asked.

"No, but I heard that the police have now also found her partner's body in the river. They are looking at whether it was a murder or boating accident. Her partner owned a small boat which has not yet been located."

"The news made it sound like Con had killed her. "

"It's just tragic," I said.

"Chloe called me. Did she manage to get you on your mobile?"

"Yes, she did, thanks. We have been texting each other about dinner. I know I must be home by 6.30 pm tonight, because she and Maria are planning a special family dinner."

"It must be so nice being a mum and having someone so excited to see you at home."

"I'm lucky, I know. I'm leaving now," I said as I grabbed my car keys and laptop and walked out of my office.

I stood in the reception area waiting for the lift. As it stopped at my floor, the lift doors opened and I was startled by two women who got out pushing a fully laden clothes rack. I said to them, "Are you sure you are on the right floor? This is a legal firm."

"Is this the office of Sarah Walters Lawyers?" they asked.

"Yes, it is. I'm Sarah." I said, clearly surprised by their arrival. The woman who had just spoken to me looked me up and down before replying, "I am sure we got your size right. Are you a size ten?"

"I am, but I did not order any clothing," I replied.

"We are personnel shoppers from the seventh floor at David Jones. Phil Thompson requested that we bring you a range of dresses to choose from to attend an event. We have brought a selection of dresses for you to look at, but if you don't like any of these, just let us know, and we can bring a whole new rack and take these back."

I was speechless. Luckily, Kate had heard their voices in reception and had come out to see what was happening. "Oh, my goodness, he did it," Kate said as she stared at the clothes on the rack.

"You knew this was coming?" I asked.

"Well, sort of. Phil thought it would be helpful if he arranged an assortment of dresses to come to the office for you to choose from, because you were so busy that it might be easier for you than to go shopping."

"This is crazy. I can buy my own clothes."

The two women holding the rack of clothing remained silent, but one of them said, "Oh no, Sarah, you have taken this the wrong way. We do this for a lot of busy working women. Mr Thompson was trying to be helpful, not pushy in any way. If you don't want any of the clothing, we can take it back, or you can keep whatever you like, courtesy of Mr Thompson."

I looked to Kate, who had started to work her way through inspecting the dresses on the rack. I watched her face as she pulled out a long, mauve chiffon dress. Kate's eyes widened as she touched the fabric and then walked towards me. "This dress would look amazing on you. Look at the colour next to your skin," she said as she held the dress right next to me.

"I chose that one," the taller of the ladies said. "It just arrived yesterday, and the colour is just spectacular."

I took the dress on the hanger from Kate and looked at it closely. It was a beautiful dress, and I knew the colour would suit me. Sensing my hesitation, the lady who first spoke to me said, "We can leave these all here for you to look at, if that is ok with you. Call us when you are ready, and we will come and collect the rack with anything you don't like." She then handed me her card with her details.

Kate said to them, "Thank you. We will let you know." She then hit the button for the lift, signalling to the ladies it was their queue to leave. The lift arrived promptly, and the ladies left.

I felt bewildered, and Kate attempted to soothe me immediately by saying, "Look, they are just dresses. You don't need to keep any of them if you don't want to. Before you react unnecessarily, why don't you head home as you were going to, and let's look again tomorrow when you are not so tired."

"It just feels odd to me," I managed to say as I headed toward the lift again.

"I know," Kate said. "You are not used to anyone spoiling you, and you may need some time to adjust to it. I will take this into your office, and you can take your time tomorrow to think about it." Kate then started to wheel the rack away from me.

"Thanks. I will have to race home now, I said," as I waited for the lift.

As I was waiting, Kate's phone rang, and I could loudly hear the conversation between Kate and Phil. She had the call on speaker. He asked Kate, "Did they arrive?"

I stepped closer down the hall to listen to the conversation.

"Yes, they did," Kate answered.

"Did Sarah like anything?" Phil asked in a tone that sounded so sweet and childlike that I could not believe it was him."

"She had to leave to get home to her daughter, but she had a quick look before she left, and I know for sure that she loved at least one of the dresses," Kate said.

"Are you still there?" Kate asked.

"Yes, sorry, Kate," Phil replied, "Sorry, I was deep in thought".

"They are the most divine selection of dresses, Phil, honestly the most beautiful clothes I have ever seen."

"You know Kate, if there is anything there that you would like to wear, please take it. I would love for you both to have something to wear to the ball."

I knew I was eavesdropping, but I had to continue listening, hoping the call would end soon, as I didn't want to be home late for dinner with Chloe.

"Thank you, that is lovely of you to offer, but nothing on the rack would fit me. Sarah is quite a different shape to me if you haven't noticed."

"Sorry," Phil replied.

"I already have a dress to wear, Phil. It's made by one of Sarah's friends, Mel, and if I didn't wear it to the ball, he would be quite upset with me," Kate said.

"Great," Phil said, sounding very relieved. "Can you let me know tomorrow how it goes? They can send more dresses if Sarah doesn't like any of them."

"I will let you know, and I am sure at least one of them is perfect, Phil, so don't worry."

"Thanks, Kate."

"Good night," Kate replied.

I quickly jumped into the lift to go home. After listening to the call, I was surprised that Phil had developed such a friendly relationship with Kate. Still, I was not going to bring it up with her. I was glad I had overheard the call, though, as much as I trusted Kate, I did not trust Phil, and his desire to get close to Kate was now concerning me.

Kate

Chapter 53

As soon as I had wheeled the rack of dresses into the boardroom, I checked that Sarah had left the office. I then called Charlie for his advice. When he answered, I commenced frantically describing what had happened, "Two women delivered a rack of designer dresses to the office, from Phil, for Sarah. He called me and said it was for the ball. He even told me to choose one. Who does this Charlie, and what do I tell Sarah to do?"

"Seriously, do you have any doubt as to what to do?" Charlie replied, soundly genuinely shocked.

"What do you mean? Yes, of course I'm serious," Kate said.

"I am concerned, Kate. This behaviour is atypical of a manipulative and controlling man seeking to make a woman feel that he is showing her, and those around her genuine concern and affection, when he is being controlling and manipulative."

"Really?"

"Why do you think he sent the dresses, Kate? Think about it. Sarah does not want or need anyone to send her something to wear to a ball. His conduct is out of line. It's the act of a man who wants to control what she wears and how she looks."

"Oh," was all I managed to say."

"Phil will appear generous and kind to get what he wants. Then he will keep being kind and generous until it doesn't suit him anymore. If he doesn't get what he wants, and is confronted, he will become mean and offensive."

"I am clearly out of my depth here," I said,

"We need to help Sarah get this guy out of her life," Charlie reiterated.

"I feel bad now because I encouraged him with the dress thing. I should have known it wasn't right. You hit the nail right on the head when you said Sarah wouldn't like it, it was the first thing she said to me, "But I don't need anyone to buy me a dress," and I thought she was being stubborn."

"It's not your fault, Kate. Phil is very manipulative. He knows you are close to Sarah. That's why he is nice to you. He is using you to get to her. He is the expert in manipulation and finding people's vulnerabilities."

"What do I do now?" I asked.

"Don't change the way you act with him. Keep him on your side, and don't let him know you are on to him. If he feels you are pushing against him, he won't confide in you anymore. Just keep updating me on what he does. I know that Sarah will work this out, and when she does, we need to be there for her."

"What do you mean, Charlie?"

"Sorry, Kate. I didn't mean to confuse you. What I mean is that if Phil sees that his overt and overwhelming actions aren't working, and he is getting Sarah's attention, he will move on to getting her to feel sorry for him. He manipulates people, so he is very clever at reading them. Right now, he is sensing Sarah's feelings of vulnerability and that is why he is targeting her with his demonstrative moves."

"How could he make Sarah feel sorry for him?"

"He will for example try to make her feel guilty about going to all the trouble of arranging the table at the ball, the dresses and flowers. He will tell her how hurt he is that she has rejected him when he has tried so hard. If she still rejects him after this, then he will turn nasty, and that's when she will need our help."

"Now I am more confused, Charlie. If someone turns nasty on Sarah, she won't need our help. She can be tough when she needs to be."

"Oh, now that's where you do not see the difference, Kate. There is a significant difference between being tough in business and being tough in your personal life. Just look at how Sarah has acted with Peter and what she has put up with from him."

"Ok, I now get it. I will keep you posted."

"Phil will stuff this up, Kate. He is not used to women like Sarah, and he will underestimate her, which will push her away. We need to support her."

"Thanks Charlie, I'm relieved I called you for your advice. I was falling for his ways, but now I can see its entrapment."

"I'm confident that Sarah would have figured this out herself in time. But the longer the chase goes on for Phil, the nastier he will be when he realises that his feelings are not being reciprocated by Sarah, which he not used to."

Con

Chapter 54

I was at the police station; my daughters were crying, and my wife was dead. My life could not get any worse. Why did this have to happen? Our lives had been good. Why did Eva want to get divorced? I even offered to forgive her so we could be a happy family again.

I believed I had tried everything to convince Eva to change her mind about leaving the girls and me. Trying to talk sense into her, being practical, all of it had not worked. Upon the advice of my friends, I sought legal advice. In desperation, I took the advice of my lawyer Neil. I cut off Eva's joint credit cards on Sunday night and withdrew the money from our joint bank account. The lawyer had told me that this reality check sometimes worked to jolt women into realising the repercussions of what leaving a financially secure marriage would feel like, or it would push her away. Whatever way it went, he said, it had to happen.

I knew it would not be long before Eva would try to use her credit cards and realise what I had done. I had been at home when Eva called me the next day to tell me she was at the supermarket with a trolley full of groceries, when her cards wouldn't work. I said I would come immediately, and when I arrived, I saw that she was standing at the checkout crying. I took out my credit card and paid for the groceries as Eva quickly pushed the trolley away and headed towards her car.

I drove around the block for half an hour before I walked into the house. I hoped that Eva would now be prepared to have a sensible discussion with me, but as soon as I walked in, she walked to the door with two packed suitcases and said to me, "I am leaving, and I will not be coming back." Instead of making her realise that she needed my financial support to encourage her back to me, I had only pushed her away.

My lawyer Neil had said to me, "If she leaves the house, that is the best result for you. We can then drag the sale out or buy her out. If she forces you to move out, she can apply for orders for the house to be sold, and you have to find somewhere else to live. You do not want to be the one who leaves."

I followed Eva to her car as she wheeled her bags beside her. She refused my help to put her bags into the boot. Her last words to me as she left were, "We will now only communicate through my lawyer. I am not talking to you again now that you have cut me off financially with no discussion and embarrassed me like this."

I said to her, "Why do you keep threatening me with lawyers, Eva." I did not understand why Eva thought that we could not resolve the situation between us ourselves.

"Because lawyers are now my only alternative," she said.

I said to her, "I was just trying to get you to understand, that to enable you to live your life as a single person means that we must separate our financial affairs. You have created this situation that my lawyer told me had to happen, not me."

In response, Eva did not speak. She glared at me before she slammed her car door and drove off.

I had expected that Eva would return within a few days, but when she hadn't, I told my family that Eva had moved out of the house, and they were all shocked. My brother George had been more upset about Eva leaving me than I had expected, remarking on how he thought it was disgraceful of her.

George and I had been close until he was in his late teens, got his license and ended up getting involved with a group of boys who were in trouble with the law. He had spent a year in and out of youth detention facilities. But instead of being reformed in there, he bragged to me about how much he had learnt about breaking the law. I had not seen much of George in the last few years, as Eva didn't like him around the girls. But we had stayed in contact. George had offered to help me by suggesting he try talking to Eva. I told him it would not work, but I gave him Eva's mobile number because he wanted to try.

The following week, George told me that he had called Eva, but she had hung up on him. He said he had been following her and knew her movements. During the week, her boyfriend drove to work at 8 am, leaving Eva with his children. Eva would then drive them to school at about 9 am. On the weekend, they had dropped the children off at his sister's house before they drove to a marina, where they got on a boat. After watching them together, he said he had agreed that she would not change her mind.

If I am honest, I accept that we had been unhappy for over six months. Eva had lost interest in the family. Gone were the days when she would cook breakfast for us every morning, pack the girl's lunches and delight in telling us what she would be preparing for our evening meal. She no longer enjoyed tending her vegetable garden at home, delighting in telling us that she had grown our fresh vegetables in the garden. Maybe I should have known something was wrong, but I thought it was just a stage we were going through in our marriage. I had never anticipated that she would want to leave our family.

Since saying she wanted to end our marriage, Eva had just heated takeaway meals or left the girls to cook. She had also moved into the spare bedroom and had little to do with me. She had stopped even watching TV with me in the evenings.

My criminal lawyer, Rupert, believed that the police did not have enough evidence to charge me. That could change, he said, if the police found further evidence. I had told Rupert the truth; that I had not killed Eva. I had, however, not told Rupert that I was relieved that she was dead. It relieved me of finding a way to keep the home for my daughters to live in. I had done the maths with my accountant, and at 67, there was no way I would be able to finance a 20 year mortgage from a bank, to be able to pay her out.

My accountant was not concerned. He had pointed out to me, that even if I was convicted of Eva's murder, the maximum time I would get in jail would be ten years; half the time it would have taken me to repay a mortgage to keep the house. He saw the situation as a win/win as far as he was concerned.

I was very relieved when I asked Sarah, and she had confirmed that her boyfriend could not make a claim against me seeking a share of the house or my assets. Because Eva had not commenced Family Court proceedings for a property settlement before she died, negotiations regarding the divorce could not be continued by anyone else on her behalf. Now that Eva was dead, there was no longer an entitlement to my assets under the Family Law Act by her or her estate.

My criminal lawyer had not asked me what I thought had happened to Eva. If he did, I would never tell him that I thought George may have had something to do with it. I had not discussed it with George, but I hadn't heard from George since Eva's body had been found in the river. I had tried calling and texting him, but he had not returned my messages.

The police told me I could not arrange the funeral until after the autopsy. This was distressing for my daughters and that upset me. I could only keep thinking that this could all have been avoided if only Eva had changed her mind and come home.

Debbie

Chapter 55

As I sat nervously in the waiting room of my lawyers' offices, I was still shocked. When I had initially called to make the appointment, I had not realised how nervous I would be. I had nearly hung up when the receptionist answered my call. It was only because my brother had been standing right next to me, assuring me that this was the only sensible approach to take, that I did not hang up. I trusted his judgement more than anyone.

I had only been waiting a few minutes when a lady who introduced herself as Kate, led me into a conference room. Sarah walked into the room moments later. She introduced herself, and I was so nervous I felt like vomiting. Sarah noticed that I looked anxious and asked, me "Are you Ok?"

"I'm sorry, I am just a little overwhelmed." I then burst out crying, despite my best efforts not to.

Sarah handed me the box of tissues on the boardroom table, and after drying my eyes, I said, "Thank you for seeing me. I am so embarrassed about my situation. That makes me more nervous than usual if that makes sense."

Sarah replied, "Please do not feel embarrassed. I have been divorced myself, and I understand how hard this is. You have a highly emotional situation and are sitting in a lawyer's office, which is also new and stressful to most people."

"Thank you for understanding, but my situation is unusual and has taken me by surprise. My husband does not yet know, but I have discovered he is a cross-dresser. Apart from making me feel like I do not know him, this revelation has made me concerned about his role in our daughter's life. I need your advice and your help with this."

Sarah was very compassionate and said to me, "Discoveries like these can come as a shock, and you are right in seeking help on how to deal with how you manage it for both your and your daughter's welfare. I hope it comforts you when I tell you that I have helped clients in many diverse cases.

"But where do I start? I cannot even talk to my husband about this because it is all so surreal. I know that he will deny it, and then I will lose it with him, which is not what I want. I do not want to go to court. I want to work out a way to be comfortable with him spending time with our daughter. I know she needs a father, but how does a little girl cope with this when I can't?"

"Debbie, I know it must be a huge shock for you. However, I have had other cases with similar circumstances, and we have counsellors to help you work through this. I can recommend a couple of therapists specialising in this area for you to talk to."

"Really? This does not surprise you at all?"

"Not at all," Sarah replied.

"Yes, I think a counsellor could help me a lot," I replied.

"Now, about the financial aspect of your marriage, were you able to complete the list on the information sheet Schedule that my secretary sent you when you made the appointment?"

"Yes, I did. We don't have a lot, so it is quite short," I replied, handing the completed forms to her.

"Once I have had a chance to go through this, I will give you my advice on what I think would be a fair settlement range you would be entitled to."

"Does that mean how much I get of our assets?"

"Yes, that's right. I can also calculate the amount of child support you would be entitled to."

"Do you then contact him to tell him what I am entitled to, or how does it work from there?" I asked.

"That's an excellent question. There are different ways to do it. With the information, you can approach him, or I can contact him, or you can agree to go into the mediation with a mediator who speaks to both of you."

"I really want to sort this out amicably. I don't want to spend money fighting with lawyers; no offence."

"That is very sensible, and I hope he agrees to that. Once we have worked out what your entitlements are, you can begin the process to try and resolve things. You can start with mediation without lawyers, then if you both reach an agreement, lawyers can help you finalise an agreement."

If I went to a mediation with a lawyer, he would not be so receptive, particularly when I tell him what I know. If I go alone, that will show him I want to do this nicely. But what if we cannot work it out in the mediation? What happens then?"

"You will benefit from the mediator's guidance about the issues you will face regarding your daughter and facilitating her relationship with her father. You could also have another mediation with both of you, having lawyers present with you to help you both."

"I should try doing a mediation without lawyers first, but Sarah, before I call the mediator, can you tell me, have you had a case like this before? Have you had any experience seeing how kids cope with situations like this and how the courts view it? Would the court force her to go with him if she felt weird with him dressing like a woman?"

"Children are far more resilient than we think they are. They love both their parents and need them. In cases where there may be issues for the children, the court normally orders a family report. A child psychiatrist or psychiatrist would be appointed to do a report and make recommendations on the arrangements for the child with her parents. They would interview you separately and see you with your daughter when doing the report. Everyone will work together to help make this work for you and your family and be there to support you if any issues arise and any of you need help with."

"That sounds promising. I suppose I am not the first person this has happened to, am I?"

"No, you are not, Debbie, and there is no need to feel embarrassed."

"Thank you. I feel much better about this now. I want to work this out and reach an agreement between us, so I will work hard towards that. But at the same time, I will do the right thing for our daughter financially and as a parent."

"That's a great approach to take. Let us go through your financials. After that, I can give you a guideline to have in mind when you are with the mediator."

"If we reach an agreement with the mediator, what happens after that?"

"The mediator may be a lawyer but is not acting as one when they are meditating. So, if you reach an agreement, they will give you both a copy of the terms you have agreed upon. Either your husband's lawyers or I will draft them up into court orders for you both to sign."

"That's good. I want to see you before I finalise anything and get your advice."

"The court requires that a lawyer signs off on the agreement to protect you. I will get my secretary to come in and give you the details of a few mediators to consider. I should have advice for you in the next week or so."

"So, we might be ready to go to mediation in a few weeks?

"Yes, you will be ready, but do you need to check with your husband before booking the dates?"

It's best to book the appointment and then let him know. He will go."

"Kate can help you book a date with a mediator if you like. I think anytime, two weeks from now, you will be ready. We will do everything we can to help."

"Thanks, Sarah. I like this approach and am so glad I came to see you."

"I hope it works out,' Sarah said. 'Call Kate or me anytime at all."

Sarah

Chapter 56

I quickly chatted with Kate, to check my diary for the morning before I left the office to drive to Hillary's house for an early dinner. Hillary had invited me to meet her accountant and have dinner to discuss the School Scholarship Fund.

As I left the office, I realised that I felt better about myself after my conference with Debbie today. Having met another woman with a husband who also had a secret life, made me think I was not the only woman dealing with surprises after years of marriage. I was impressed with how Debbie had managed the situation and was placing her daughter's welfare as her main priority.

I had always found the drive to Hilary's house relaxing, but I especially enjoyed driving alone. I enjoyed the solitude and found having time to myself the most rejuvenating thing I could do for myself. Thoughts were racing through my head. Although, the thought of losing Hillary to her illness was upsetting, I was honoured that she wanted my assistance. For the last couple of weeks, I reflected on Hillary's generosity to the scholarship fund and the girls she helped, including me. It was humbling that she had done this for so many decades without acknowledgement when most people sought public accolades for their charity work.

On my arrival at her home, Hillary was her usual graceful and elegant self. She was dressed in a beautiful flowing chiffon dress, with her hair in an upswept style that highlighted her magnificent cheekbones. She wore a single strand of pearls around her neck, drop pearl earrings and a beautiful broach of diamonds and aquamarines. Her accountant Brian was charming, suitably well dressed in a three-piece suit, tie, and matching handkerchief.

Hillary introduced me to Brian, and after a brief introduction of himself and his firm, he assured me that the scholarship trust's financial side was secure. He told Hillary and me that with the funds her estate would be leaving to the scholarship fund, it could continue indefinitely if it was well managed.

I could see that Hillary was pleased that Brian and I were getting along well. At dinner, Hillary said to Brian, "I chose Sarah to help you manage the trust, because she will help identify the girls, we need to help the most. I came from a home where things were perfect, so I relied on others who had a radar, like Ms Kris, to find the vulnerable girls who need our help. Now Ms Kris has left, we need someone like Sarah to help us."

It never ceased to amaze me how insightful Hillary was, and how much thought she put into everything she did. After this meeting with Brian, I knew exactly how I would honour Hillary's work and continue to grow her legacy.

As soon as we finished our meals, Hillary left the table for a moment and returned with two photo albums. "I have some photos I would like to show you," she said. As she opened the album's first page, I saw the photos of me at school. I was immensely touched as Hillary went through each page, remembering precisely the events that I had been photographed attending.

Brian had not realised until now that I had been a beneficiary of the trust created by Hillary. In one of Hilary's last official events as a Judge, she was the person who had handed me my law degree at my graduation. After closing the albums, Hillary gave them to me and said, "I thought I would give these to you to keep. I'm sure your daughter will enjoy them."

"Thank you so much. Once Chloe sees these photos, she will insist on meeting you."

"I would love to meet her too," Hillary replied.

"Let's make it soon, then."

"I wish I had done this all sooner. I wish I had got to know you both earlier," Hillary said.

I walked over to Hillary and hugged her. "Thank you for going to so much trouble to record all those memories for me. I will do everything I can to ensure the beautiful legacy you started will continue. Because of you, I have the life I have today. Without you, there is no doubt my life would have been quite different."

Sarah

Chapter 57

As soon as I arrived in the office this morning, I could tell that that all the staff were excited about the ball tonight. The receptionist smiled at me whilst answering the phone, and she pointed to a dress, which was hanging behind her chair.

As soon as Kate saw me, she walked over to show me her the schedule for the staff to have their hair and makeup was done by hairdressers and makeup artists that she had arranged to come to the office for the, "Let's get ready for the ball party." She had created a wonderful feeling of camaraderie and excitement in the office for the event.

For the first time in a long time, I was enjoying the thought of, and not dreading going out to a function. The ball had reignited my desire to put on an evening dress and feel special, and it felt nice. Hillary had said to me, that she had noticed how happy I seemed when I discussed my dress with her. She said to me, "If Phil had done nothing else, he had at least made me interested in going out and enjoying myself again."

When I had recalled the last black-tie event that I had gone to, I realised that it had been my wedding. With that thought, I felt guilty as I recalled how much I had been distracted by one of my cases at the time. So much so, that Peter had said to me, the night before our wedding, that our wedding seemed more like an inconvenience than a celebration to me. With hindsight, he was right. That was how I had felt at the time.

As I sat in my office, Kate showed me the list of hire cars that Phil had booked to take all of us to the event. Two minivans had been ordered for the staff and a hire car for Kate and me. All the vehicles were arriving at the office at 6.30 pm, to take us to the ball. Phil had been in constant contact with Kate about the arrangements, and Kate had told me that he had said how excited he was to see me wearing my new dress. I knew Kate was watching me to see my reaction to her last comment, but I let it slide.

I quickly checked my emails and then headed to the Family Court for my matter which was listed for hearing before a Registrar at 9.30 am. The lawyer for the other side had called me yesterday to let me know his clients, the grandparents who had applied for custody of the grandchildren, wanted to negotiate about settling. I said to Kate, as I left the office, that I hoped to be back by 3 pm, but would call with updates during the day and let her know how the case and/or settlement negotiations were progressing.

"If you could get back by 4 pm, that would be perfect timing," Kate replied. "Your dress is hanging up in your office, and you are booked into the hairdresser and makeup artist between 4 and 5 pm."

Walking along the street towards the Family Court, I saw my clients who were about 50 metres in front of me. As they stopped in front of the court, they both turned around and saw me approaching them. My client said to me, "Sarah, I have wonderful news, Mum called me last night. She and Dad are going to settle the case with us today. They aren't going to push for the kids to live with them anymore, and they have accepted that Brian and I are together."

"That's great news," I said. "What changed their minds?"

"I did," Brian replied. "I told them that if the problem was that we were not married, we would get married as soon as possible. After I said that to them, they seemed to change immediately and even started discussing settling."

"That's incredible" I said. "Did you have a feeling that was their sticking point? I had no idea it was."

"I woke up that yesterday with a light bulb moment. I just had a gut feeling and went with it," he said.

"I am so glad you followed your intuition. It should never be underestimated. Now, let's go in and see if we can get this sorted out for you both."

As we walked into the courtroom, the lawyer for the grandparents came up to me and handed me a document. He said to me, "My client's called me this morning and asked me to put together draft terms for today. They cover everything from time with the kids with my clients, schools, religions and special occasions like Christmas & Easter, and we are no longer pressing for the kids to live with us. Let me know what you think, but I think it gives both our clients what they really want."

Brian said to me, "Did I just hear right? Are they seriously asking for orders about Christmas and Easter?"

I said to him, "It's the usual terms, that's standard really. They want to know if they give up having the kids live with them, that they will have secured periods of time that they will see them. We will work through all of this, but the main thing is that they are no longer seeking that the kids live with them."

"Of course, we would let them see the kids at Easter and Christmas. I just can't believe we have to have court orders about it."

The Registrar appeared in the courtroom. We informed her that the parties had decided to proceed with negotiations to settle. She agreed to adjourn our matter in the list, until we were ready to hand up the finalised terms.

We walked outside and set ourselves up in a meeting room to go through the details that needed to be finalised. I called Kate quickly to tell her I would be back in time for my allocated hairdressing time slot.

By 3.30 pm, the terms had been finalised, and we appeared before the Registrar to approve them. She congratulated the parties on reaching a sensible and detailed settlement for the care of the children and wished them the best. It was an excellent way to finish the week for everyone, and we all left the court with a huge sense of relief.

As I walked back into the offices, I noticed no one was in reception. Walking down the hallway, I saw that the boardroom had been transformed into a beauty salon. It was lovely to hear laughter and excitement from my staff while they were having their hair and makeup done by professional stylists. When Kate saw me, she handed me a glass of champagne.

"Time to relax and be pampered," she said.

"Thanks for organising this, Kate. It was such a great idea."

"I don't want to hurry you, but if you want to shower quickly and change into this robe, you can continue with your drinks while they do your hair and makeup."

"That sounds great. I'll be quick," I said.

The process of having my hair and makeup took up the next hour in the boardroom. All the staff had been pampered while drinking champagne and enjoying cheese and canapes.

When my hair and makeup was finished, Rob said to Kate and me as we sat in our robes, "Ladies, you should both put your dresses and shoes on now. Then I will know if I need to make any last-minute touch-ups or changes to your hair or makeup."

I smiled as she walked back into my office to change my gown. Stepping into my new dress and shoes, I felt wonderful. I looked to Kate, who had sashayed into my office and said to me, "Don't we look amazing?"

"Yes, we do Kate. Your dress looks beautiful."

"Mel did miracles altering it to fit me, when it was really made for one of his 5'9, size ten models."

"Well, whatever he did, it looks like it was made for you. Your shoes are perfect too. Honestly, I had really forgotten what it was like to wear a long dress and how much fun this is," I said.

Rob had walked into the room and stood with his hands on his hips as he said to us, "My beautiful girls. You are both breathtaking." He then made a few minor adjustments to our hair and makeup before announcing to us, "Now you can go girls. You both look perfect!"

"And it's perfect timing," Kate said, "I just got a text that our car is waiting downstairs."

Sarah

Chapter 58

As soon as we sat in the back of the stretch limousine, the driver offered us a glass of champagne. "I could get very used to this," Kate said.

"It's been a long time since I travelled in style like this, and it is very nice," I said.

The doormen opened the car door, and photographers had lined the hotel's entrance. I felt like I was floating on air as I walked into the hotel's foyer. I was so surprised at how much I loved the feel of the dress that Phil had given me. I felt tall and glamorous, and I was enjoying it.

Kate was walking closely behind me, and I saw how happy she looked. "I can't believe how many people are here," she said. We continued weaving through the crowd into the ballroom.

"I heard that over 1000 people are coming to this event tonight," I said, as I scanned the room, trying to see if I could see Phil or our table number.

Kate asked, "Sarah, before we sit down, can we go to the ladies' room to touch up our hair and makeup?"

"Sure," I said, as I felt a hand on my shoulder. When I turned around, I saw it was Phil. I was surprised at how different he looked in his black tuxedo. "I almost didn't recognise you," I said. "You look terrific."

"You look stunning. Absolutely gorgeous," he replied.

Kate laughed as she said to Phil, "Your jaw has hit the ground, pick it up."

Phil looked towards Kate and regained his composure. "Thanks for that, Kate."

I said to Phil, "You should wear a suit more often, Phil. It really suits you. You look very handsome tonight."

"Thank you. If I promise to wear one, will you go out with to dinner with me?"

Realising she had to intervene, Kate interjected, asking Phil, "Which one is our table, Phil?"

"Right there," he said, pointing just in front of the stage. "It's table 100, right next to the stage."

"Thanks. We will be back in a minute. We are just going to the lady's room."

"But you just got here," Phil remarked.

"We won't be long, don't worry."

"Can't you go to the bathroom on your own, Kate? There are so many people I would like to introduce Sarah too." "It's a girl thing," Kate said as she gently placed her hand on my arm to lead me off to the ladies' room.

As Kate dragged me away, I said to her, "What is going on?"

As Kate continued to usher me towards the bathroom, she replied, "As we walked into the ballroom, a lady came over to me and asked me if we could meet her at the ladies' room in ten minutes. She knew our names, and I recognised her face, but could not put a name to it. She said it was important."

"How strange? I wonder who she is?"

As we walked towards the bathroom, the lady was waiting for us. I recognised her immediately as one of Phil's ex-wives. "Hi, Sarah," she said as we approached her.

"Hello, Jan," I replied. I was surprised to see Jan, who looked as beautiful as ever. I recalled Jan as one of Phil's easier ex-wives to deal with. Jan had been straightforward in the settlement conferences, clarifying precisely what she wanted and settling quickly as soon as Phil agreed to it."

"I love your dress, Sarah. Let me guess, Phil bought it for you?" Jan said.

"Why do you ask," I replied.

"Don't worry; only I would pick up something like that. Phil loves to dress his ladies, particularly when he is courting them, and I know his taste in clothing. He has the same plan of seduction every time."

Jan could see that Kate and I were looking confused, but she continued, "Let me guess, he sent a florist shop of flowers and a rack of designer clothes? If you have not received it yet, it will be jewellery next."

Kate looked at Jan and said, "Why are you telling us this?"

"Because watching Phil seduce women, is like watching an out-of-control car careering down a street and smashing into people. I like you Sarah, and I hate what he does to women."

I was taken entirely by surprise by what Jan was saying, mainly why she was saying it to me when she was an ex-wife. I said to her, "I remember you saying to me during the settlement negotiations that you believed that you still loved Phil, which is why it was so hard for you at the time. Is that where this is coming from?"

"I am trying to warn you because I like you, Sarah. Yes, I did love him, but I realised he loves no one. He keeps hurting women because we women let him. We need to warn each other to stop this."

Kate interjected and said to Jan, "Out of interest, have you tried to say this to any of his other girlfriends since you and Phil broke up? Did you try to warn Stacey, for instance?"

Jan laughed at the mention of Stacey. "You can only warn women who are smart enough to understand what you are warning them about. Poor Stacey, she was a sweet girl, but she could barely read and write, let alone be warned about a serial killer like Phil."

"A serial killer is a bit harsh, isn't it?" I asked.

Jan turned to me and said, "Some girls may need the ride, but you don't, Sarah. You are a trophy, which would make him attractive to you. It's just a game. I'm sorry, but that's all it is. You are a trophy on his arm, so he is interested in you. You are just a new angle. But he never stays interested, and then he will hurt you."

I felt uncomfortable with the discussion, but I wanted to end it politely. I said to Jan, "Thank you for your concern, but I really must get back to my table."

Jan touched Sarah's arm gently before she replied, "I know you are going through a tough time, and that is the only reason Phil got anywhere near you. I know at no other time would you have given him a chance to be in your life. He has the sense of a vulture – he knows when someone has a weakness, and he hits hard. I will leave you with that," Jan said as she walked away.

Kate looked at me and said, "Wow, Sarah, I am so sorry. What a weird thing to happen."

I knew how excited Kate had been about the ball, and I wasn't going to let Jan or Phil ruin the evening for her. "Let's forget about that hiccup and have a good night. We can't let a little noise from an ex-wife of Phil's upset our evening."

"You're amazing and right as usual," Kate replied.

"I am taking Hillary's advice. We all look great, and the room is amazing. There is fabulous food, champagne, and entertainment. We are here to have a great night and give to charity. Let us not forget what's important."

"And my bet is that Phil will be donating big time tonight to impress you," Kate said,

I certainly hope so," I replied. "We should touch up our lipstick and go back to our table. Our absence will be annoying Phil by now."

The evening went to plan from then on. I sat chatting to Phil all night, ignoring Jan's conversation. During the night, I picked up a book of raffle tickets on the table to purchase them; but Phil paid for them immediately. Then I looked at the brochure of the auction items for sale, and as I flicked through it, Phil asked me if there was anything I wanted.

As the night went on, Phil was earnest in trying to impress me. He bid on auction items and made a generous donation of $100,000 to the children's hospital. I appeared appropriately impressed by Phil's generosity.

At the end of the charity auction, the MC announced that it was time to relax. A band appeared on the stage, and it was not long before most of the people in the room were up and dancing. Phil asked me to dance immediately.

On the dance floor, Phil materialised as a surprisingly good dancer. He remained focused entirely on me, holding me closely. I noticed that Jan had walked onto the dance floor with a male partner. They started to dance next to us, and we had no choice but to acknowledge each other.

The evening was an enormous success, and no one wanted to leave as the MC announced that the band would be playing their final song for the evening. It was a slow romantic love song. As Phil danced with me in a close embrace, he asked if I would like him to take me home in his car. I politely reminded him that tonight was not a date, but a function with my staff and that it would be inappropriate for me to be seen leaving with him when I had arrived with Kate. Phil appeared annoyed that he had not predicted this as a problem earlier, and his disappointment was obvious. His mood changed instantly, and he stopped dancing and took my hand to lead us off the dance floor."

We walked back towards our table, but as we reached our seats, Phil turned and walked away.

Kate had been seated at the table and had sensed something was wrong after observing our abrupt departure from the dance floor. She walked over to me and asked, "Why did Jan dance next to you two?"

"It was so weird," I replied. "They couldn't get any closer. Phil had his back to her, and she was staring me up and down. She and her partner could have moved to the other side of the dance floor and avoided us completely, but they didn't. She was trying to get Phil's attention by steering her partner in front of him. After failing to catch his eye for a few minutes, she physically touched him on the shoulder until he acknowledged her."

"What did he say to her?"

"He was polite. He said how beautiful she looked and even commented on her dress, to which she replied, "Do you remember when you bought it for me." Honestly, it was like she was flirting with him."

"That's just nuts," Kate said. "Anyway, our driver has just texted me that he is waiting outside. Are you ready to go?"

"Yes, that's perfect timing since Phil has stormed off."

As we got up to leave, Phil arrived back at the table. I said to him, "It's been a lovely evening Phil, but our driver is here, so we should go. Thank you so much for a great night."

Phil had recomposed himself and was gracious enough to insist on walking us to our hire car.

He was the perfect gentleman, both opening the car door. As soon as the car pulled away, we both burst out laughing.

"You were amazing. I don't know how you kept yourself together through that," Kate said.

I put her finger to her lips as she motioned towards the back of the driver's head. Kate suddenly realised that I had indicated that the driver might be listening to our conversation. She picked up her mobile and sent me a text message. *Do you think he would report back to Phil?*

I replied by text. *Maybe. I wouldn't put it past Phil. Better to be safe than regret it.*

Kate smiled and then shouted to me, "Isn't it lovely the staff are texting to say what a great night they had."

"Yes, it is. Phil was so generous inviting us all tonight, and with all the donations he made during the night," I replied. The driver looked back at us in the rear-view mirror, which confirmed my suspicions that he had been listening to us.

When we arrived at my apartment building, the driver opened the car door and escorted us to the entrance foyer. He said, "I have something Phil asked me to give you." He handed me a card with a small box which he took out of his jacket pocket.

"Thank you," I said.

As the driver walked away, Kate asked, "Can I come up and have a drink? I really need one."

"Of course, I have a bottle of champagne in the fridge, waiting for us."

As we walked in the front door, Maria greeted us and asked, "How was your night? You both look beautiful."

"It was a fantastic night, Maria," I said.

"That is good. I am so glad. Chloe is asleep, and I will head off now and see you tomorrow."

Kate had walked into the kitchen and reappeared in the lounge room with a bottle of champagne and two glasses. She saw me staring at the open box and asked, "What is it?"

"It's a necklace from the silent auction tonight, the diamond heart pendant. Phil had asked me what I thought of it, and I had said it was sweet. I knew he wanted me to ask him to buy it, so I tried to sound unenthusiastic."

"But it didn't work," Kate replied.

"His note says, *I had a lovely evening, and this is a small gift to thank Chloe for sharing you with us tonight.*"

"He is so good he is scary. Thank goodness we bumped into his ex-wife tonight, or we may have fallen for this stuff he comes up with."

"I love how you use the royal "we", Kate."

"If he is trying to get to you, he has to get through me, too," she said.

"You know, I am not sure about Jan's motives. If she was concerned about my interests or hers," I said.

"What makes you say that?" Kate asked.

"Rhonda told me that one of his wives is still in love with him and wants him back. What better way to do that than to scare off the women he pursues? Thinking about it, it was weird how she came up to us tonight. Why would you bother if you were an ex-wife? I would find doing such a thing embarrassing."

"And what about her and her partner dancing next to you and Phil on the dance floor? That was weird. She was definitely trying to get Phil's attention onto her, and away from you," Kate said.

I handed Kate the necklace and asked, "Should I give this back to him? I don't think I am comfortable with giving it to Chloe from him."

Kate frowned as she said, "I'm not sure. It's a gift to Chloe, so technically, it's hers, not yours to reject, isn't it?"

"I suppose so, but then she is a child. I'm also worried that he may take offence if I return it. I don't want to be appear rude."

"You are impossible sometimes. Always doing the right thing even though we are dealing with an impossible man."

As Kate refilled our champagne glasses, she said, "You will have to be careful in how you reject this man. He will find your rejection of him more of a reason to pursue you because he is a man who is used to getting what he wants. Not sure of the angle of your exit plan, but you need one, and it must be good."

I stood up and walked towards the window. Staring out at the darkness of the night, I remembered waiting for my parents to come home, until one night, they didn't arrive home. I saw Kate was watching me, and she knew I was ruminating on what to do next.

"What will you do?" Kate asked.

"I will be pleasant to him but keep my distance. He will become bored with the chase."

"Do you think so?" Kate replied.

"I do. Remember, Phil was interested in me years ago, and then he went away when he realised, that he was getting nowhere."

"But you were married then, which makes it a different challenge this time."

"What matters to him the most is that he gets what he wants. He decides what he wants when he sees it, and he can detect vulnerability in a person. That ability enables him to work out how to pursue the woman he is after. It's all about the chase that matters to him. Sometimes if a woman is married, it makes the chase more interesting for him because there is more at stake for her."

"What do you mean by that?"

"If a married woman has an affair with him and leaves her husband, then she has just put everything at stake for him. He likes that because she depends on him, giving up her relationship with someone else for him."

"Gosh, I didn't really see it that way. Why did he invite us to the charity ball then? To impress you?" Kate asked.

"Of course, we were impressed that he was buying tables at a children's charity function, weren't we? Some other women would be more impressed if he just gave them a Hermes handbag than spend $50,000.00 on a table for them to go to a charity event."

"Why didn't I see this before?" Kate asked.

"I only saw it when Jan pointed it out to me. She was right. I have been feeling less than my best lately, as much as I hate to admit it. With all this stuff with Peter, he has noticed that. For years I have rejected Phil's advances, and it is only because of how low I have been feeling that he had any chance with me. I just enjoyed his attention instead of analysing it for what it really was."

Kate poured more champagne into our glasses and said, "Who said champagne doesn't fix everything."

"Well, I, for one, have certainly found that it helps the healing process for me, that's for sure."

Kate said, "I have to say, I can see how he manages to lure women into his web. He has a seductive process going on there when he courts a woman. I can imagine that life after Phil would seem quite dull and inadequate. I mean, if the next guy who came along sent you just a bunch of flowers instead of a truckload of flowers, it may seem disappointing."

"That's why his exes still chase him like Jan was tonight. They mistake his courting process for real love and are now unhappy with what is normal. Jan used the guy who was her partner tonight, who seemed charming by the way, just to get Phil's attention."

"I was angry with her, but now I feel sorry for her. She must be tortured by watching him pursue women as he pursued her," Kate replied.

"It's up to her to break the cycle. She has the means to do it. We have enough to do to look after ourselves, Kate."

"Yes, we do. I am so glad we have figured out Phil. It's a huge relief for me, and I know for Charlie too, who was very worried about you."

"I know he was. I will call him Monday and reassure him that Phil is not a danger."

"Well, it has ended up an eventful night. I will head home now happy that all is now sorted. I have just ordered my Uber, and it's about here."

"Goodnight, Kate. Thanks for being my wingman tonight and always. Have a great weekend."

Jim

Chapter 59

The night of the show was fantastic, and we had all agreed it had been the best performance the theatre had ever produced. By I got home, I was still on a high, but it was late. I walked into the bedroom and was asleep in bed.

The next morning when I woke up, I was still on a high, but Debbie was in a strange mood. She had got out of bed without even looking at me and had walked straight out of the bedroom. When I followed her into the kitchen, she told me that she had arranged to go out with Ashley for the day to see her brother. She proceeded to then walk towards the bathroom and jump into the shower.

For the next few days, Debbie's moods alternated between being distant and then teary. When I discussed this with my mates, they all advised me that she sounded like she was going through menopause. As a result, during dinner I tactfully tried to raise it with her suggesting perhaps she should see her doctor for blood tests; but that was met with a loud silence.

The next week, when I came home from work, Debbie told me that she had moved into the spare bedroom, telling me she needed some space. I had exhausted the advice of my friends so I decided to call her brother to ask him what I should do, but he said he was unaware of anything being wrong.

Yesterday, finally, Debbie told me that we had issues. She said that we needed help; but would not tell me why. She said that she had arranged a meeting with someone to help us. I was shocked and asked why we couldn't talk about it first, but she was determined not to discuss anything without help.

So here we were, sitting in the office with a mediator and Debbie. I was not happy. What had changed in Debbie these last two weeks was beyond me. I was confused as to why we needed to see a mediator, but I was willing to try anything if it would make Debbie happy. The mediator walked into the room and introduced himself. Then he said to me, "I know why Debbie is here, but can you want to tell me why you are here?"

I was surprised at his question but responded. "Debbie said we needed help. She has been acting weird at home lately, not telling me why, and insisted on this. This has been going on for two weeks now."

Debbie said, "That's because I have been scared to say what I have to say to you alone."

"What are you talking about, Debbie? What do you mean you are scared?" I said, feeling embarrassed.

Debbie started to cry as said to me, "You think that leading a life that is a lie doesn't hurt me?"

I needed clarification. *She couldn't know*, I thought to myself. "What do you mean?" I asked.

"Jim, I know. I have seen you in a show. I followed you and filmed you. I have gone through our bank accounts and credit card statements. I know about your double life, and I don't understand any of it."

I was shocked. I had expected something else. All I could say was, "I'm confused."

"Please, Jim, don't look so shocked, and for goodness' sake, don't try to deny it. Don't make this any harder for me."

I looked at Debbie and saw how upset she was, and I felt awful. I had never wanted this to happen, but I did not know how to respond to her distress.

"Jim, we need to sort out how we bring up our daughter from now on. How do we weave your lifestyle into ours? Therefore, I needed a counsellor present so he could guide us on how to do this."

"I never wanted to hurt you," I said.

The mediator interjected and said to me, "I know this is a difficult time, but my understanding is Debbie would like to try and reach an agreement about parenting arrangements?"

"That's what we must do, as well as a property settlement," Debbie replied.

"This is news to me," I said.

"To help you both, I would like to start with putting an agenda on the board with issues we will work through to form the basis of an agreement which you will be taking to your lawyer, Sarah Walters, I understand?"

"You have a lawyer already?" I said, taken by surprise.

"I do, Jim, and she is a very good one, so for all our sakes, let's sort this out now."

I reached over to touch Debbie's hand as I said to her, "Debbie can we talk about this before we go straight into ending our marriage? Can we at least discuss this?"

Debbie started crying again and said, "What is there to talk about, Jim? You lied about where you went, you wear women's clothes and dance in shows as a woman with other women, and before now you didn't think that we should talk that through?"

I stood up, walked over to Debbie, and tried to put my arm around her, but she pushed me away.

I was horrified that I had caused Debbie to be so upset. I walked back to my seat and sat down. "Did you think I liked keeping this a secret from you? Of course, I didn't want to, but I knew this was how you would react. I love you; I love our daughter and our life. I love cross-dressing, so I did it in a way that didn't affect you. I never wanted to hurt you, nor did I want to lose you."

Debbie had been sitting with her head in her hands, looking at the floor as I spoke. She looked up at me and suddenly stopped crying.

"Are you telling me you that are not bi-sexual, homosexual or having an affair or something?"

I stood up and started to walk towards Debbie again, but then stopped, remembering her last reaction to me touching her. "I am not bisexual, homosexual, or having an affair. I understand you think I may be, but I am not. I love you and I have never been interested in another woman or man. I love dressing in women's clothing and performing on stage. I tried to stop it, and I was miserable. It's just part of me, and I wanted to have it in my life. If there is no way you can accept it, I will give it up. I would be more than miserable if I lost you. I would be nothing."

Debbie stared at Jim and saw the love he had for her. She saw the hurt and fear in his eyes and knew he was not lying about his feelings for her and their daughter. She said to him, "Jim, how do we explain what you like to do to our daughter?"

I almost laughed and caught myself. I realised that not all people were as open-minded as I would like them to be, and that I had to be patient with my wife while she was still prepared to ask questions. "Debbie, if we love each other and live with this, we will find a way to explain it to Ashley, and she will accept it. If she knows I love you both, she will cope. I am more concerned about you and if you can accept it."

Debbie stared ahead as she replied, "Jim, I don't know if I can ever accept it. It was a shock seeing you dressed like that and dancing that way. I felt like I didn't know you, and that was weird. When did this happen? Why didn't I know, and how long have you been hiding this from me?"

I felt overwhelmed by Debbie's shock, and I sat back in my chair and recoiled. I put my hands over my face as I bowed my head. Debbie sat beside me and put her arms around me and said, "Honey, I just need you to tell me why and when this started so that I can understand it all."

I lifted my head and looked at Debbie and then at the counsellor before explaining, "It started when I was about five years old. When my dad was drunk, he would pick on me. Sometimes he would come home late at night and wake me up by dragging me out of bed. He would tell me he had to teach me how to be a man, which meant to play football or arm wrestle with me. It would always be rough because he was drunk. He would end up having me in a headlock or belt my arm down so hard on the table in an arm wrestle that I thought he had broken it."

"That's terrible," Debbie said.

"He would tell me I was acting like a girl if I cried. Once, he bit my ear so hard it wouldn't stop bleeding. Blood was pouring down my neck, and I was so scared that I wanted to wake up my mum. He told me I was acting like a girl, and he got one of my sister's dresses from the laundry and told me to put it on. After I put it on, he started laughing. When I saw him laughing, I was relieved, so I began to dance around like a girl, and he laughed even more. Eventually, he walked away from me laughing, much to my relief."

"I am so sorry, honey. You never told me that your father did this to you. I wish I had known. How long did this go on for?"

"Years. After that time, it became a thing with him. After waking me up, he would tell me to put on a dress and then laugh at me and tease me. Once, he asked me to walk around and pretend I was a girl. When I did, he started laughing, and then he asked me to pretend I was doing a striptease, and when I said I didn't know what he was talking about, he made me watch a scene from a movie where a woman stripped. He told me to copy it. The movie is called Striptease, with Demi Moore in it. I watched it so many times until I could copy her strip tease exactly."

"It was so wrong of him to do this to you, honey."

"A week later, he woke me up in the middle of the night. He had a couple of his mates with him. He told me to put on a show for all of them. I didn't want to, but he yelled at me and I was scared, so I did. They all laughed at me while I did a striptease, and then dad told me I could go back to bed. He stopped hurting me as long as I made everyone laugh because I was dressed like a girl."

"I am so sorry," Debbie said.

"I wanted to make my dad happy, so I started to plan my shows for him and his friends. The better I got at it, the more he liked me, and he stopped trying to make me play football or wrestling. I don't know when, but I realised I enjoyed wearing dresses and liked the entertainment. I would look at my sister's dresses when they weren't home and plan which one, I would wear for the next show. My sisters never blamed me when they couldn't find a dress and never looked in my room. They just accused each other of years."

Debbie said, "I don't know what to say. I had never expected this. I knew that your dad had been a drunk and a tyrant because of the stories I heard from your mother and sisters, but I'm blown away by what you told me.

I looked at Debbie and I let go of my hesitation, walked over to her, and put my arm around her. When she didn't flinch, I moved closer and hugged her. We both collapsed into each other's arms and hugged tightly. "I'm sorry, Deb, I'm really sorry. I love you. Please can we try and work through this. I should have told you earlier, I should have done many things, but now we are here, can we try?"

Debbie started to cry again, sat down, and put her head in her hands. Shaking her head, she looked up seconds later and said, "I am so sorry for what happened to you. I don't know how we work through something like this, but I will try as hard as possible. I don't know if I can accept you are wearing dresses for the rest of our lives. Still, I know I love you, and because of that and our daughter, I will try to keep our marriage together."

The mediator walked over to us and touched us both on the shoulder. "I can see that you both love each other deeply, and right now, I can see that although you have difficulties, you both want to try and work through them. I am happy to help you with that and to move forward."

Debbie said to the counsellor, "Have you ever helped a wife accept her husband's cross-dressing fetish before?"

"I know this may be an extraordinary thing for you to accept about your husband, but let me tell you, I have had to help couples work through tough situations. In many cases, we have succeeded and kept the marriage together."

Debbie asked, "What kind of tough situations? Were they harder than this?"

"I have had to work through fathers' finding out they are not the natural parent of a child they thought were theirs. I have had to work with adopted children who were unaware of that until they were adults. I have had women who have found out their husbands had other wives and children they were unaware of – there have been many complicated situations that I have helped people work through. Love is the main thing that gets couples and families through this, and seeing the love between you today, I can tell you that I believe you both have a chance."

Debbie said, "Jim, I need some time to work through this. I want some time at home to take this all in. Will you give me a couple of weeks? Can you stay at your mum's or somewhere to just let me process this?"

I smiled and replied, "Of course. I will do whatever it takes for you to work through this, and if it's two weeks or two years, I will wait on whatever terms you want. Please understand. I know this is my fault, and I must try to make this right."

Debbie stood up and said, "Could we come back to see you again after we have had time to absorb all of this and think about how we will sort this out?"

"Of course. Take your time. I wish you all the best and look forward to hearing from you," he replied.

Debbie and I walked out to the car park. I walked Debbie to her car and said, "Should I come home now and pack a bag, or would you prefer to pack it for me, and I'll pick it up later tonight?"

"I don't know," Debbie replied.

"I'm sorry, Debbie. I never meant this to hurt you. It's killing me to see you so upset."

"I'm sorry too. You will need your stuff, so come home now, and we can have dinner with Ashley first. You can tell her you are going to your mums for a visit. At least then she will know why you aren't home."

"That's a good idea. Let's do that. I want to follow you home, so I know you get home safely. I am worried about you. I don't like it when you drive and you're upset."

Looking at Debbie, I could see that she still loved me, which made all the difference. I still had a chance.

"Ok, that's the plan. See you at home," she said.

Sarah

Chapter 60

I woke up the morning after the ball feeling relieved. I had been confused about my feelings for Phil, but Friday night had finally opened my eyes to the mistake I had been making. I knew I had faced what my psychiatrist had been saying to me about myself, and I had decided that I would start therapy with him again. My psychiatrist had been right when he warned me that emotions not dealt, with could cause equal and opposite reactions in my life. My choice of Peter as my husband was clearly a result of my troubled youth and my ability to just set aside what I didn't want to see about a person.

I had promised Chloe that we would spend the weekend together, and I felt the most relaxed I had been in years. I had realised that it had been the first weekend in months since I had not worked at least one day of the weekend at the office, and how unfair this had been on Chloe.

Whilst we were relaxing after breakfast, as a surprise, I decided to give Chloe the necklace Phil had bought her at the auction. I handed it to her, trying to explain that it was a gift from one of my clients who had purchased it at an auction to raise money for the children's hospital. She loved the necklace and squealed with delight as I put it on for her.

Phil called as I watched Chloe look at her reflection in the mirror wearing the necklace. After some general chit-chat about the ball, he asked if Chloe liked the necklace. I commented on his timing, letting him know Chloe had just put it on and loved it. Phil surprised me by asking if we could get together with Chloe over the weekend. He said he wanted to meet my daughter and see how beautiful the necklace looked on her. Initially surprised by his request, I quickly realised why Phil had bought Chloe the gift – to make her feel that he had a connection with her. I had underestimated Phil and his art of manipulation; Charlie had predicted it accurately.

When I said to Phil that I had plans to spend the weekend having quality time with Chloe, I knew he would be disappointed. Still, I was taken aback by his terse reaction when he said, "Don't you think you should give Chloe a chance to meet me and thank me for such a generous gift? Are you too busy this weekend to teach your daughter some manners?"

I replied, "I am sorry I have disappointed you. Thank you for being very generous with your gift to Chloe and inviting my staff and me to the ball. But I can't change our plans for this weekend."

"Enjoy," Phil said before hanging up.

I walked into the kitchen and made myself a coffee. I sat in one of my new large leather armchairs, enjoying the morning sun streaming through the window. Somehow, I was feeling more relaxed about my life. My call with Phil had resolved any prospect of a relationship with him. I also thought I had come to terms with Peter and the implications of his friendship with Anthony. Trying to anticipate things with Peter was impossible, as was avoiding any fallout from his actions.

I reflected again on what Charlie had said. I had been unfair and emotional with him, even walking out on him during a session. As I stood up to the kitchen, I saw Chloe walking towards me. She said, "This is so much fun just hanging out together, mum. Can we stay in our pyjamas all weekend, watch Netflix and order Uber Eats? It will be the best weekend ever."

"That sounds wonderful, honey, and if you get bored at any time, we could do whatever else you want to do. I am yours for the whole weekend."

Chloe sat at the table with me and asked, "Can I have a coffee too?"

"Sure, honey," I said.

"I want to talk for hours with you, Mummy, hours and hours."

"Really?" I replied.

"Yes, I want to just sit here and talk to you."

"Ok, me too. Can I tell you all about my friend Hillary and her charity, or is that boring?"

"You mean the lady who gave you the photo albums of you at school? I want to hear everything about her Mummy. She sounds amazing."

I enjoyed telling Chloe all about Hillary and her charity. Chloe was really looking forward to meeting Hillary. I knew that Chloe and Hillary would get along well, and that Chloe would love her home. Spending time with Chloe, I felt wonderfully happy. I realised just how busy I had made my life and that I had to do this with her more often in the future.

Sarah

Chapter 61

It was Monday afternoon, and I had just arrived back at the office after finishing my hearing for the day in the Family Court. As soon as she saw me walk in, Kate came into my office and handed me a bundle of phone messages as she said, "Sorry, there are so many messages. It's been one of those days when everyone wanted to speak to you. I put the most urgent calls first."

"Thanks, Kate," I said as I started to sort through the messages.

"Marci is the most urgent. She called a couple of times, desperate to speak to you before you spoke to her ex-boyfriend's lawyer."

"I get it Kate; you want me to call her now?"

"Please?"

I called Marci immediately and she answered promptly saying, "Thank you for calling me back, Sarah. I really appreciate your offer to help me. I'm very embarrassed that my affair with a married man, has resulted in such a mess."

"I am not here to judge you, Marci. Gary asked me to help you, and I am sorry that things have turned out the way they have for you."

"I called you today for two reasons. The first is, that I have some good news. I got a call this morning, and they told me that I was not hepatitis B positive. Apparently, Gary, my doctor, had received the wrong blood results when he told me that I was hepatitis B positive."

"I can't believe that could happen these days, but that's great news." I replied.

"Either could I," Marci said. "I had gone to the clinic at the hospital two days ago to fill out the forms for an appointment with a specialist for my hepatitis B diagnosis, and I had to have another blood test. The clinic called me the next day and asked me to come in for another test as they were confused about the results. Then I got the call from my doctor that I had received the wrong result initially."

"I'm sorry that you had to go through that," I said.

"It's great news for me, but now my doctor has to tell one of his other patients that they are positive, when they thought they were negative. I know it's not my fault, but I feel bad about that too."

"That is not your fault, Marci. I'm so sorry that your relationship was ruined because of this. You know this does not change your rights to stay in the unit, and we can still proceed with sorting that out for you?"

"Sarah, I never want to hear about or see Bruce again. He can have his unit and everything in it. I am healthy, and I now know what matters to me. I am healthy enough to work and look after myself. He lied to me about the unit being mine, and then when I was sick through no fault of my own, he tried to throw me out of the home he promised he had transferred to me. I am leaving Sydney tomorrow to live with my parents in Byron Bay until I work out what to do next with my life."

"You sound like you have made up your mind and are comfortable with it, Marci. It's wonderful that you have your parents' support."

"I know I won't change my mind. I have realised now that how I was living my life was just a temporary situation. I don't want to take Bruce to court, and I don't want to hurt his wife, who is pregnant. I wish I could apologise to her, but I know I can't. Life is too short and precious to have regrets and waste time on things I can't change. Thanks for your help, and I want to pay you for your time."

"Marci, we really have not done anything for you. There is no charge. Have you spoken to Bruce to let him know the result was wrong?"

"I tried contacting Bruce, I don't know why, but even before I told his lawyer about my hepatitis B result, he stopped answering my calls or responding to my text messages. I sent a text to him saying that the result was wrong, but who knows if he will believe me."

"Do you want me to contact his lawyer for you?"

"No, I don't want to take up any more of your time. I will send him an email now that I have spoken to you. Apart from the wrong test result, I will let him know when he can pick the keys up for the unit."

"Just let me know if there is anything you need our help with."

"Thanks, Sarah, I will. And if you get to Byron, please call me, I owe you a drink."

"I would love that, Marci. I hear it's beautiful there."

Sarah walked straight across to Kate's desk to tell her Marci's news. Kate was pleased for Marci and said, "That's a relief for Marci. I'm glad that she can move on from that situation."

"It was terrible for her to go through, but it is probably the best thing that could have happened to her. It was not a good situation for her to live in."

Kate replied, "As you can see from the rest of your messages, Phil has called several times to speak to you. The last time, he was frankly quite rude to me."

"What did he say?" I asked.

"He said that no one could be so busy that she couldn't take the time to talk to him for a couple of minutes. He mentioned the ball, the dresses and Chloe's present and that he felt you were being rather ungracious actually."

I took a deep breath as I listened to Kate and decided it was time to call Phil and end his calls and harassment of my staff.

He replied harshly and clipped saying, "Hello, Sarah."

Realising I had to firmly lead the conversation, I said to him, "Kate said you called. It's the first chance I have had to call you back."

"Is it?"

"Yes, Phil. I have been busy today."

"So have I, Sarah, but I treat you as a priority. Clearly, that's not reciprocal even after all I have done for you."

"Is there a problem, Phil?" I asked.

"Yes, there is. I have treated you like a princess, and all I get in return is your secretary telling me that you are busy. Then you call me back hours later. Is this reasonable?"

"I believe we have a misunderstanding Phil, and I don't like how you speak to me. You have been generous and kind to my staff and me, but that was at your discretion and whim. I asked for nothing. To expect me to behave in any other way, than what I have done today is unreasonable of you. If you are disappointed, I suggest you accept this is the best it will ever get."

"You are unbelievable, Sarah," He said before he ended the call.

Kate walked into my office and asked me, "Are you ok?"

"Did you hear that?"

"I think the whole office heard it. Phil was speaking very loudly."

"That's awkward," I said, grimacing.

"No, it's great. We all hate him."

I heard my phone ping and saw that I had received a text from Phil.

Sarah, I have found a new lawyer. She will contact you for my files.

I showed Kate the text as she said, "I can't wait to tell Charlie about all of this. He will be proud of me. Oh, and I have already packed up Phil's files. Can you text him straight back with, *Your files are ready for collection now.*"

"No, but you can," I said.

Sarah

Chapter 62

As a result of Anthony's allegations against Peter, it had been several weeks since Chloe had seen her father. Now that the police had dropped the charges against him, Peter had asked me if he could start seeing her again. Peter told me that he was prepared to work with me to develop his relationship with Chloe slowly. So that we were all comfortable with slowly integrating him back into her life.

As Chloe's birthday approached, I decided it would be the ideal time to have a family dinner. I had booked Chloe's favourite restaurant, which she loved because it was on a beach. I wanted to invite Hillary and was relieved when Peter agreed to it. I knew Chloe would love meeting her, and her presence would help ease the tension with Peter at our first lunch after a long break from each other.

When I arrived at the restaurant, I was surprised to see that Hillary and Peter were already seated at the table. I looked at my watch and checked that I was on time. As I approached the table with Chloe, Peter stood up and excitedly hugged her. They were so happy to see each other, and as I looked towards Hillary, I could see how pleased she was that the dinner had started so nicely.

"I am sorry that we were not here first. I usually am," I said to Hillary.

Hillary smiled and said, "We arrived half an hour early to beat you here. We knew you would be on time."

"So, you colluded with Peter to be early?" I asked.

"Colluded is a serious word Sarah," Peter said as he and Chloe sat at the table. "We just wanted to ensure we got an outside table here on the beach."

Hillary said to Chloe, "Happy birthday, darling, it's lovely to meet you, and I hope it's ok with you that I am here tonight."

"Oh yes, it's lovely to meet you," Chloe said. "Mum has told me all about you."

Hillary handed Chloe two wrapped gifts and said, "I hope you like them. It's a long time since I bought a present for a young lady."

"Thank you very much," Chloe replied.

As Chloe was taking her time unwrapping the gifts, Hillary interjected and said, "I hope you didn't mind, but I contacted Peter to ask his advice on these gifts. You gave me a hint Sarah, but I needed some help arranging it's execution."

Peter was smiling as proudly as I had ever seen him smile.

Chloe had unwrapped the more significant gift. She opened the box, and although smiling, she was clearly embarrassed when she saw that it contained a beautiful pink dog collar and leash. She said politely to Hillary, "Thank you very much, but I don't have a dog."

Peter excitedly interrupted by saying, "Well, you do now, as he placed a large bag in front of Chloe. "Look in there, Chloe," he said.

Chloe opened the bag and pulled out a stuffed toy grey French Bulldog. Although she tried to look happy, she was clearly disappointed when she said to her father, "Thank you, dad."

"You can put the collar on him, can't you?" Peter said excitedly.

Seeing her disappointment, Hillary interjected and said to Chloe, "I have a second present for you darling," she said as she handed it to Chloe."

The box had several layers of wrapping, and when Chloe opened the lid, there was a photograph of a grey French Bulldog puppy. When Chloe stared at the photo Hillary had placed in a beautiful silver frame, Hillary said, "Would you like a puppy like that one?"

"It's my dream that one day I can have a puppy just like that," Chloe said.

"Sometimes dreams do come true, Chloe," Hillary replied.

Moments later, a lady walked up to their table with a puppy. Chloe squealed excitedly as the lady placed the puppy in her arms and said, "Happy birthday Chloe." As Chloe was excitedly hugging her new puppy, Hillary said to me, "I asked Peter to help me find the puppy and to arrange to bring her to the restaurant tonight. I hope you don't mind me asking him for help, but I am not as mobile as I used to be. I remembered you telling me that Chloe would love a puppy and that Peter had wanted to get her one for years."

I didn't even recall talking to Hillary about it, but Chloe could not have been happier at that moment. "Can I take her onto the beach?" Chloe asked.

"Sure," Peter said. "I will come with you. Mum and Hillary can chat while we play with your new puppy."

"Her name is Gracie, not puppy Dad."

"That's such a beautiful name for her," said Hillary.

"It's because she's grey," Chloe said as she giggled and walked towards the beach.

The waiter poured Hillary and me a glass of champagne. We watched Chloe playing with her new puppy Gracie, on the beach. As I looked out to the water with the sun setting, I remarked what a magnificent sunset it was and that there was nothing more beautiful than watching a happy child with a puppy playing on the beach."

Hillary replied, "I will never get over losing my daughter, but being here with you and Chloe is the first time I have felt like I'm starting to fill the huge hole that losing her left in my life. This is just such a beautiful night. Thank you for inviting me."

"It is just a perfect night," I replied as we continued to watch Chloe on the beach.

"That's a beautiful boat out there," Hillary said.

"It looks amazing. I love the table on the deck with all the beautiful flowers and candles," I said as two waiters walked past our table carrying large platters of seafood. They walked onto the beach, delivering the platters to two men waiting near a speed boat. After delivering the food, they walked back to the restaurant, and Hillary asked them, "Is there a special occasion?"

One of the waiters had stopped to take a photo of the boat, while the other responded and said, "No, it's just Phil Thompson having a romantic dinner on his boat. He loves our seafood platters. Sometimes he even comes into the restaurant and has dinner, but tonight he is dining on his boat with his girlfriend. He has pulled out all stops, flowers, champagne, and our best seafood. He is a legend."

"The bloke has some style," the other waiter said as they both walked away.

I smiled at Hillary and said, "Raise your glass, please. I want to make a toast to dodging a bullet."

"You didn't dodge a bullet Sarah. You caught it and threw it back."

The end